Archangel

MICHAEL VORHIS

DEDICATION

This book is dedicated to the people who have made the biggest influence in my life—including initially my sisters and brothers, and now my wife and child. Most especially, this work is dedicated to my Mother and my Father, who I will always love beyond measure, and who each uniquely inspired the values to which I hope this story is true.

CONTENTS

ACKNOWLEDGMENTS

A very special thanks to Alan, Bernie, Will, Bob, Liz, Donna, Gopal, Shelly, Matt, Marc, Greg, Max, Linh, and my Father, for their varied and individually invaluable input in bringing this work into being.

CHAPTER ZERO

It was a pathetic collection of defenders, as sieges go. And of course they had no hope. The handful of filthy men peered frenetically over a dirt embankment, small-gauge shotguns and broken pick-axes clutched in their dirt-caked hands.

Night had not yet given way to early dawn, although that deep in the narrow mine shaft it held perpetual dominion anyway. Its only challenge was a rusted kerosene lantern, flickering where it stood low and unsteady on a sloping pile of dirt. A Hispanic man in his late twenties, his intelligent expression compromised by a day's growth of beard and bloodshot eyes, bent to the floor and turned down the flame. "Keep this light down or blow it out," he muttered. "They'll pick us off by our damned silhouettes."

Three of his companions, rough-looking men whose high cheekbones revealed their American Indian heritage and whose waning courage came mostly from the anger of youth, didn't respond. A slightly built Caucasian man well past fifty years, with jacket and white shirt collars both open, stared from the lantern to the other men in alarm. He tried in vain to adjust wire-framed spectacles, and settled on blurting his fears aloud. "Are they coming?!"

"We knew they would, just keep it down low."

The old man pulled from beneath his collar an austere black rosary, distractedly kissed its crucifix, and waved it mechanically across his face and shoulders. One of the Indians re-seated the shotgun he held resting upon the crest of the dirt embankment, not far below the mine shaft's ceiling. He looked to be readying himself for an impending onslaught.

Another of his tribesmen grimaced in anger, an ugly facial scar contorting as he hissed at the Mexican. "You said you knew these goddamn tunnels! Bring it down, bring the goddamn mountain down, you said. We've done nothing!"

"We were stupid," the man balancing the shotgun said. "Nobody knows we're here."

*   *   *

In a wider tunnel, two other men were talking with more purpose. They kept their flashlight beams pointed at the shaft's floor as others in their party loitered nearby or brushed passed them on one side. Both were tall enough that they had to pay attention to the ceiling height.

Daryl, a powerful man with cold eyes, sneered carelessly. "They're back in there 'bout fifty yards.

2

They never got to the dynamite. We can end this now." He hooked a thumb over the handgun in his holster, enjoying the feel of the cold grey metal.

His companion's face was shrouded in shadow. Square shoulders and jaw, aristocratic in more genteel settings, here seemed gaunt. "Do it," this man instructed with the practical manner of a construction foreman. "Not that damn thing. Engine exhaust or smoke. Then have Rowe dig one big hole with the 'dozer, up top, somewhere back in the tailings—should still be places." He paused, then curled the darkness imperceptibly with his lip. "But bring the two to me. Alive. Just you."

Daryl lit a cigarette.

Thirteen months passed.

CHAPTER ONE

The beat-up '66 Landcruiser rattled itself across the expanse—a lonely road, shared only with the wind. Except for the absence of trees, he thought, the intensely rugged Dakota Great Plains would have long since earned the title 'mountainous.' As it was, it went by the simple phrase 'open road.'

Mick rubbed his eyes and pulled his jacket collar tighter against his neck. With a driver's side window permanently stuck down, it was times like these he almost regretted owning what amounted to an open-cockpit vehicle. He'd been on the road four days in the decade-old machine, watching the terrain change from civilized to tamed to ignored, and now it had changed again. It sang its own glories. It held dominion. The early September morning light spilled and darted through bottomless twisted gulches and along steep shadowed slopes, oblivious to his existence.

Boxes and luggage rode behind him in the truck's cargo area. A 20-foot-long bagged thing was tied to the top, the fabric fluttering in the 50mph chill. At least this jacket was thick. At least this collar wasn't Roman.

Mick fished a solitary fig bar out of a knapsack behind his seat and pondered the unfathomable developments that had propelled him west. Back in Boston the old Bishop had called him in. For a chat about the stairwell, he'd thought.

"My long-time friend and former classmate Bishop Cole has asked for our help," the old man had droned in his soft voice, "given that he has no one left to send, and he himself has taken ill." Mick had squirmed uncomfortably in his chair across the ancient desk. "I'm sending you out to replace his Father MacArthur because I sense this is the right thing."

"...I..."

"You came to us late in your life, Father Mick. You've led a...hardy...existence. Not without its share of mistakes. And I've always suspected, what with your war experiences...and your hard Appalachian origins...that you've seen some real pain."

"...Bu..."

The Bishop's expression had cut Mick's words off as surely as if he'd continued to talk. Mick had tried again, unsure of what was going to come out.

"Excellency...uh...."

"You're," the Bishop had continued again undeterred, "you're not the... holiest scholar...I've ever met. But you just might be what the people out there need right now."

"Is there no one else...?" Mick had managed to stammer.

The Bishop evidently hadn't heard the question. "I have seen the many letters that Father MacArthur sent to his Bishop—to my friend Bishop Cole. Father MacArthur was perhaps not right for that parish. I've been told he's sent nothing for a long time now, and Bishop Cole fears it was too much for him."

Mick knew nothing of this Father MacArthur, which wasn't the point anyway. This was all going in the wrong direction. "I'm not ready for a parish, Excellency," he'd pointed out as gracefully as he could. "I'm happy painting walls and mending stairs around here for you. My church-building skills are best served with a hammer."

The Bishop had smiled the smile of a man distracted by his own thoughts. "Many have used cathedrals for sanctuary over the centuries," he'd intoned. "But the Church can never be a sanctuary from ourselves." He'd gazed at the walls around them in a wistful way, then directly at Mick. "And I know you're really not cut out for this big cathedral thing. You belong...out there."

Gravel in the westbound lane brought Mick back to the present, and he shook the recollections off in favor of reliving the road itself. Michigan, Iowa and Minnesota were now respective blurs of traffic, corn, soybeans, and more soybeans. He'd grabbed a nap in the dugout of a little league baseball field outside of Pipestone. He'd taken the Interstate through most of South Dakota. Now he was in its western stretches, mixing good lands with bad.

Within wishing distance of Rapid City he stopped for gas and supplies. He filled the Gerry can too—this was remote country, and he knew all too well what it could mean if he ran out of gas. He walked across the street and back, stretching out a cramp in one hip, then strapped in again to devour more westward road. After staring down 60 miles of Wyoming winds, he limped into Buffalo and found a cheap hotel. As tired as he was, the glorious early autumn Bighorn sunset had to be watched, with breath partly held.

Morning sneaks late into twenty-dollar rooms, he thought as he rose and checked his watch. In a man's late forties, he reflected, bones are octogenarians at first light, in their prime during the day, and ready for retirement as the sun sets. He washed quickly and grabbed a greasy breakfast of biscuits and ham at the diner two doors down, then aimed the truck once more toward Montana.

The difference between a thousand Ponderosa Pines and ten thousand is nine minutes, the average time between tumbling clumps of wind-driven sage nine seconds. He drank in the free air and rolled on. High windy plains rose to plumes of steam and sulfur, then slid headlong into the Yellowstone River.

Open valleys grew smaller, more intermixed with ranges of higher country. One more dusk turned to night. Idaho claimed to lie up ahead somewhere, another hour or two...and the tall, deep green labyrinths of the Kootenai. Short of that, a small exit off the Montana state highway marked Mick's turnoff, and he took the single lane country road up a long alluvial plain to the edge of a town, stopping to read a wind-whipped sign of welcome: "Terradise Valley." The claim-to-fame line added, in smaller weather-worn letters, "Heaven on Earth."

It was past midnight, although it really didn't matter. Streets were deserted. Not surprising, he thought, considering the town's size, which he'd read days before to be about four thousand. It looked to be a highly inflated number. Old-west style boardwalks lined both sides of the main street. A church's spire loomed over an avenue two blocks off the main. Homing in on that, he pulled into the church's parking lot and stepped out, the scraping of his feet against gravel and a distant coyote duet the only two sounds available to hear.

Now what? What was he even doing here?

A glance at the church building revealed a small side door, with a piece of torn paper pinned to it, curling slowly in a single silent breath of breeze. Mick walked over to inspect. Printed over-large in pencil, the note said simply, "House door not locked, bed room left of can. Elmer." At the bottom there was a cryptic afterthought: "Conf 8," which Mick knew didn't refer to any conferences, but rather that he would have to preside over confessions scheduled at eight the next morning. He was out of practice, he thought, although he knew his distaste for the task ran deeper and more personal than that. He turned and saw a tiny house across the small parking lot, with a somewhat dilapidated porch hanging off it leading to a plain wooden door, and decided it must be the priest's residence building.

Leaving all but a small bag in the truck, he lumbered quietly up the creaking porch steps, opened the door, and entered, closing it softly.

Behind him, the streets remained peaceful. Those who walked them by day hadn't seen him arrive, and could not yet know he had been sent to save them.

CHAPTER TWO

Twenty-seven-year-old Gabriella and her small boy sat in the fourteenth church row. The child, between three and four years old, faced backward, lips hooked over the back of the worn wooden bench seat, intently watching two elderly women pray. His young mind knew that a moment ago, one of them had struggled to light a too-short wick at the little bank of flickering indulgence candles against the side wall, and that now she was kneeling some rows behind him, head bowed in reverent silence. He also knew her hat had small feathers in it.

It was a decent showing for a weekday morning; Gabriella and the others gathered in church hadn't attended morning confession for many months, ever since the previous pastor had disappeared and the occasional day-trip fill-ins from parishes in towns to the south had stopped being sent up. A rumor of a new full-time pastor was the reason for the turn-out, although up to now it looked to be a false alarm.

Several of the rag-tag attendees had already departed, leaving a small handful soon to follow suit.

The boy noticed that far behind the feathered hat, the church main door opened quietly, letting in a shard of morning light. A strange man dressed in a black robe tried to squeeze inside quietly, accidentally kicking a low metal trash can, spoiling all chances he'd had for stealth. He was a large man, Angelo noticed, although not a giant. He looked rugged. His face was strong but not mean. His hair was sticking up.

Out of the corner of her eye, Gabriella caught sight of the new priest as he bumbled up the side aisle. He was twenty minutes late. Nodding apologies to people and walls as he shuffled, he couldn't help but strike a comic figure. His black cassock was wrinkled like twice-used aluminum foil. Clearly he'd just awakened. Gabriella stifled a chuckle and pretended to keep her eyes averted.

Mick found the lone two-compartment confessional booth, opened the rickety wooden door of the main compartment, and entered, bumping his knee loudly on the wood once inside. Swallowing a muffled oath, he sat, breathed a sigh of embarrassed relief, and waited. Almost immediately he caught the staccato clack of hard-heeled women's shoes, which began from the front of the church, paused while the wearer bent knee to floor, then grew louder as the noise approached his position. "Slight limp," he thought instinctively. A woman in her sixties peeled back the corner of the side compartment curtain and knelt by the semi-opaque screen to his left. "Bless me,

Father," she began. Mick cleared his throat in dread and waited.

The specifics were typical to the point of being mundane—not that that helped him relax. This woman was no seminary student, no fellow ordained, no deacon candidate versed in the game. This was a real parishioner, found in the wild so to speak. Real world, real lives, and he was supposed to give them what they needed. He choked back an urge to bolt and run.

The woman shared her secrets and he offered what prefabricated guidance he could think of, and she exited. He rolled his eyes at the triteness of his own words. But one down; maybe he could get through this without hearing serious problems calling for wise solutions.

Two more came and went; Mick tried to get away with more listening than speaking, hoping it would provide what they came for and still help contain his ineptness for this stuff.

A full ten minutes passed, and then he could tell by the shadowy profile that the side booth was occupied again. A young woman this time. He waited but heard nothing. Peering out through a crack in the door frame, Mick confirmed that the small boy was sitting alone, swinging his dangling feet on the bench seat. This must be the dark-haired young mother that had not looked up as he'd entered the church.

A soft voice found its way through the screen. "Bless me, Father. I would like to confess my sins."

"Of course," he mumbled, his airborne hand moving as taught years before. "Would you tell me how long it's been since your last confession?" There was something a little mysterious, almost alluring, about the voice, and the long pauses that hung from it.

"I have not always been patient with my son, and I would like to show more tolerance."

He noticed she'd moved past his question, going straight to the point, almost as if to get the thing over with. With the others it was a sentiment he'd have shared, but he felt a subliminal urge to get this one right. He thought about his first answer and tried the obvious. "Patience is something we could all nurture more of. If you know your child is a good boy, and should have a good patient example, if you know he deserves...courtesy, then I'd suggest you don't think of this as a sin. Your heart is in the right place. Just give him the example he needs, on average. I'm sure you're a fine parent."

"I would also like to be more kind in my thoughts," she forged on, again seemingly intent on rapid progress...and yet not saying much. "I am sometimes harsh in my judgments."

"Well, that's the other one we all struggle with. Again, I'd say just do your best." By now he knew she was stalling, and he didn't rush to assign a handful of prayers to ice a garden-grade absolution. He awaited the real reason she'd come here.

"I..." there was a long pause, "...hate."

Mick sat back from the screen. Not something one expects on one's first morning in paradise. But he had to say something. He took a deep breath, making sure it could serve as an audible alibi until he could

14

think of some reply. "Hmmm, that's...pretty strong," he tried, stalling. "We all know hate is never an answer. Doesn't solve anything—never did. We must never let ourselves sink into the pit. I know it's often tempting. And it sure seems at times like a situation might call for it. But...would you like to talk about whatever it is that pushes your emotions so far?"

"In my dreams I punish...the deserving...and I use my hate. I feed it, in those dreams, and out. It's enough to admit it; a priest would not understand."

"Why not?" This was almost conversational. He could do this. Just speak from experience. No, he thought...not that.

"Do you know what it feels like to unleash evil?" she asked in challenge. She waited, but Mick was staring into a deep space in his memory. The woman sensed his distance and brought him back. "Even in dreams? I think you do not. So then there's no need to discuss this. It's enough that I confess."

Mick cleared his throat. "I...think hate mostly begins with fear."

She allowed a long silence, perhaps to consider what he'd said. But then she changed the subject again abruptly. "I will try to be more worthy, if God will give me the strength."

"Worthy...how?"

Gabriella hesitated, then replied simply, "This he knows, and if I am to be tested then it's my place only to try harder, to find a way."

She left the confessional so silently he wasn't sure she'd gone. Intrigued, almost alarmed, Mick tried to see again through the thin gap in the door frame, but another sound beyond the screen interrupted him, and a voice like the tomb rattled him back to a seated posture. It was the woman who'd confessed first, the one with the slight limp, back again. This time instead of sharing personal flaws, she was offering to bake him a pie.

"...and I grow my own peaches, I canned so many of them this summer you wouldn't believe, Father, not many can do it, they're small but oh they make the best pies, I've been making pies all my life, my mother made them too, that's where I learned, she died years ago, I believe it was 1949...."

Mick nodded, forgetting that she could see his silhouette leaning forward as he peered again out through the door frame. The bench the young mother and child had occupied was empty.

"...and I thought you might like one Father, and I could bake you two if you really think that would be better, and..."

"That sounds, uh, sinfully tasty! Uh, so for your penance...ahhh...one pie! And then I think I'll have to do some jogging penance of my own." The woman twittered, delighted, and went on to recite the recipe. Mid-litany, Mick extricated himself with hurried grace from the booth, and strode back to the main church door. He caught up with the young mother as she was descending the front steps and cautiously tapped her on the shoulder.

"Thank you for coming today," he said, extending his hand. "I'm Father Calahan, Mick Calahan, the, uh, new pastor. Just got in late last night. Sorry for this morning's tardiness...it was a long drive from the eastern seaboard."

Gabriella extended her hand enough to shake the tip of Mick's fingers. "Welcome to our town Father Calahan," she said civilly. "Gabriella Cielo...and this is Angelo, who is normally braver than this." She indicated the boy hiding shyly and silently behind her.

Mick nodded, smiling to the child, who retreated further behind his mother's leg. "Cielo..." he mused, unsure why he wanted to keep the conversation from ending. It was probably only concern ignited by her troubling confession. "Is that...are you of a Latino family?"

"My mother was of native blood—tribal blood—and grew up in this area," she said off-handedly. "My father was Mexican. And my married name is also Mexican." The latter was a warning, Mick recognized—an automatic if somewhat vague 'husband reference,' instinctively used by women when talking to men. That it was used on him, a priest, was actually a compliment of sorts, and he nearly smiled to himself.

Gabriella began to turn away, helping Angelo down the steps. Mick smoothed the conversation's end. "Yes, I was going to guess Mexican, but...well, guessing can get one in trouble. Anyway it was nice meeting you, Mrs. Cielo." He flashed his most priestly smile.

"For us as well. We hope you enjoy the country air...while you're here." There again, thought Mick, a comment mildly curious. Out of place. He let it be.

Gabriella nodded an impersonal farewell, and walked down the sidewalk holding her child's hand. Thumb in mouth, the boy stole a long glance back at the priest, his expression somewhere between afraid and unafraid. For an instant Mick imagined he saw a request in the child's eyes.

The few remaining parishioners, along with the pie woman, had gone. Mick re-entered the now-empty church and walked back up the aisle. At the bench where Gabriella and Angelo had sat, he stopped to retrieve a small toy Jeep that had rolled under the seat, smiling as he realized how closely it resembled his old Landcruiser. He pocketed the trinket and walked to the side door, looking around himself doubtfully in the unfamiliar church, stopping for a long while at the bank of indulgence candles to watch them flicker, as he had always done in the past.

CHAPTER THREE

Changing the wrinkled cassock for a pair of jeans and a faded sweatshirt, Mick ignored the unpacking of his truck in favor of embarking on a first walk through the town. Redemption Catholic Church—what he supposed he should be trying to think of as 'his' church—was two full blocks off the main street, but was otherwise set close enough to daily activity, such as it was. A survivor by nature, he took instinctive note of practical basics first—community features that, he told himself, could be as useful to him in the short term as they were to residents who actually intended to live here.

He noted a gasoline station at the beginning of the small business district, with a single service bay around which a half-dozen ailing or expired junkers reclined. Car bodies appeared to last just short of forever in this clean air and on these salt-free roads, he observed, despite what was surely a reasonable supply of rain and snow; some of the machines still expecting to be repaired had outlasted the companies who'd once made parts for them. Half an original Indian motorcycle, leaning against a cedar fence post on one side, bore ignoble testimony.

On a side street partway up the main thoroughfare stood a barber shop, single chair empty as he walked past. On the primary street and further up yet, he found a tiny hardware store that looked through its single window to be filled to near bursting with dusty shelves, obscure parts, hand tools, and small boxes that hadn't moved in decades. Behind the building were larger items no doubt considered necessities to a rural community, including rolls of fencing spanning various mesh sizes, stacks of metal and cedar posts, pipe, and a few oval galvanized troughs. Two doors from the hardware store, a grain and feed store offered similar items from its own back yard, although it stocked more and larger troughs, plus grain hoppers and other equipment, much of which by the height of the weeds had sat unmoved for some time. The front of the feed store implied it carried rope of various kinds, and tack such as saddles, bridles, and halters for equestrian use.

A mom-and-pop grocery store and what was probably passed off as a historic main street hotel enjoyed more central positions, as did two diners, several small clothing shops, and other assorted establishments. An abandoned realty office with a faded window sign had obviously been closed down for a long time. Mick thought it interesting that the store space had never been reclaimed for other use; evidently there were not many visitors and little if any growth.

There were buildings here and there seemingly used for nothing, and slat fences and storage sheds mixed in occasionally with the storefronts. Wooden exterior walls were weathered; many had never been painted, their natural cedar color adding to the visual flavor of the town. A dingy saloon displaying the faded, unhinged name "Inferno" sat balefully across from the small market. Another, more rundown and evidently without need of a name, sat a block off the main street at the town's far edge and looked to be permanently locked. A tiny sheriff's office was situated a block from the gas station. The post office adjoined the hardware store.

A small town hall, with a sign reading "Mayor" hanging askance by a single nail, seemed to be closed for renovation. The carpenter in Mick knew there had been no work done on the building in a long time.

Fronting all the centrally situated shops was a covered wooden boardwalk, reminiscent of the Old West and of towns trying hard to recapture that image. Vehicles were few and travelled slowly on the main street, angle-parking if they stopped. Pedestrians, what there were of them, moved at a somewhat more purposeful pace than did vehicles, getting straight to what business they had and disappearing. Some were town residents, others from ranches sprinkled throughout the valley, coming into town for parts or supplies. Yelling, honking of horns, and general over-exuberance were not part of the picture. "Peaceful; quaint beauty; fresh air; big sky," Mick decided he would tell them back east, when he told them.

He walked up the side of the street that received the morning sun, feeling like a tourist. What was he supposed to do here? For what reason had he been sent? He'd been bundled off with just enough advance notice to pack his things, and nothing was ever very clearly spelled out. "Just go and be of service," his superior had instructed. Men with so little experience in parish work were never sent alone to any town, much less to a remote place like this, where he didn't know the culture and would have no support. What was so important about this assignment? Was he simply being gotten rid of? Was it some sort of strange test?

Near the market he looked across the street and spied two Caucasian men loitering in front of the Inferno saloon. They leaned against the overhang's wooden upright, carelessly cradling bottles in their hands, watching him. He nodded in their direction; they continued to stare but returned no acknowledgment. One of them leaned back toward the open saloon doorway and murmured something inside, without taking his eyes off Mick. Within the dark interior Mick could only make out the orange flare of a cigarette.

Further on, he stopped for a moment to watch a large bird soaring overhead, gaining altitude slowly in a column of rising air. He smiled. It was a majestic creature—it looked like a Northern Goshawk, a species Mick knew he'd never seen back East. He admired the fluid expertise with which the falcon worked the light lift.

Bringing his eyes back to earth, he noticed a thin, dark-skinned man, evidently a member of the local indigenous tribal population, ambling toward him up the boardwalk, staring at him as the distance closed. He'd have to get used to this, to being the conspicuous outsider, to drawing wordless stares. The thin man eventually dropped his gaze, and before passing the priest turned quickly down a gap between two buildings, raising his eyes for one more extended look at the stranger before disappearing.

After several hours of aimless wandering, navigating partly by the church steeple and partly by the high ridge behind the town, Mick made his way successfully back to the priest's residence. The afternoon had given way to early evening, bringing a small but noticeable drop in temperature the moment the sun dipped behind the 200-foot Ponderosa Pines that lined the mountain ridge. Lights leaked from inside the house; creaky porch boards gave away his approach.

Barely mastering the sticky latch and shouldering open the door, he saw a large old man in his sixties, his back to the entrance, wielding a broom on the far edge of the living room. The man was taller than Mick, and as broad. He wore faded denim overalls over a shirt of thermal underwear. What was left of his hair was grey-white, and disheveled. A loud regular thumping almost sounded as though he was using a bare stick instead of a broom.

Mick approached, cleared his throat to announce his presence, and extended his hand. "You must be Elmer, the man behind the note."

The man turned to face him, and Mick realized the thumping sound came from a wooden leg made of a long, straight, rough plank, covered by the overalls except at the bottom.

"And you must be the bastard who tracked mud all through this house."

Elmer's scowl caused Mick to retract his hand awkwardly. "Did I? I'm sorry, it was dark and...here, allow me." He reached for the broom but the old man turned away and continued the chore himself.

"Well I'm happy to undo what I've done," the priest offered. "Didn't mean to make any work."

Elmer snorted. "Who d'ye think keeps this place livable? And that church too? It ain't elves, and it ain't the damn redskins, that I kin tell you."

Mick changed the subject. "I'd have said hello this morning, but...well, didn't want to wake anyone. I suppose I could have taken a peek in your room...maybe I wasn't sure who I'd be peeking at."

Elmer continued to sweep the corner and did not reply.

"You probably get peeked at too much anyway," Mick added, venturing a bit of levity.

Still no answer. The old man jabbed the broom under a chair and drew it out.

The priest tried a different approach. "Look," he offered, "I didn't mean to get on your wrong side. Last thing I want. I'm pretty much un-briefed here. I was sent out with almost no instructions at all. I didn't even know there would be a housekeeper, or a house for that matter."

Elmer paused the broom to peer silently and critically at Mick, then turned back to his work.

"Well, anyway, good to meet you Elmer. I'm sure I'll get the hang of how you do things around here. If I booger something up, don't be afraid to let me have it. I'll carry my load."

"Had my fill of Easterners." As cantankerous as it was, it was at least an opening.

"I'll try to be more Western. Maybe...learn to spit."

But the caretaker seemed immune to humor. He grumbled himself off to a back room, whisking the broom here along the base boards and there across the worn rug as he went. "Damn city folk, whites, outsiders, injuns...." Mick heard him muttering his litany of dislikes until long after the words were no longer discernable.

It had been an eye-opener of a day, the priest admitted with a sigh. He thought back to how it had begun—a troubled young mother simultaneously crying for connection and avoiding it. Then he'd explored a community he knew nothing about that seemed to half-resemble a ghost town. He was also running an abandoned parish with no idea what it was supposed to need, what to do, or how to go about it. Finally, his caretaker hated him and all who rode in like him.

At least there was the peach pie, due any day.

He shuffled into the kitchen, hoping to find something with which to make a sandwich, and was shocked to discover on the table a dainty dinner already set out for him, complete with the full array of polished utensils lined up on a clean linen napkin according to proper rules of etiquette. A tall candle and an elegant goblet of sparkling water stood back from the plate. He smiled and sat down.

After dinner, to avoid the wrath of the old man he made sure to wash the plate and fork, then retired to his room—a small chamber with a too-short but reasonably firm bed, a stack of faded wool blankets, a single well-flattened feather pillow, a closet he didn't bother to open yet, a chest of drawers with one stunted leg that had seen some years of wear, a window with thick curtains that faced east, a ceiling-mounted light with a wisp of cobweb clinging to it, a wooden chair, and on a tiny wobbly table, a little lamp partly made of deer antlers next to a black rotary phone. A large faded circular rug covered the lion's share of the wooden floor, leaving the floor's corners and edges exposed.

The long drive west had finally caught up with him. Recalling an early Mass scheduled for the next day, he tossed his clothing onto the chair, drew the curtains together, doubled the blankets, and sank into an exhausted sleep, with nothing but uncertainties flowing through his dreams.

*   *   *

Early next morning he awoke with a jolt, fearing that once again he'd overslept. He grabbed his wrist watch and held it up to catch a thin seam of light sliding into the room between the curtain halves. Seven and change—could be worse. Rubbing his eyes, he sat up, recalling the look of the room. He stretched and almost threw back the blankets until he noticed that while he'd slept, Elmer had evidently been in the room and had laid out a set of formal priest's vestments on the corner of the bed.

He slid out from beneath the covers and found the bathroom in the hall outside. There was no shower, only a basin and free-standing tub. In the interest of time he washed hurriedly with a cloth, shaved, and returned to his room to put on the items Elmer had prepared. He could barely button them. Father MacArthur had clearly been a short and slightly built man.

Mick slipped outside onto the porch, intent on the church's side door, and was surprised to find his small array of bags and other belongings stacked on the porch deck. Elmer was bringing the last heavy carton from the Landcruiser. The long bagged item that had been tied to the top was already lying against the side of the house; how the tough old man had done it with a wooden leg was a mystery.

Mick strode toward the church, clapping Elmer on the shoulder in thanks as they passed each other.

"I know what that damned long lunatic thing is," Elmer called over his shoulder. Mick smiled.

The church was nearly empty. Only four old parishioners were inside, mostly in the back. They sat or knelt anonymously and Mick went through the standard progression as he'd done countless times before. Admittedly this was only a weekday, he thought, but the sparse attendance was a relief. Not much different from the solo services a junior priest working in a diocese office holds every day; a little one-man chapel with no audience was what he was accustomed to.

He finished the Mass in well under an hour. Unprepared, he'd dispensed apologetically with a sermon and stayed behind the altar, partly because sermons were not common on weekdays anyway, partly because of the tiny and inattentive attendance, and partly because the clothing Elmer had rustled up for him barely hung down past his knees. He was painfully aware that his bare ankles, black socks, and sneakers were visible below. Not the most dignified entrance to be making here, he thought. Well, when a little of his own stuff was unpacked he could remedy some of the problem, and for the rest he'd simply have to find someone who could wield a needle and thread...or maybe just live with the situation. It wasn't as though he'd be here very long.

The service ended normally with Mick exiting to the back room sacristy. He removed the primary vestments and dutifully made his way out to the front steps, resigned to play the obligatory role of gracious host. The four attendees were less inclined. Mick made a half-hearted attempt to greet each as they left, but one by one they slipped out spending as few nods and smiles as four people could. By the time the last one darted past he'd stopped trying.

He shuffled back to the house, neither tired nor hungry, and certainly not inspired. What in God's name was he doing here? These people didn't need an outsider like him. What could he possibly offer a place like this? The main thing was, he reminded himself, it would be irresponsible for a man like him to get involved.

He closed the door behind himself and paused to lean against it once inside. Elmer had brought his suitcases in and had left them at the top of the short hall. He glanced at them wistfully. They were still packed. He could reverse this whole bad idea.

The house was quiet; Elmer was out. Mick took a short nap; since he'd driven out to this state instead of flown, he was getting in sync with the local time zone quickly, but the extra sleep still helped. He got up again an hour later, revived himself with a quick bath, and made a sandwich with some bread and cheese he found in the kitchen. He fished a fresh shirt out of his luggage, taking care to leave the bulk of his clothing folded in the bag. His cheap camera fell out a side pouch and he stuffed it into his jacket pocket, tossing the jacket on the bed. Then for want of a better plan, he set out for another stroll through the town.

The outing started as a carbon copy of the previous day. The few locals he saw went about errands reservedly and quickly. Other than the men who drank inside it and then loitered at its door, there seemed never to be anyone along the stretch near the Inferno saloon. He found himself opting to take a side street instead, unsure why. Maybe the place just felt strange. Maybe, he mused ironically, he was simply becoming a local.

The barber shop door was ajar; on a whim he stepped in. A completely bald man standing less than five feet tall stood on a small box trimming another man's hair. The barber noticed Mick in the wall-mounted mirror and inclined his head without turning or locking eyes. "Trim sir?" he asked a little stiffly.

"Anyway I was just sayin' to you Marv," the patron in the barber's chair addressed the short man, "that there Mr. Knox is a leader we all admire, and that's a fact." He said it a little like every ear should hear it.

The barber cleared his throat and nodded, trying not to be caught studying Mick in the mirror, then repeated his question in a small voice: "Trim sir?"

"No thanks," Mick replied with a smile, "just wanted to meet you and introduce myself. Mick Calahan...the, uh, Catholic church...new pastor...uh, temporary...new pastor." He gestured with one thumb up the street in the general direction of the church. "Guessing you're Marv, then, and...?" He held out his hand.

The two men froze with mouths agape, until Marv released a held breath, stepped off the box, stuffed the scissors under his arm to free up a hand, and shook Mick's. The patron in the chair nodded with a weak smile into the mirror.

"Well, don't let me interrupt your conversation about your friend Mr., uh...who was it?"

"No, we wasn't...nothing, just...seems cooler than...yesterday...." Both barber and patron cleared their throats and fell silent, until there seemed little else for Mick to do but nod and back out the door.

He crossed back to the main street and more out of boredom than anything else stopped at the small grocery store, picking out a couple of pears and a bag of cookies and taking them to the counter, where he stepped behind a dark-haired woman in her thirties carrying a full basket of food and other necessities. The proprietor, an older woman with white hair, was just beginning to tally the items. A short, lean Caucasian man sauntered in through the door, stepped in front of the dark-haired woman and grabbed a carton of cigarettes. He cast a confrontational stare at her, Mick, and the proprietor, then reached across and took another carton, and without paying strolled lazily out and across the street with the boxes tucked under his arm. Mick knew enough to say nothing, noticing that no one else commented either.

He returned to the priest's residence in early evening. Hearing Elmer making a small commotion with a skillet and lid, he stepped down the hall to wash his hands before heading for the kitchen. But Elmer had evidently finished by then and stepped out. Mick saw a simpler but equally appreciated meal set out for him—chicken in some kind of aromatic sauce, steamed carrots, and what must surely be baked Idaho potatoes—and he dug in.

Later he sat for an hour looking at the walls, feeling like a man exiled. He hadn't even brought anything much to read; he'd assumed there would be people here with whom he could talk—with whom he could interact.

He decided to seek a solution. Grabbing the phone in his room, he sat on the corner of the bed, ran the zero full-circle around the rotary dial, waited for the operator, and gave her the long-distance number. "Yes, I mean no, it's Boston, not New York City," he acknowledged to her. He waited, rehearsing how he'd say it. Surely the Bishop would see sense, after hearing how disconnected—how undefined—the situation was.

But a woman's voice answered. "Archdiocese office," she twanged with the nasal tone Mick hadn't heard since he'd left the East Coast.

"Could I speak with Archbishop Truello please?"

"His Excellency is not in would you care to leave a messagggge?" she asked as if reading, elongating and stringing the words together without punctuation or pause.

"You're with the night answering service?"

"Yes sir would you like to leave a messaggggge?"

"I see. Yes...I'd forgotten about the time difference."

"It's 1:20am sir," she confirmed.

"Yes I'm sorry. Well could I leave you a message to pass on to the Archbishop?"

"What is your messagggge?" The nasal pitch made it difficult to know whether she was asking a question or attempting to sing.

He persevered. "Yes, okay, please tell him Father Mick Calahan has called again...I called from the road a few days ago...I've made it all the way now, but...tell him...tell him I said this might be a mistake..."

"...And His Excellency will know what you're referring to?"

"Yes, he'll know what I'm referring to...tell him I think it may be a mistake, and that I think maybe I should return to speak with him and...help him find someone else. And...uh..."

Mick trailed off, uncertain whether to add some other comment. Suddenly he drew the receiver from his ear and stared at it. A dial tone droned its relentless hopelessness into the air. Either the line had gone dead or she'd felt the message was long enough.

He hung the receiver back on the phone and set it quietly on the night stand. He sat in silence, looking awkwardly at his hands, then at the phone, trying to think of what to do now.

CHAPTER FOUR

Morning arrived the way the last one had, despite the fact that Mick had pulled the curtains together more tightly. He rose and shut out the thin seam of light, then dressed and walked to the church to preside over the morning Mass, certain that he was looking at the same four attendees he'd seen the morning before.

Service over and eager to put corrective action in motion, he dispensed with the charade of greetings at the front steps and hurried back to the house, where he changed into jeans and a T-shirt, shaved, and hopped into his truck. Now that Elmer had emptied it, he could begin to see to some arrangements.

Instinctively taking side streets even though there was no one from whom to hide his intentions, he arrived at the garage at the far end of the main street. The same collection of old vehicles he'd seen before crowded the building on all sides. A single gasoline pump island stood in front, with a middle-aged woman—probably the mechanic's wife—walking out to operate the pump whenever a motorist came to fill up.

Mick stopped the Landcruiser in the gravel to the side of the limited paved area, got out, nodded to the woman, and waited until she signaled the mechanic, who stepped out to meet him. The man had been up to his elbows in a reservoir of old motor oil when Mick had pulled up, and now was wiping a rag over his arms only enough to keep from dripping oil as he walked. He was small and spry, wore greasy overalls, and carried a crescent wrench, still coated in thick dark liquid.

Mick extended his hand. "Hi. Mick Calahan."

The mechanic, still wiping his dirty hands on the rag, looked quizzically at Mick's extended hand, then up at the priest's face. Chuckling, Mick withdrew his hand and put it into his own pocket.

He inclined his head toward the Landcruiser. "Could you give this thing a good checkout? It's a heap, but maybe you could get it ready for a long drive?"

The mechanic peered at the Landcruiser with squinted eyes, then nodded.

"Sign says 'Hawkins.' That you?"

Nod.

"Well, I guess engine, brakes, water pump, the major stuff. Look it over please. Um...charging properly...take a look at the compression if you would...I'd hate to blow a head gasket out on the prairie. One thing I can tell you, the clutch has been feeling...well, loose."

Again Hawkins nodded silently, squinting. Mick held out the keys and the mechanic accepted them with a soundless smile, moving with small-man agility to the truck's cab. He gave his smeared arms one more wipe, then spiked the oily rag onto the gravel and hopped into the driver's seat. He moved the truck directly to the front of the repair bay.

Mick decided to wait a few minutes in case there were any initial questions, and sighed in satisfaction, glad to be taking some kind of sensible action. He'd write and let the Bishop know he was ready to start the long trip back as soon as he was given the word. As crazy as two back-to-back week-long drives seemed, everything else made even less sense.

The low morning sun warmed his shoulders. He walked out to the sidewalk, gazed up the main street, and smiled. The scene was truly quaint, he admitted—the kind of town people might visit on vacation. He chuckled to think that someday he too might return to a place like this as a tourist. It would be different if he'd not been sent—if he'd not been handed an undefined job interwoven with real peoples' lives. It spoiled—he spoiled—the rustic charm. There are better men to send on such missions, he thought.

Putting his hands in his jacket pockets, he felt the small camera he'd stuffed there the day before, and on an impulse drew it out. Sighting through the viewfinder, he panned left and right, trying to get as much as he could into a shot. The single focal length lens didn't afford many options. He snapped one pointed straight up the sidewalk, then took two steps back and aimed again, trying to frame one angled slightly to the far side.

Something caught his eye in the viewfinder, and he paused to watch. It was a couple of blocks away, and hard to tell, but...it almost looked like a scuffle of some kind. Two small figures—maybe kids?—were lying near the center of the pavement. Mick pulled the camera from his eyes and peered up-street, shielding out the low rays of the sun. Had the kids been fighting? Was that someone taller in the gap between that building and that fence? Was it a parent disciplining children?

He heard Hawkins approaching him from behind, and turned to see the mechanic had brought a clipboard and pen. Mick peered up-street again, then glanced back at Hawkins, half looking for an explanation.

"First rule o' gettin' involved in this town is don't," the greasy little man advised him, breaking silence for the first time.

Mick turned his back to the confusion up-street and took the clipboard, glancing quickly over the blank form, which had the single phrase "check truck" scrawled on the top line. He started to reach for the pen in the mechanic's hand, thinking to add his name at least to the top of the form.

But he couldn't shake the idea that something was wrong. He turned and glanced again over his shoulder. The two small figures were still lying in the road. He looked at Hawkins, then handed the clipboard back to him and began to walk slowly, then more briskly, finally breaking into a quick jog up the street.

It was a distance of about three blocks, and Mick arrived still at a loss as to what had occurred. He found two tribal boys about eight years old sprawled on the pavement. One—the taller one—made a weak sound and moved his leg; the other was breathing but lay still. Mick approached them immediately.

"You boys okay? Are you hurt? What happened?" There was no sign of major blood or visible wounds other than a badly bleeding knee beneath the taller child's torn trouser leg.

He tried again. "Can you boys hear me?"

Neither boy opened his eyes or spoke, and after taking cursory note that the taller one had no obvious arm or leg breaks, Mick moved quickly to the one who wasn't stirring, fearing the child's fall to the pavement more than whatever had made him fall.

A noise above and to the side of the street caused him to glance up. He noticed an elderly tribal woman peering at him through a bedroom window. He tried to signal to her, but she moved behind a flimsy curtain and stood motionless. He called out, first to her, then to anyone within earshot. "Do you know these boys? Can you help me please? Can...can anyone help? Can someone call a doctor? We need a doctor, there are injured children here!"

No one answered or came. More than a minute passed. The smaller boy began to stir. The other one opened his eyes for just a moment.

Two white men walked idly out from the far side of the closest building. Still kneeling over the younger boy, Mick turned to face the two men. "What happened here?" he called in an increasingly urgent tone. "Did either of you see what happened here?"

"Those boys was there when we come along," one of the men replied. His unconcerned manner caught Mick off-guard.

"Probably tripped over their loincloths," the other man added.

"What? What did you...?" Their responses were unexpected, and Mick was torn between confusion and anger. He stood and called out to the woman still behind the curtain. "Did you...did anyone... see what happened to these boys? Is someone calling a doctor?!"

The woman disappeared completely from view. Mick watched the window and the ground-floor door of the house for a moment, hoping she might reappear, then turned back to see that the two men had also left.

Kneeling again, he tried to inspect the children. They were both crying softly now, which he knew was a good sign. Glancing over bloody abrasions, he looked more carefully for broken bones. He found none. He checked the backs of their heads and considered how he was going to keep them immobile and still fetch a doctor. He decided he was going to have to move them carefully to the side of the street. He lifted the smaller one and turned. A middle-aged tribal man was standing in front of him.

"Is this your...?" Mick began, but there was no reply. The man took the child from him quickly and walked across a small dusty front yard and out of sight. While he was doing so, a younger Indian man and woman had appeared also out of nowhere and were similarly removing the other child from the street, half-carrying, half-dragging him. None of them said a word.

Assuming these must be family members or neighbors of the injured kids, Mick tried to follow. "Can I help? Are they hurt? I don't know what happened, I was too far away to see. Can I...?"

They looked at him with a mixture of suspicion and surprise, and their reaction stopped him in mid-stride. He stood helplessly as they quickly left, never taking their eyes off him. In a few moments he was standing alone in the street.

Unsure what had transpired, he eventually returned to Hawkins and finished filling out the form, aware that the mechanic was quietly studying his face. He added a written mention of the clutch inspection, to make sure it wouldn't be overlooked. The sooner he was ready to leave this place behind, the easier he'd breathe. He walked home, again unclear why he was giving the Inferno saloon a wide berth.

CHAPTER FIVE

Three days passed. Mick heard nothing about the children, despite his several inquiries. He'd revisited the street where the incident had occurred, but no one was ever there, and no one answered his knocks at the door where he'd seen the woman in the window. He had found no evidence of a town doctor yet either, and had to assume there was none, and that residents were compelled to make the drive to a larger community for pharmaceuticals or medical attention. He'd visited the sheriff's office twice but could never find the lawman in. And Elmer, who he'd hoped could be a sounding board for some of these questions, was an ubiquitous but unseen ghost of beautifully prepared meals and folded towels.

The Landcruiser check-out was still unfinished, although Hawkins had assured him it was now mostly just a matter of replacing some leaky ignition wires and topping off brake fluid, and that it would probably be done by week's end. Aside from the one bit of cautionary advice Hawkins had given him when they'd first met, the mechanic was a seemingly observant man of almost no words.

Mick had heard nothing from back east as yet either. He'd also made no friends here as far as he could tell—not that there would be any point in it. There were the morning Mass rituals, the unwelcome restless dreams replaying answerless questions, the uncertain near-term plans, and the daily undercurrent evidence of a town in strange and constant tension.

*   *   *

Saturday arrived on its own. Clouds covered the valley long before sunrise. Two figures moved quickly, quietly, and efficiently up the main street, making occasional forays a little way down side streets as they drifted from point to point. They were Washokki high school students; one carried an armload of hand-made posters, the other a staple gun. They moved as though their route was pre-planned, affixing posters to building corners and poles, lingering only momentarily at each point, always looking over their shoulders before making the jump to the next spot. They did not pass in front of the Inferno. By the time there was sufficient light for someone to identify them they had disappeared up a side street on the east end of town.

By mid-morning a light breeze had set up, but then subsided as the weak front moved past. Stretching, Joel and Thad stepped from the Inferno saloon out onto the boardwalk. Thad lead the way.

Short and slightly built, he had always felt like a somewhat unlikely bad-ass, yet a bad-ass he knew was his calling. Since even before the Central American days, a thinning scalp necessitated the longer individual hairs through which he now ran his fingers. He rubbed the thick web-like flaps of flabby skin that cruel fate had substituted on his head in place of earlobes. He'd spent most of the night drinking in the Inferno and the rest of it passed out across the worn, splitting vinyl cushions of a maroon-colored booth, despite there being a room in back with cots that he and his associates could use. Having been awakened by a shard of light slicing through the black window paint and chancing to impale his face, he'd dragged himself back to the bar and begun the day with beer.

Thad knew his paymaster Lucius Knox frowned upon abject drunkenness. After all, any given day there may be work to do. A short man in Thad's line of work had to be sharp—a professional, an intellectual. No, like he decided most days, lest he blow this sweet gig, a shot of Kentucky Straight would have to wait. Until mid-morning, anyway, a beer would do.

Now he and Joel strolled lazily into the street, looking for nothing in particular. A handful of tribals were gathered by a utility pole half a block up-street, and Thad stared, hoping they would notice him doing so. They did not, and Joel grinned at him as the two approached the group from behind to have an idle look at what was on the pole.

Like a malevolent shadow a taller man wearing a holster appeared from nowhere. A two-way radio protruded from where he'd carelessly stuffed it into his hip pocket. He stood a handful of steps further back and stopped to light a cigarette, cold eyes absorbing the scene. "What the fuck is that," he finally muttered, not even bothering to make it sound like a question.

Thad whirled around. "Daryl! Uh...some damn poster. Never seen it afore. We're on it though!" He turned back to peer over the heads of the tribals, who were now aware of the whites' presence and were one by one already trying to disperse casually without being personally called out.

Joel read slowly, while Thad, agape, mouthed the words. "Tribal Unification Day. A...celebration...of the joining of the Washokki and Tissoma tribes."

"Unification!" Thad tossed the word over his shoulder in Daryl's direction. "More like Unifornication."

Joel laughed over-loud at that. He pointed to one of several photos glued to the poster. "Lookit that old fart there. Must be a hunnert. And bakin' in the sun most of it too, I'd say."

Thad suddenly spat in dramatic, intellectual disgust. "I don't remember nobody issuing no permit for this shit." Stepping forward through the tribe members and grabbing it near the top staple, he tore the poster down and tossed it in the street, glaring authoritatively at those he'd shoved aside. The poster spun like a Jack of Clubs and came to rest face-up on the pavement.

Daryl, expressionless, expelled smoke from flared nostrils and regarded the gathering, including Thad.

Joel spoke to the air around them all. "You know, Thad? I feel like declarin' a day myself. I guess anyone can declare a day. I feel like makin' today a...uh...'Buffalo Hunt' day!"

"Now that's a good idea Joel," Thad rejoined, eyes lighting up. "That is a good one. I don't believe we've had one o' them fer...."

"Couple o' weeks!"

"Not since the last big herds!" Thad cackled and took another gulp of his warming beer.

"How shall this day be marked?" Joel asked dramatically. "How does one best celebrate a Buffalo Hunt day?"

"Well...first...." Thad purposefully avoided glancing in Daryl's direction while he sought a response that would differentiate him. He could see the tribal scum was beginning to drift away, and that didn't look very respectful. And he knew the answer was division and disruption. "First we gotta give the white people of this town the day off. Honor this day properly. All these doors gotta close!" Thad indicated the shops lining the main street.

"Well now that goes without sayin' o'course," Joel agreed again. "You're a genius Thad, you'll be mayor soon, I know it! That is if ol' Lucius don't get his spooky ass in gear and pump us some money outa that damn mine."

Thad spat again, then finished off his beer. "Long as he pays me, I already got a job." He turned toward the feed store near which they stood, and to the middle-aged man who had been sweeping the boardwalk in front of its door. "Hey, you there, business is closed for the day!"

"I was...just...cleaning...."

"What?" Thad asked aggressively, taking two menacing steps toward the man. "Did you hear me? Then whyn't you jump?"

The man scrambled quickly into the shop and closed and locked the door, the sound of the thrown deadbolt echoing like a rifle shot to the street's far side and back.

Daryl continued to watch the pageant, having barely moved since he'd appeared. He now heard footsteps on the boardwalk behind him and turned to see Mick, out for his morning stroll, this particular day uncharacteristically still in his black cassock.

Their gazes met briefly, but Mick, as yet unaware of the power of the other man's presence, disengaged in favor of first scanning the overall scene. Daryl held his stare longer, the remains of the cigarette still curling smoke from his left hand.

Thad felt certain he was on a roll. He and Joel began to move back down the street, looking for businesses to close. They passed the saloon again, where Joel stuck his head inside. "Who wants to have some fun?" he called. Raam, a hooked-nose hot-head in his mid-forties with more passion for confrontation than he had brains, scrambled out, unbriefed but game. Mister cigarette cartons, Mick thought to himself. Raam was followed by the fleshy Ofstedder. The four wandered along both boardwalks in high spirits, ordering all shops not in the business of hunting buffalo to observe the holiday by closing business immediately. Store patrons were ejected without explanation. They milled about in confusion on the boardwalks trying to figure out what had happened. The shop doors were locked quickly behind them. Faces of proprietors flashed briefly into view from store windows but vanished as quickly as they had appeared.

Four Washokki men expelled from the hardware store stepped off the boardwalk into the street and began to whisper inaudibly to each other, pointing to the poster lying in the gutter. Their voices rose until caution began to ebb. Mostly they spoke in the unique hybrid Nakota-Kalispell dialect of the region, but at one point the English phrase "white bastards" echoed up and down the sidewalk, as if deliberately turned loose. They became quiet again immediately and shuffled slowly toward the nearest side street.

Two Caucasian women stood bewildered a few feet from Mick, lamenting more quietly and with more caution.

"Now how am I going to get my errands done?" one bemoaned softly. "Everything closed, and nobody's going to have the nerve to open up later on, you know that. And tomorrow's Sunday. We've got things to do! I've got children and my husband has dogs. What am I going to feed them the next two days? Dried turnips?"

"It's their fault," the other whispered sternly, nodding toward the disappearing group of four Washokki men and implying the tribes in general. "They're always stirrin' up some kind of trouble. They must have done somethin' or none of this would've happened. Always somethin'."

Blame was being assigned at random up and down the boardwalk. The tribes and whites each avoided confronting each other overtly, but sentiments were clear. It resembled great wars fought over the centuries, Mick thought, after which the downtrodden invariably accused those equally unfortunate just across the river or mountain or border. No one ever placed the blame on the strong—on the cold-blooded muscle that had swept through like fire, fuelled by pride or greed. He knew why: The downtrodden didn't have the heart to risk calling that muscle back. Better to denounce someone who has also been obliterated—condemn them for doing something foolish or unlucky, or for displeasing some god.

Tension on the street remained high, and other than the path of discretion and acceptance had no vent for release. Adults, in general able to understand the continuing threat and risk, took no action. But the young had mastered no such restraint, and a new incident now ignited itself ahead of the wave of store closures. An unsupervised group of Washokki boys had noticed the sheriff's car parallel-parked in front of the café two blocks ahead, and had begun to pelt it with stones from a short distance. The dull, reverberating clank of impacted fenders turned the heads of those within earshot, including Thad, who paused his game to enjoy this new show. One of the younger kids overthrew, and a small rock struck the café window. The glass didn't break, but the café owner, unaware of the shop closures as yet, came storming out. "Hey! Beat it! You goddamn red vermin, I'll beat the piss out of you!"

The boys retreated a few steps but laughed. An older Washokki teenager hollered, "Watch your mouth mister!" Ofstedder, up to this point a lesser player in Thad's game, now walked ahead of his compatriots, sensing an opportunity for action. He approached the sheriff's car.

The café owner continued to rail. "You punks think it's open season now, with your wild punk-ass boy getting out of prison! I'll show you open season, bigod!" The café owner bolted back into his shop and returned a moment later waving a shotgun. The children began to flee; he aimed the barrel as if to fire over their heads. Ofstedder stepped up behind him, knocking him down with a skillful, brutal elbow to the back of the head. The shotgun discharged into the air as the café owner slumped to the ground. "We do the shootin', grandpa," Ofstedder said, spitting on the man.

The sheriff made no entrance on the scene.

Mick heard the gunshot from his vantage point further along the street. "What now?" he muttered aloud. It was more a statement than a question, and a nearby elderly Washokki man offered to expand on it.

"Knox's men do what they want," he said, unsolicited. "Nobody stops them. The sheriff...hell, the sheriff takes orders from them. It's tearing this goddamn town apart, the violence, fear...greed. Both sides fan the flames."

But two younger tribal men within earshot had more to say. One, long-haired and tall, commented, "They fear Aak, and because of him they fear all of us."

His younger associate replied, "I can't wait."

The elderly man drew closer to Mick. "Sorry I said 'hell' and the other thing to you, Padre," he murmured.

Fascinated, Mick reflected as he returned the man's nod; a place could be disintegrating into barbarism and the instinctive solution was to keep the language genteel. It was a little like wearing cuff links to a lynching.

Pedestrians evaporated like vapor in the late morning's increasing heat; Daryl had mysteriously disappeared as well. Thad and Joel grew bored with their sport before they reached the end of the street where Hawkins' garage sat, and wandered with their compatriots back to the Inferno, dropping warm beer bottles in the gutter along the way. Mick watched from the street's opposite side as they disappeared within. Two disheveled women, sitting on the boardwalk outside the saloon's door, dragged themselves to their feet and followed the men in. The second one, about thirty years old, took a surreptitious half-glance back over her shoulder at Mick, the last figure left in view, before disappearing inside.

CHAPTER SIX

Other than a comparatively packed house at the morning services—twenty percent of seats were occupied instead of the usual handful—Sunday came and went without event. Mick cheated by merely introducing himself for a sermon. After the service he walked again down to the Hawkins garage but found no one there, no gas dispensed at the pump, and no apparent change in the location or condition of his truck. He returned home and, unable to find any reading material in the house, spent the day cleaning wax from the candle holders in the church, and later walking partway up a nondescript, sage-covered hill at the south edge of the town. In his slightly expanded field of view, green velvet ranges of the Kootenai forest roamed over the land to the west and north. He could see a water tower at the town's north end standing guard over a larger than normal one-story building, and made note of its general location. Later back at the residence, he left another message for his Bishop before retiring.

Monday morning he walked around the town's east end, out of curiosity making for the structure he'd seen the evening before. As he'd surmised, it proved to be a small school building. The sign identified it as a facility for the lower grades; a semi-circular turn-out in front marked where school buses, if there were enough kids to require them, could load and unload. Cedar and juniper shrubs lined the wall in front. He'd detected from the hilltop what looked like a fenced playground in back, but could not see it from the street.

He mounted the two steps in one stride, entered the unlocked front door, and paused while his eyes adjusted to the darkness. Hall lights were off, and this being already September that probably meant classes were in session. He walked softly up the hall, noting the small lockers along both sides, feeling like a first grader late for homeroom. He spied an open classroom door by the light streaming onto the hall floor, and half-approached it; a teacher was conducting arithmetic class inside, asking for an answer to something she'd written on the board. Mick tried to slip past but she caught sight of his motion and, mildly surprised, halted the lesson mid-sentence. "Can I help you find something?" she asked, drawing him forward from the hall's shadows.

"Sorry. Father Mick Calahan. Hi." He stuck his head into the classroom. "I was just looking for the Principal's office. Didn't mean to interrupt the class." The small group of children peered at him quizzically from wooden desks.

"No problem, I think they like a little excitement. This is our second grade." She addressed the class. "Children, this is Father...um...?"

"Father Mick."

"Father Mick. He's come to see how we learn. Do we remember how we greet visitors?"

The children attempted to address the stranger in unison, but failed miserably. "Hello...Father...M...."

Mick smiled and tried to nod graciously to the entire room, waving apologetically to the teacher for the interruption as she pointed further down the hall. "Last door on the right," she whispered, smiling.

He found the principal's office and poked his head inside. A middle-aged administrator looked up from her desk.

"Hi," he began, "Mick Calahan...Father Mick Calahan, new to the Catholic church. New to town actually...I...just thought I'd introduce myself."

"Yes, we heard, come in Father Calahan. What can I do for you?"

"Nothing, really, just...wandering aimlessly. Mick." He stuck out his hand. "Thought I'd see how the other half learns."

The principal rose, came around her desk, and extended her hand. "Well we get by. Always a resource shortage but we do what we can. Andrea Burton."

"Hi Andrea." Mick shook the hand, looking around the room as he did so. Her desk was surrounded by waist-high stacks of documents and metal filing cabinets with open drawers. A well-cared-for fern at the window spread its fronds a foot in all directions.

The obligatory round metal wastebasket sat neatly beside the desk.

He noticed a bookshelf, nearly ceiling high, stocked with a variety of used volumes. "Now this is nice," he commented. "Your personal collection?"

"Oh, closest thing to a library we have here in the school I guess. I know that must sound awful...I mean it is only a single wall. The state sometimes makes old high school and college texts available to backwater places like us. Occasionally they send a truck from town to town, and I grab what I can. It's worth the trouble...sometimes one of the teachers finds their way in here looking for an old algebra or history text to check if they're really telling it like it is. And a lot of what we have is out of print. There's another low stack over there at the end; we sort of ran out of shelf."

"You have eight grades here?"

"Yes, one through eight all together, like they used to do. Classes aren't very big; we often put different ages into the same room. Children go from eighth here to High School—ninth. But that's in Kalispell; they send a bus."

"I see. Well...I don't want to be an interruption. I really just dropped by to introduce myself. Thank you for the tour. Tell the second grade children it was nice meeting them. I'm a little out of place here, but let me know if I can...I don't know, maybe have a postcard sent from back East or something, anyway...."

"Then you're just visiting Terradise Valley?"

Mick just shrugged and smiled.

"Then a postcard would impress them I'm sure," Andrea responded with aplomb, seeing him to the door. "Nice of you to drop by, Father."

Mick left her office, started the wrong way in the hall, caught the error and made for the front door. He exited the building unsure why he'd gone inside in the first place. He was neither qualified nor particularly intent on getting involved with education here. Well, he could do a cursory assessment of the infrastructure and general state of the town, and add it to his verbal report to the Archbishop when he saw him again. It might be useful in identifying someone with the right skills and nature to run the parish.

In any event, what now? He had nowhere in particular to go. He wandered down to Hawkins' garage by residential streets, noting the overall small size and low structural quality of the houses. A carpenter sees neighborhoods differently, he realized—everywhere there were construction techniques and materials evident that had been abandoned elsewhere in favor of improved methods. The residents of this place clearly lacked resources. Roofs were patched instead of being replaced, and often with homemade shingles of split cedar, nailed over cheap worn out asphalt material. Driveways were dirt, or absent. Garage doors were jammed open or missing. Chimneys were often just an aging once-galvanized flu pipe.

He arrived at the garage; Hawkins had finally finished his work, cautioning only that the clutch pedal may now be too "touchy." The mechanic added that he'd also replaced the belts and that the compression was "almost up to snuff." Mick thanked him and promised to bring cash down later in the day, which was good enough for the curious little man, who handed over the key, gave a wink and a handshake, and like always regarded Mick with interest until he'd pulled out onto the side street.

Mick angled straight east this time through different neighborhoods, again skirting the dubious main street corridor, certain that he could find the church without seeing familiar landmarks. Near the town's northeast edge, he caught sight of an unusual old residence set amid a collection of blighted cedar trees. As an excuse to give himself a moment to gaze at the place, he tested the truck's brakes at the corner.

The house was old. It was situated roughly in the center of a very large yard walled with stone, to which reclaimed brick had been added in places, brought in long ago from somewhere else. Dead or ailing moss covered much of the stone. The grounds were relatively bare except for the trees themselves and the dead branches that littered the dirt around them. Below the tree branches, the house had a clear view to the perimeter wall on all sides. Despite the obvious affluence that had originally created the dwelling, upkeep now was poor. It resembled a compound more than a mansion.

The building itself was dark. A single gnarled oak tree, mostly devoid of leaves despite being still alive, stood like a skeletal umbrella trying to shield the house from the sky's light. On the structure itself, higher gables with dormered windows were bare of curtains, lending a gothic quality to the place. Was it deserted? Mick paused to gaze for a moment, then refocused his attention back onto his clutch pedal, which was indeed grabbier than it had been. He wondered if it was something he could simply get used to, and drove on, playing with it.

The next morning brought just a bit of rain and a welcome mass of cooler air. Mick found Elmer still at home when he darted out to hold the morning Mass, tossing him an unanswered greeting as he left. On return an hour later, Elmer was still there, pulling weeds by the edge of the front porch. Mick changed clothes and came out to help him, and the two worked wordlessly side by side for almost another hour, never looking at each other. Elmer finally ended the silence with a simple, "Breakfast sounds good about now." He heaved the pile of weeds in his left hand out to the side of the house, pulled his big frame to a standing position, and entered the door, holding it open in invitation.

Over flapjacks and juice, Mick opened up to Elmer, who was whipping up a second course of fried eggs; he needed to bounce his disjoint thoughts off someone with a fresh perspective.

"Thing is," he said, breaking the sound of chewing and knowing the topic would seem out of the blue, "I'm really not sure what I'm doing here or what this assignment is all about."

Elmer was silent.

"I mean, what do you think it might be about? As in, what I should be doing."

"Spam or no spam?"

"Huh? Oh, um...whatever you recommend."

Elmer fried and then replied. "You're the scholar with the schooling."

"First time anyone's called me that. My Bishop wouldn't tell me anything really...not so sure he knew. Can't get him to answer my calls, either. I guess he probably sees it as one of those personal quest things—wants me to figure it out."

"Well you could just hit the road...follow yer buddy."

The comment hit the mark, and Mick, stealing a glance out the window at his truck, felt ashamed. He presumed Elmer knew of his visits to Hawkins' garage. Okay...deserved. He had little right injecting himself into the lives of this old man or anyone else if he was intent on abandoning the post.

He realized it was also his first clue as to what had become of the former pastor. "Father MacArthur? Where did he go?"

"Who the hell cares...nailed himself up, fer all I know." Elmer, fully aware of the theologic tastelessness of the reference, slapped the fried egg onto Mick's plate and plopped two greasy fried spam slabs on top of it. But then he reached behind him, produced a dainty sprig of parsley, and laid it over the spam, meticulously positioning it for best visual impact. Mick smiled.

"What's the deal with this town, Elmer?"

"Ain't no damn good."

"Were you born here?"

"Not the 'here' yer seein'. Born in this valley, sure. One time, you'd-a not pried me out of these parts with a railroad tie. This place was somethin' to see, too, and so wuz I. Warn't a job I couldn't do nor a man what didn't tip his hat to me then. Worked the line from Fort Benton to Coeur d'Alene and beyond, and logged some too. Even was a deputy once. They sure tipped them hats. Not now, no...." He wiped the frying pan clean with a rag, scowling, lost in thought.

"What happened?"

Elmer thought long, deciding whether to share any of it, then replied simply, "Tried to help a kid once...never shoulda bothered." He went silent for a full minute, but eventually reopened the original subject. "Got a picture...somewhere...of me when I was deputy sheriff. Got a whole pile of newspapers and such from them days, and even some from the beginnin', gimme by my Daddy, still got 'em, and this was the place to be, bigod. More folks arrivin' from back East all the time, ever'thing hoppin' in all these hills, minin' claims galore. But ain't no damn good no more. I'd go, anymore, I'd go now...too old to learn a new place though."

"I see. What happened here?"

Silence.

"What has happened more recently?"

Silence.

Mick decided they had accomplished a lot and thought it best not to press too hard. He glanced to the window sill, where sat the little toy Jeep he'd found in church a week earlier. Thinking a moment, he said, "Well, I have to call on someone this morning—return something very important. Cielo family, I think they pronounced it. Know them?"

"Know most folks."

"If I asked a few questions about Terradise Valley while there, do you think I might get an answer or two?"

He waited this time for Elmer's reply, and eventually it came. "If I was you I'd keep my nose outa some peoples' lives. People is caught in the storm as it is. You ain't gettin' no help from me findin' folks fer you, that much I'll say...nobody out North Fork Road 'bout seven mile, anyways. Purty little farm as y'ever did see."

Mick smiled his unspoken thanks and rose from the table. He tried to wash his plate but Elmer elbowed him gruffly out of the way. As he left, the caretaker added, "Don't go bringin' trouble to them that's got enough already—best not let them outsiders see you visitin' folk they got business with."

CHAPTER SEVEN

A late morning after a light rain in mountain country is alive with smells—sage, pine, cedar, juniper, coffee-colored earth, and the myriad varieties of grass that carpet small meadows and open plains. Mick was happy the driver's side window was still stuck in the down position, reflecting that the aromas of the forest must be the reason he'd forgotten to mention it to Hawkins.

A day like this made him feel strong, made him forget who he was. A day like this injected a dose of Divinity, he decided. He didn't know if the small child would remember him, or the mother either for that matter. And if they did, he didn't know what kind of reception he'd get, especially after Elmer's curious warning. But he'd do his best.

He knew he came to them less as a priest than as a man. He didn't know he was the first to visit them in friendship since the child's father had been lost.

Rural North Fork Road ran serpentine from the town's edge roughly eastward. It crested several low spines and crossed short stretches between them. The little farm lay, as Elmer had described, just past seven miles from the church, in a small valley. Mick decided it was the place he sought partly by the distance and partly because he saw no other houses.

The lane ran off the road to the left about 150 feet, into a yard between a small house and an outbuilding to which a rough log fence was attached. The fence went on to enclose a shady green meadow of about two acres, lined with tall Ponderosa pines. Mick knew the fence meant livestock. A handful of chickens roamed the grass and gravel. He pulled in slowly, stopping behind a rusting 1965 Ford sedan parked in the dirt driveway, its four doors dented beyond caring, the vinyl of its bench seats cracked with age. As he opened his truck door, a friendly Border Collie barked twice from the porch and bounded out to greet him.

Mick did his best to walk comfortably to the house, tripping only twice on the enthusiastic dog. Before he got to the steps the door opened and Gabriella Cielo stood before him, holding a large spoon, momentarily stooping to stand something long and thin behind the doorframe out of his view. Mick knew it was a small rifle. She waited for him to speak first.

"Hi. Father Mick Calahan. You...might remember."

"Yes, I remember." A moment of cool silence passed—all too familiar an experience with the people of this town, thought Mick. "What can I do for you, Father Calahan?" she asked pragmatically.

In his most disarming manner, Mick held out the toy Jeep.

"Ah, thank you," she said, stepping out to the edge of the steps and reaching to take the toy, one hand still propping open the screen door behind her. "Someone's been looking all over for it." Mick noticed the child standing close behind his mother's jeans. "But...surely you didn't drive all the way out here for this," Gabriella added.

"Well I was just...driving...no actually...." Mick shrugged and started again. "Just trying to get to know...people."

"I see. To be shaking hands so far out from the town center already, you must...work very fast."

"Touché." Mick grimaced and tried to change the subject. "Sure is a pretty place. Peaceful."

"Peace is easier to find the further out you go."

"I guess it is."

"You can go seventy miles east before you see another settlement. Just you and the wind...if that's what you're after."

Mick began a third time. "Mrs. Cielo, quite frankly there don't seem to be any hands in this state that want to be shaken. I've met almost no one, in town or out. I was sent here from nearly three thousand miles away, I don't know why, or what to do, nobody including my own caretaker will say much to me, something's strange about your world here, and you seem like somebody perhaps not exactly in league with everyone else. That's why I came."

Gabriella nodded, thought, and looked away. "It's not the most normal place in the world," she acknowledged reluctantly and quietly. "There are the whites and the tribe, always suspicious of each other, and then those damn men Knox pays to keep what he calls order, brutes mostly, nobody knows from where. And nobody knows you, either, including Elmer...nobody knows who to trust. Not surprising it's all a mystery to you I guess." She seemed understanding, but a touch nervous too, habitually glancing past him up and down the road.

"Knox? I've heard his name mentioned. Who is he?"

"I really need to get back to my chores, Mr. Calahan...sorry, I mean, 'Father.'"

"Of course, I understand. Didn't mean to interrupt normal routines. Uh...maybe sometim...." But Gabriella had already begun to recede behind her screen door, giving him a partial smile and a courteous but definitive wave as it closed. He'd been in the military; he knew what it was to be dismissed.

The dog escorted him back to his truck. As he walked past the Ford sedan, he noticed it was listing slightly to one side and saw that the left rear tire was flat. He glanced back toward the house, but Gabriella had disappeared inside. He had no schedule pressures...surely he could do a good deed before heading back to town. He popped open the car's trunk and began to hunt for the spare tire amid the collection of crumpled feed bags, empty buckets, rubber boots, frayed lengths of rope, toys, and other assorted items that had clearly been tossed inside over a long period of time. He didn't hear the door reopen on the porch.

"Can I help you Father Calahan?" Gabriella called; she was standing apprehensively at the porch's edge now. Angelo held her hand.

Mick extracted his head from the trunk so she would hear him. "Sorry...you...you must have picked up a nail or something. I assume you knew it was flat?"

"Is it? You must mean the rear one there...no I didn't, but it's been bald forever. It even spins out sometimes in the gravel driveway. I drove it there, but the tire must have gone down in the night. I guess I should have gotten around to fixing it."

"Where is your spare?" Mick called to her, head and shoulders again buried in the car's trunk.

"There's no spare...well, that was the spare."

Mick's shoulders slumped in obvious defeat. Then he hauled himself out into daylight again, stood, shook his head and laughed. He regarded Gabriella momentarily and considered admonishing her procrastination, but realized there may well have been financial issues that had left her little choice. He looked down at the flat tire and thought for a moment. "It's a six-lug hub...wheel well seems like there's enough clearance...I'm going to loan you the spare on the back of my truck. It's a small one anyway...I don't have the right one either...and it won't be that different in size I don't think. Might work...better than what you've got anyway. Just until we can get it done right."

"No, I couldn't...."

"Look," he assured her, "it's not safe being out here...with a child and all...and not able to get around. And you've got animals to feed I expect. This is workable. Might be why fate sent me out here today. Believe me, I've got no one else I need to lend it to."

Holding the child's head and shoulders to one leg, Gabriella whistled for the dog and hung onto its collar with the other hand, then observed soundlessly while Mick jacked up the car at the bumper and removed the threadbare old tire, laughing aloud at its condition when he got it into the light. He went back to his truck, rummaged for the tire tool, and removed the spare from the rear chassis panel, then rolled it back up to the Ford and wrestled it into place. A grin tossed hastily toward the porch let Gabriella know it was on the lug bolts successfully. He applied and tightened the lug nuts, dropped the bald tire into her trunk, and finally let down the jack, then stood back admiring the result, holding up filthy hands like a surgeon being gloved. "That one oughta grab better in a gravel driveway," he said with satisfaction, catching and almost meeting her suddenly serious gaze.

She looked at him for a long time as though looking through him—wrestling, she knew, between apprehension, doubt, and something far more disturbing...hope? It had been a long time since anyone could be trusted. Yet...anyone can change a tire, and caution seemed more...cautious....

Sensing some internal struggle he didn't yet understand, Mick gave her time to return to the moment. Eventually she did, reached behind without relaxing her probing gaze, and opened the screen door. "You'll want to wash those hands," she said at last. "And I'll bet you're hungry."

He followed her into the kitchen and scrubbed his hands at the sink, while Gabriella cleared space at the small table with one forearm while whispering into Angelo's ear. The boy ran into a nearby room and peeped shyly from around the doorframe. Trying to appear nonchalant, Gabriella pushed the little .22-calibre rifle, still standing against the doorframe, back among a small array of brooms and out of sight. Through the screen door the Border Collie watched Mick sit down.

The kitchen was rectangular and small, but had the quality of making a stranger feel welcome. Central to the action was the wooden table covered with a clean, simple yellow cloth. Twin windows along the wide outside wall opened onto the porch and partly faced the roadway beyond. A small refrigerator stood against the narrow wall opposite the screen door. Three small wall-mounted pine cabinets held chinaware essentials, overtop of which a quaint decorative shelf lined with small photo frames, a few Catholic statues, a collection of geodes, two separate vases of small dried lupine blossoms, and a diminutive lantern, circumnavigated the entire room. Wallpaper from a bygone age covered what the cabinets did not.

Two small rooms and a bathroom adjoined the kitchen at the inside wall. The kitchen windows faced southwest, positioned to let in the gentle afternoon sun, even in winter. A carpenter's eye could see the house was designed by someone who understood snowy environs.

Gabriella set before him a simple lunch of garden greens she'd evidently picked that morning. Sweet carrots, radishes, spinach, arugula and juicy red tomatoes, which he heartily sprinkled with salt and pepper, covered the plate. A slice of cheese and a clear glass of cool water completed the fare. She had the same, pausing a moment in apparent silent prayer before eating. Mick appreciated that she did not press him into service to recite some pre-memorized rhyme for them both.

"Good tomatoes. Mmmmm...really good."

"You mean the red thing you buried in salt?"

"Aha, you saw that. I thought it would..." he took a moment to enjoy another hearty bite, "...would bring out the flavor, but these don't need bringing out."

"There are about three weeks in the late summer when they get enough sun here to be this good," she said.

Mick lingered another few moments on a forkful of arugula, then commented, "You have quite a strange town here, if you don't mind my thinking so."

"There's no one here who wouldn't agree with you. Nobody trusts anyone, nobody ever does anything about it."

"But...I mean, does anything about what?"

"Surely you've seen all those men wandering around, those strangers, making everyone miserable."

"I don't know who are strangers and who have lived here all their lives. I thought maybe they were the Kiwanis Club or something—until you said earlier something about nobody knowing where they came from."

"They're outsiders. Knox pays them. Started bringing them in a few years ago. They've got no authority...but intimidation serves just as well. We only have one legal sheriff...they tell him what to do and he does it."

"Doesn't the mayor or the town council or someone have anything to say?"

"There isn't any town council. We had a mayor at one time but she resigned when they closed the town hall, where her office was. Renovation, they said, but it's been nearly three years. Nobody wants to be the mayor."

"No resident council at all...don't know if I've ever run across that. Back in Boston, when we hear about that kind of thing we generally have a tea party."

"The tribes sometimes get their elders together, but their focus is only their people, not the town itself."

Mick wanted to drill down a bit. "Tell me about this Knox," he asked boldly. "Knox who?"

"Someone who controls things."

"How so?"

"He brought a lot of money into the town when he first arrived. A couple of years ago. Nobody knows much about him. He's the richest thing anyone around here ever saw. Maybe he feels that makes him king, because he's tightened his grip from the day he showed up. Took a big interest in the old slide mine north of town."

A memory is a terrible thing. Ignited by as little as a single word, it turns a man's past into his sentence for having once lived it, and condemns him to repeating the living of it for eternity. It had been a 40-year failing endeavor to try to bury the image of a seven-year-old boy standing terrified at the mouth of a filthy mineshaft in the middle of the night. Mick could still see the swinging arcs of the adults' flashlights as they milled around him in confusion, could still smell the foul, cool, malevolent air belching lightly from inside the earth.

"I don't like mines," he said at last.

"People want what the earth gives away for free," she responded, not noticing the personal tone in his words. "The mine here gave birth to this town."

He thought about how she'd put it—the giving earth. He knew the earth relinquished, and sometimes it swallowed.

"How does this Knox figure into the mine?" he prompted, returning to the immediate subject.

Gabriella stood and glanced out the window without realizing she'd done it, then reseated herself. "He arrived here supposedly with the deed already in his hand, and now is reopening it—hiring outside crews for shoring, digging, blasting—and security. Those mercenaries are here mostly because he's afraid the local Indian tribes would sabotage the mine."

"To keep order."

"To control."

That larger perspective rang more true, he knew. Still, sometimes an industrialist's paranoia is justifiable. "Is it a reasonable concern? Are the tribes claiming or threatening the mine?"

"One side is as bad as the other—they all smell money—and they all enjoy clashing horns."

Mick brought it back to the town itself. "I don't recall meeting or even seeing anyone that those men seem to answer to. Just one...."

"Knox stays in shadow. But his arms are long. He has his captains."

A noise to his left turned Mick's head. Angelo was still peeping at him, one ear, one brown eye, and one little hand visible around the edge of the painted white doorframe. Mick pretended not to notice momentarily, then suddenly darted the boy a bold smile, watching him duck out of sight with a giggle. He played the game another few identical rounds, then returned his attention to Gabriella.

"I've stumbled around for days and understood nothing, yet learned more that makes sense in the last two minutes than I picked up on my own, or from anybody else. I guess I now see why no one speaks to me...I generally walk around without the robes on, and they just see another white man stranger. My first day, I think the barber probably mistook me for part of that crowd—went on about some wonderful guy named Knox until I mentioned I was the padre. The darkest mysteries sure fall apart when we get a spec of background, don't they?"

"It isn't your fault; but you can't blame them either; no one can afford to speak to newcomers."

"I understand. Even my caretaker, Elmer...do you know him? He's been pretty tight-lipped...and he knows who I am." He paused a minute, figuring how best to give a delicate sentiment its rightful voice.

Finally he just said it straight. "I want to thank you for trusting me enough to explain some of this."

He was impressed at how gracefully Gabriella sidestepped the gratitude by defending the old man. "Elmer has his own way. Give him time. Things haven't been easy for him."

"I gathered that, by the angst he seems to have. Seems so angry. I think he could help me understand things a bit, maybe, but I get the feeling he's clouded by...hate or fear or something. Do you know him well? Where does he stand in this seemingly divided town?"

"Well, let's see: He hates Indians, despises the other whites, and resents and fears Knox and his associates."

"How about puppies?"

"Probably hates them," she half-smiled.

"A lot for one old guy to be carrying around," Mick observed, returning to sobriety. "What happened to his leg?"

"There are different versions of the story, and I can only repeat what I've heard...but it had something to do with him stepping into a fight to protect a young kid, a Tissoma tribe kid. Somehow Elmer was shot either during or after the fight...and it was the boy's own father who shot him. Elmer was a very strong man, but the law—the same sheriff we have now was part of it—left him locked in a cell for two days without medical treatment. I believe that's what cost him his leg." She finished with, "He doesn't drink—still has his pride—but I think he's never been the same since."

"That's...well it's a hard story to hear, much less to live," Mick replied quietly. "I'll see Elmer in a different light now I think." A moment's silence reigned, and Mick chanced to glance again toward where he last saw the boy. Angelo was still peeping quietly from the same doorway, this time from down near the floor. Mick stared without smiling, then flashed the boy an eye-popping expression, chuckling aloud when the child emitted a squeak and ducked again out of sight.

Gabriella asked the priest if he was still hungry.

"Oh no...thanks...really a very refreshing lunch," he offered as graciously as he could, knowing he'd eaten the fare she'd planned to have that night for dinner. "Thank you." He crunched a final mouthful. "They say those things in the eastern supermarkets are vegetables, but they don't stand up to your home-grown fare. I think they make them out of some kind of synthetic vegetable...looking...stuff."

Gabriella smiled, eyes on her own plate.

Mick probed for more information. "You know, there was some strange incident on the street the other morning, and I...."

"What incident?"

"Just bullies throwing their weight around...the same people you described I'm sure...I didn't catch how it had begun. But I heard someone shout something about some inmate being released from the state prison at...would that be in Deer Lodge?"

Gabriella nodded, knowing where he was going.

"...and how much trouble the guy is expected to cause. What's that all about?"

"Wayne Aak," she nodded, stepping on his last few words.

"Some sort of local villain...or...hero?"

"Both," she confirmed, "depending on who's talking. Even just his name makes whites and the elderly nervous, and many others from the tribes...almost hopeful."

"But how is he woven into all this? Because I think...because I have this strange feeling he's connected somehow to my...mission...here."

"Wayne was...an orphan, they say," she began, "which is not common among the tribes. Someone usually is there to take children under their wing, but Wayne wasn't as lucky. He grew up rebellious—and that part is common." She paused to take a drink of water. "A couple of years ago he attracted the attention of Knox's men when he got drunk one night—in his early 20's by this time—and refused to be bullied by them. Three of them jumped him with sticks, but he was rash and lucky, and beat them all...instantly becoming a local hero among the youth of the tribes—who are as stupid as the whites...."

"You said that already," Mick smiled.

Gabriella nodded self-consciously, and continued: "One of the men died of head injuries from that. So not only was he a local hero with the young and foolish, Wayne Aak also became a marked man in the mind of Lucius Knox. He represented the notion that Knox's control could be challenged, even beaten."

"I see."

"Other tribal gangs who were prone to trouble anyway were made bolder by his luck...his short-lived fame...and trouble brewed again between the whites and the Indians. And naturally against the law. Some shops were damaged, vandalism..." she trailed off without finishing.

"Was he...tried for that man's death, I guess?"

"They couldn't make it stand up, so they set him up not long after. He and...someone else, another marked man...were framed for the murder of a different Indian boy, although it was most likely the Law and Knox's men who'd killed that kid. Wayne Aak was sent to state prison, where he's served...maybe less than two years. I guess there's been some kind of appeal, or they questioned some of the evidence or something...anyway he's supposedly being released." She paused. "They've all built him up to be some kind of superman who will somehow grab that mine for them—God knows how they expect that to happen."

"What other 'marked man'? The former pastor? Is that how he disappeared? Went to prison, or went on the run?"

"No. And that priest was a coward. Elmer said he just left. Everyone probably expects the same from you." She gave him a long glance, and Mick saw in it both an accusation and a plea.

He cleared his throat. "I...find it...hard to believe a priest would abandon his post and not seek the help of his diocese. And my superior and his both spoke well of him. But they don't seem to know what happened."

"People confided in him," she said, without being specific. "They looked to him for guidance, or at least example. He deserted them, and the priesthood. One morning he wasn't...he just quit." She looked inwardly angry.

"Maybe something happened to him. Were you one of those who had confided?"

Gabriella gave no reply.

"Who was the other marked man, Gabriella?"

She hesitated, and Mick knew they were peeling painful layers that could begin to reveal her personal story.

"Someone whose land they wanted. Someone who they say ran away to escape the law. But they always lie." She rose again and paced to the kitchen window.

"Who?" He decided it was worth pressing.

No answer came; Gabriella froze at the window, instinctively taking a step backward away from it. Mick half-rose and caught sight of a dark primer-red truck passing very slowly out on the road. The truck stopped and idled at the lane, in view of Mick's vehicle.

Gabriella abruptly ended the lunch. "I have to ask you to leave now, Father. I'm sorry to make this so sudden but I have a lot of work to do."

Certain that something was amiss but unsure what exactly, Mick stood. He made one last goofy face to Angelo, disarming the tension for sake of the child, who finally smiled at him. Then Mick took a step toward the screen door, but Gabriella's instinctive hand on his arm bade him pause. She continued to watch earnestly through the window until the red truck outside revved and oozed out of sight eastward;

then she composed herself and again faced him, hands clasped together to help keep them still.

He said simply, "Thank you for the lunch, and the visit. Keep that tire on there as long as you like...I'm not planning on any long trips." His statement, intended to reassure the woman, surprised himself.

The early afternoon sun still shone over the top of the high tree-lined ridge immediately to the south of the road. He tossed the jack into the Ford's trunk on his way to his truck, taking his own lug wrench with him. The Border Collie escorted him again, and he gave the dog an appreciative scratch behind the ears, then climbed into the Landcruiser cab and started the engine.

Driving westward toward town and cresting a low hill at the first spine, he momentarily spotted in the rear view mirror a flash of primer red color near the side of the road a half mile the other side of Gabriella's lane. Then he was over the rise and the color vanished from view.

He slowed and drove awhile in second gear, but no vehicles approached or passed him.

That night he had a dream. He was a child, and could not find his toy Jeep. He was digging for it in his yard. He called to his father for help, but no one came. A man told him to stop. He ran away but the dream kept bringing him back. He looked up at the man, and then became him, standing over a child digging in the dirt.

CHAPTER EIGHT

Four men met in the back room of a saloon in Gunnison Colorado. The door was barred and the saloon keeper was paid two dollars to stand outside the door with a shotgun. The year was 1896.

Captain Aaron Briskamph, decorated Civil War captain and trained civil engineer-turned-entrepreneur, had called the meeting. He had managed to bring together well-heeled but little known capitalist Ernest Broum and seasoned geologist and operations specialist Rufus Smithy. Broum's accountant also attended the meeting.

The men already knew what they were here to discuss; they had previously agreed in the abstract, by telegraph and hand-carried letter. Smithy had visited the site in Montana the month before, and now presented at the meeting his opinion in a verbal report: The location bore sufficient mineral evidence to convince investors and to begin construction.

In three hours they had drawn up a timetable, bill of needed materials, and responsibilities, including when, where, and how to contact markets back east, and how to set up agreements and security for transport of gold.

Then they left the saloon in different directions.

Each was vested 30% of net. Broum was a silent partner—he would finance development without publicity, and also would have his expenditures covered before percentages were calculated. Smithy, given his technical value, would oversee operations on-site. Briskamph would assist with operations as his schedule permitted and would also attach his name to the project in its East Coast promotion. He also claimed most of the remaining 10% for having made the initial find and created the project. Broum's accountant, Thomas L. Wrightson, in addition to his normal salary, would lay personal claim to 2% of net as an incentive for secrecy.

Over the next 16 months supplies poured into Cheyenne Wyoming and Missoula by rail, then north to the western Montana site by mule train. Crews were hired, shafts dug, track laid. The mine was readied for sizeable production. Veterans of cavalry units were hired for protection.

Smithy, then an inexperienced player in the field of ore extraction, had managed a small gold mine in the Dakota Black Hills not quite twenty years prior, in 1879 through 1881, at the tail end of the frenzy there. The mine was largely unproductive, but Smithy earned a name for deft management of information by continuing to win and keep backers long after the mine's heyday had been past. It was there that he met Briskamph, a former cavalry lieutenant in the

Civil War and the wars against the Sioux, who had through family connections in Washington D.C. narrowly escaped being assigned to the ill-fated Seventh Cavalry under General George C. Custer. Briskamph had been released from military service over continuing complications with an old knife wound he claimed to have received in battle in east Texas in 1874, and Smithy's geologic knowledge and general experience with mining operations had caught the former cavalryman's attention. The two men kept an association over the next twenty years.

Smithy spent three years in the Dakota Territory prison system, first in Yankton South Dakota and later at the penitentiary in Williston North Dakota, beginning August of 1881. He was released in January 1885 when the temporary jail facility extension in which he was incarcerated collapsed under a heavy snow load. He ventured south as far as Texas over the next decade, engaged in nothing particularly noteworthy, until Briskamph contacted him in 1895 regarding a project in Montana, and discussions commenced.

Now, with supplies and crew arriving weekly, Smithy put the new and well conceived plan into motion. Local forests were harvested for shoring timbers and track ties. Blasting began for three shafts simultaneously, to meet schedules. Cattle too were brought in, and canvas, to feed and house the crews. Between the first winter of 1896-1897, the reckless blasting and destabilization of the main slope, and the not uncommon skirmishes between the crews and the native Flathead and Sioux (and also violence between crew members), forty four men were lost the first year. But for every fallen worker, four more arrived ready to take his place.

During that first winter and the following spring of 1897, Briskamph was busy circulating photographs and gold production projections among investment-minded circles up and down the East Coast. He sold shares into private investment funds and held invitation-only promotion events in clubs where New World industrialists and ambitious European investors congregated, from Boston to the nation's capital and in Philadelphia. Sizeable operating cash was raised to offset and replenish Broum's initial seed money. The new capital was set aside in a series of San Francisco accounts. Information as to the amounts and the numbers of shares sold was known only to the partners, and was zealously guarded by Wrightson on behalf of Broum, now based in San Francisco.

The growth of the mine's own infrastructure spawned the birth of a ramshackle town, which was originally called Brisk or Brisk Mine. Besides being on the edge of the mine, the town had the additional advantage of being on a well established trade route for tribes of the western plains, which came to be universally traveled locally by merchants of all races. Brisk quickly established permanent structures for primary services, local governance and law enforcement, a reliable supply chain, and boasted a permanent population that included women and families, in addition to the exploding transient male population who came for wealth or work and who could be found encamped in large numbers semi-permanently in huts and tents throughout the valley.

The smell of gold, ignited by the rapid build-up of the Briskamph Lode, caused a flurry of other claims throughout the local hills. Prospectors hoped to find what the primary players had already announced, and expectations ran high. It was these peripheral excavations that occupied the energies of most of the transient population, as the Briskamph Lode itself had staffed itself early on and had not yet begun production.

With the establishment of a permanent population came the influx of culture, especially religion. At the height of its growth, Brisk boasted over forty thousand residents and thirty seven churches of various sizes and degrees of affluence, from permanent structures to makeshift tarps where services were provided. Civic leaders, encouraged by primary Christian constituents, changed the town's name to Paradise, and later to Terradise amid fundamentalist objections. (In 1947 it was again changed to Terradise Valley, to include surrounding ranch and smaller community populations).

By 1898 an unforeseen development changed the landscape. Gold had been discovered in the Yukon Territory and speculative investment began to shift to Alaska. Sales of additional shares of the Montana "Briskamph Lode" fell off sharply, yet production had not yet ramped up. Wrightson and Broum realized what was happening before Briskamph did, who was promoting in Philadelphia and Baltimore that year and recognized the fall-off in interest but did not see first-hand the pace and scope of the Alaskan gold fever spreading through San Francisco. And Smithy, on-site in Montana, was also in the dark, compelled to rely on his partners to keep him apprised of any new financial concerns.

It was Broum who first saw the end coming. He hatched a plan to not only recover his investment but to embezzle additional amounts from the mine's general fund. His mistake was to give his accountant Wrightson cause to suspect. Wrightson, who stood to lose his own meager 2% if Broum succeeded, secretly reported the plot to the other two partners by telegraph, hinted at the possibility of his own demise at Broum's hand, then arranged travel aboard a steamer for himself, sans Broum, and was not seen again.

Operations halted at the Montana site, and following one more bloody clash with local tribes in September, crews dispersed. Broum, Smithy and Briskamph had one additional meeting in autumn of 1899, at which point Broum acknowledged the disappearance of most of the money but managed to reconcile his own actions and intentions with Smithy and Briskamph. The partnership was dissolved pending two more necessary actions.

Briskamph and a man named Simeon Colter traveled briefly to Central America in that winter.

The following spring, a major slide of the hillside obliterated the shaft entrances. The slide was blamed on rampant destabilization combined with heavy snows and subsequent torrential melt.

Briskamph and Smithy both died violently, as poor men, roughly a decade later, in separate incidents. The mine was abandoned but remained in the possession of Briskamph's and Smithy's respective family estates until 1969. In later decades it became known locally simply as the "Slide Mine."

Following the closure of the Slide Mine, the town itself continued to grow slowly for well over two decades, mostly due to continuing influx from the East, as the West was becoming generally settled, and established services were in scarce supply, and highly valued. The town's growth persisted also due to continuing optimism over gold discovery and extraction, inspired by strikes elsewhere and rationalized by the ready availability of the supply chain infrastructure already established in Terradise and the relative ease of access (as compared to the Yukon Territory for example). Small peripheral claims were filed, re-filed, worked and reworked throughout the range, on the general belief that the potential of the area had not yet been tapped. But interest eventually waned due to the lackluster production of the region and as the realities of the Great Depression took hold; by 1929 the town's population decline was in full swing and its size contracted substantially, bottoming at less than a thousand people by 1938. In the next thirty years it grew slowly as tribal populations expanded and as transportation costs made rural living slightly more viable.

CHAPTER NINE

The primer red truck pulled around the back of the old mansion, where the soil was packed hard. It parked next to a black van with dark-tinted windows and another old pickup truck, also black. Daryl got out and went in through the back door without knocking. Inside, a brief discussion ensued.

"Been watchin' him," he reported.

"So have I."

"Him showin' up now can't be coincidence...you gettin' closer to startin' the heavy work and all."

Silence.

"Got anything you want me to do?"

"He's just a priest, wouldn't you agree?"

"Okay...long as he knows who god is and who ain't."

The gaunt figure to which Daryl spoke considered a long moment. "Perhaps we should find out his intentions."

Daryl left the way he had come. As he went, alert eyes watched him go from a bare upstairs window.

*　　*　　*

Mick walked to the post office. Still expecting word from his superior, and increasingly impatient to wait for Elmer to bring the mail to the house in the evening, he'd taken to checking the parish inbox daily himself. As usual he extended nods to the few pedestrians he encountered, but today noticed a slight difference in that, at least from Caucasians, he was getting some acknowledgment back. Maybe three weeks was the magic length of time. And maybe being accepted as part of this town was not what he wanted.

Nothing from back East. Had his letter not arrived there? Had his multiple phone messages been misplaced? Not likely. And considering he could never seem to call when the Archbishop was said to be at the cathedral, he had to assume he'd get a response when he got one, and not before. Didn't seem to be much point in continuing to call or write; he'd take notes for a later status report, but hang on to them for the time being. Anyway he knew what this meant—no quick exit. The uncertainty and his own undefined apprehension were beginning to erode his patience.

Leaving the post office, on an impulse he ducked into the cluttered hardware store two doors up. A group of Washokki—or were they Tissoma? ...he was sure the only way to know would be to know who was part of what family—stood behind the checkout counter, watching him with expressionless faces. Three generations and both genders were represented—two young men, one older man, and a woman with a child of about ten years. Mick nodded and continued past them. He looked around for a few minutes without success, and was compelled to return to ask for help.

"Hi, sorry to bother you...I was looking for a hammer. Can't seem to spot where you keep them."

One of the young men turned his back, shaking his head in ridicule. The other took an even less respectful tack: "This is a tribal store, white man," he said humorlessly, "they're right by the tomahawks."

The woman, who had avoided Mick's question by leaning to attend to her child, now looked up and admonished the young man softly. "Thomas, you know where they are. You can answer a courteous question with courtesy." Her voice carried no emotion, nor did she address or acknowledge Mick. But she had used English, Mick noted, most likely for his benefit to serve as a kind of apology. She turned again to speak softly with her child.

The older man pointed down the last aisle and nodded. Mick acknowledged without words and left, returning in a few moments carrying a large heavy claw hammer with a long hickory handle.

"That...is a hammer," the old man said appreciatively. The younger men, probably his sons, leveled sobering looks at the big tool, which seemed to improve their attitudes somewhat.

Money was settled and Mick cradled the tool in his left palm. He then extended a thick calloused right hand. "Mick Calahan, thanks, good to meet you," he offered, as though the previous exchange had never transpired.

They stared blankly from his fingers to his face momentarily, until the old man grabbed his hand and gave a hearty shake.

"I'll be back in a day or so," Mick predicted amicably. "Not sure, but I think I'll need a wood rasp."

"They will be in the next row from the hammers," the old man said. "There is a good one there, for very dense grains." Then, "What does a man need a hammer like that for?"

"To scare nails into the wood without having to hit them," Mick replied, drawing more than one broad smile.

He took the direct route home. It led him straight past the Inferno. Curious and emboldened by his newly acquired knowledge of the town, he stepped to the door and peered into the dark interior. He would see just what this place was. Two pedestrians on the street's opposite side froze in disbelief.

Roughly a half dozen white men of various ages sat in chairs in the dirty, dimly lit room, or leaned against the bar, drinking. Mick scanned left to right, observing as much detail as he could, as his training long ago had taught. The men drinking paused in their conversations to stare at him. Some seemed blankly surprised; others, probably less drunk, traded that surprise for smirks more quickly. And some no doubt saw only his silhouette against the brighter world outside.

Behind the bar stood a sour-looking fat man in his
fifties, balding, with blotchy skin and thick spectacles.
He knew the silhouettes of his constituents, Mick
presumed, so he at least recognized the intrusion.
Among those inside Mick also recognized Ofstedder,
Thad, and Joel from the main street business closures
of the week before. The mean-looking one who wore
the grey metal handgun was not among them. Three
prostitutes, laughing overloud or standing with near-
catatonic expressions, killed time with the men.

A worthless billiards table sat in the near left
corner by the blacked-over windows, with junk cues
standing against the wall near it. Raam—probably
mid-forties in age, scrawny, and also one that Mick
recognized—was bending apathetically over a pool
stick, dripping cigarette ashes on the threadbare
maroon felt of the table top. He half looked up but
continued his play, cursing at a shot gone awry. The
oldest of the three women, a chubby middle-aged
Caucasian with a triple chin and a well-used trashy
look, tried to console him by rubbing a fleshy hand on
his back, but Raam swung the thick end of the pool
cue at her. She let out a fake squeal; her too-small,
too-young, too-tight clothing made her resemble a
rubber pillow bound in straps.

A very thin Washokki girl in her mid-teens,
shoeless and dressed indecently in a tiny dirty
negligee, sat on Ofstedder's knee at a small table, with
a mixed drink in her hand. Her sunken eyes gave her
the look of a drug addict. Joel sat with them on the
corner of a nearby table, nursing a half-consumed
shot of whiskey. Ofstedder glared unabashed at the

dark figure in the doorway and downed his own drink in one swallow.

At the bar were three other of Knox's men, Thad among them. They leaned as though glued to the dusty counter top. Thad looked blankly at Mick or at the wall near Mick...it was hard to tell. The other two men had their backs to the door and did not turn. One of them was wearing a uniform, and Mick assumed he was the town's sheriff. The holster on the right hip was empty.

Leaning against the lawman's back was a third woman—Caucasian, roughly thirty years old. Fallen from a different kind of life, known to Knox's men simply as Sheba, her large sad eyes contrasted with the thin curl of smoke from her cigarette and the provocative attire. She had been attractive once, most likely.

Mick took in the details in a matter of seconds, ignoring the stares of Knox's men. If there had been any noise before, a hush now prevailed. The bartender finally broke it in a slow, insinuating, sing-song tone. "Somethin' we can do fer yew?"

Mick's eyes brushed briefly over the bartender, but his eyes moved on; that wasn't where any significance lay. He looked at the youngest prostitute, still sitting on Ofstedder's lap. She stared back at him, but sensing the strength of his eyes, hers darted away; she let out a nervously defiant giggle. Mick turned to the two older women. "How old is she?" he asked about the teen, adopting a very controlled voice, his eyes switching from one woman to the other.

"Why? You don't do statutory?" the young girl answered brashly for them, still smiling nervously, still punctuating with the girlish giggle, still looking at the floor. "I thought all priests molested little kids."

So they knew who he was.

Sheba, who continued to lean against the drunken sheriff's back, stared soberly at Mick, just a hint of guilt in her eyes. He directed a second question quietly at both her and the older woman. "Is this dignity? This what you want to do with your lives?"

Sheba averted her eyes and shifted to stand on her own feet. The older prostitute retorted, "I don't see you doin' nuthin' heroic with yours." The men, inebriated and outclassed, said nothing.

Mick turned away from the door and was gone. After he left, Ofstedder and Thad began to laugh. Sheba remained quiet.

CHAPTER TEN

Impatient days stretched into even more dreary weeks of waiting. Still no word from the Bishop. Mick could find nothing to do but exist, observe, and hope to be allowed to return and deliver his report soon. He had to assume that observation and reporting was what he was sent here to accomplish...surely it wasn't to play pious confessor and prayer meeting leader to a rural parish; if they'd wanted that they'd have sent someone cut out for it.

To inject a token measure of sanity into the waiting and help make hours pass, he busied himself doing what he knew. There were benches, doors, exterior walls, roof sections and other areas that needed repair, in the church and residence both; his carpenter's eye had spotted them nearly from the moment he'd arrived. Elmer did what he could, but had neither the mobility nor the skill to handle many of those tasks.

He'd bought the hammer with this in mind, and had gone back the following day for the rasp, a small hand plane, an assortment of wood screws, some filler and glue. Varnishes and paints he'd have to decide upon as he needed them. Sandpaper he'd forgotten up to now.

He spent a day pulling church floor boards under the rug to the left of the small golden tabernacle that sat atop the altar; he'd heard the creak and felt the soft wood each time he'd stepped there during morning Mass. Although the weather was more or less dry at the moment, he found as expected that water had been accumulating from somewhere, probably seasonally, over a long period of time. He pried out a dozen boards and followed the trail of damage until it led to a low vent where winter snow probably drifted against the outside wall. "Not up to code," he chuckled, measuring for replacement of the vent cover and removed wood. He found a hand saw in the residence with Elmer's help, and the following afternoon managed to complete the basic repair. Instead of applying varnish, temporarily he simply pulled the rug overtop, noting with satisfaction that the patch was flush and the floor now held firm underfoot.

The two days had gone by without the usual knot in his gut, and he decided to keep up the craftsmanship routine as long as there was work to do. He affixed three hooks to the roof overhang in back of the residence and suspended his 18-foot-long bagged gear from short loops of hemp rope, to keep the synthetic bag fabric off the ground, away from gnawing rodents, and protected from the sun. Noting some rusted breaks in the residence's front screen door, he stretched new screening and stabilized the old wood screen frame with a long thin diagonal strip of molding. Elmer frowned when he saw the makeshift repair, but then noticed how well the old door swung, closed, and latched, and his silent grimace softened.

The next afternoon, Mick attended to the usual errands after lunch, then before it got too late changed into work clothes and grabbed his tools, stuffing them into an old dark grey cloth bag he'd found in the broom closet. He wanted to take advantage of the daylight while there was still some left. He walked over to the open front church door and dumped the bag of tools just inside on the floor. A few people sat here and there inside, but he didn't expect he'd bother anyone. He'd noticed the front door was sticking—the wood door frame had probably swelled over time; and he was determined to make it fit again.

An elderly woman walked past him to leave, and he made an apology and room for her to pass. Inspecting the door edge and frame again carefully, he marked the areas that needed attention. Tapping with the hammer let him know there was no dry rot problem yet. He began with the warped part of the door edge lowest to the floor, planing off a very thin, tiny curl of wood on a single light pass, then testing again.

Crouched low, he worked for a minute or so, then stood and stretched his back, glancing as he did out the door and down the long wide row of steps leading out to the street. Something to the side of his limited field of view caught his eye, and he set his tools on the floor and leaned out for a better look. The elderly woman who'd left the church a few moments before was lying on one of the lower steps. Immediately fearing she'd fallen hard on the cement, Mick leaped out the door and scrambled down the steps to assist, passing someone to his left without waiting to see who it was.

He reached the woman, knelt beside her, and urged her to stay down. "Mrs. Julian, is it? Are you alright? What happened?" he asked her, partly to distract her from attempting to rise.

"I'm all right, just let me go, let me be..." the woman protested weakly. She was disoriented at the very least; had she tripped, perhaps hit her head? Or maybe become dizzy and sat down? It occurred to him this was the second medical situation he'd come across and still didn't know if the town even had a doctor.

A voice from above and behind him on the steps interrupted. "Now what we got here? Somebody who's got no license to be practicin' medicine on old bags."

Mick looked up to see Thad. And behind him, on the top step against the wall just outside the door frame, leaned Daryl, silent, watching, smoking.

Thad was descending the steps slowly toward Mick. "You knock the old bag down and then act like yer helpin' her, or what? Knock 'em down and then pick 'em up? Ain't right. I mean, most men, men who's men anyways, don't knock 'em down, they knock 'em up!" He grinned over his shoulder at Daryl, who was scowling at the sky.

Thad's vulgar, tasteless levity and the accusation that Mick had accosted the fallen woman surprised the priest, and he rose in momentary anger from his kneeling position over her. "How do you come to that?" he returned. "Were you trying to help? Either of you?" He shot a look over Thad's shoulder at Daryl, still leaning against the wall, still smoking. "Have I gotten in your way of helping this woman?"

"I'll ask the questions, mister," Thad retorted, calling Mick's attention back to himself. He had to demonstrate control. "I see you stoopin' over a helpless victim here. Now what am I supposed to think?"

"What you think, 'mister,' is of no interest to me, unless you're offering to help! No, I take that back, just back off. Did you knock her down?" He turned from Thad to the woman. "Mrs. Julian, did he knock you down?"

"I'm okay...it's Jillian...I'm okay, I just want to go home, I'm not going to answer any questions," the woman protested. She rose stiffly to a sitting position despite Mick's firm protests, supporting herself with one straight arm, still breathing heavily. He noticed she kept her face averted from Thad and Daryl. Two people in a car slowed on the street to look.

Daryl now spoke, short butt of the cigarette still in his mouth. "Leave her be," he instructed without looking at Mick. Then he gave Thad a sideways glance that said to get on with the business.

Thad began again on cue. "How long did you plan on yer holy ass bein' in this town? 'Cause nobody needs you here."

Mick did not acknowledge him, instead focusing on simple triage questions he'd been trained to ask in the military long ago. He checked whether the woman had hit her head, whether her back or extremities hurt, whether she felt weak or dizzy. He checked for dilation of her pupils, fluid coming out of the ears, and any breaks in her extremities, especially including hip or back pain.

Thad knew it didn't look good if he allowed himself to be ignored. "Look at me," he said in what he hoped was a commanding tone. He took a menacing step toward Mick. The priest rose without speaking; he was on a step lower than Thad but still looked down at him. His glare made Thad lean back.

Daryl took over from the top step. "Why're you here?" he asked, breaking his silence a second time.

"I'll ask you the same question," Mick replied, again switching focus past Thad to Daryl directly. There was no reply save a cold stare and a flick of Daryl's cigarette butt backward through the door into the church.

Mick knelt again and helped the woman to her feet, then up the steps, brushing Thad unceremoniously out of the way with the back of his hand when the way was not cleared for him. He ignored the small man's over-dramatic reaction and continued slowly up the steps, passing Daryl without a glance to him either, and on into the church. He ignored the smoldering cigarette butt. He helped Mrs. Jillian to a seat in the last bench, walking slowly, thinking as he went. He'd been the target here, that much was clear. The woman had merely been bait—

an attempt to provoke him or catch him off-guard. He also knew there was no intention to arrest him for any kind of assault. The confrontation was staged to find out why he was in Terradise Valley, and probably to intimidate him into abandoning his intentions...whatever they were.

So...there was something about his arrival, or about himself, that bothered these men—bothered their employer. He'd really done nothing except keep his mouth shut and try to leave, yet still he'd somehow caught their attention. Maybe it was just that he was an outsider. Maybe they connected him to whatever the other pastor had been up to; maybe they didn't realize just how much in the dark he was.

One thing was clear: This was a milestone—an escalation. It was the first time they'd brought trouble to him personally. They were willing to risk getting him involved. It was a sentiment he wasn't prepared to match.

These thoughts ran through his head in a troubled instant's time. Evening light now prevailed. He returned to the door to close it, bending to move his tools out of the way. A dark shadow flowed into the doorway, filling it. Instinctively and slowly Mick stood; locking with the cold eyes of Daryl inches from his face.

The cruel man's words smelled like snarled tobacco smoke. "You don't listen."

Mick stood in his way what seemed a full minute, staring into those eyes, yielding no ground. Finally, as slowly and calmly as could be done, he replied, "Try me at eight on Thursdays. Confessions.

Otherwise, get off my church steps." He closed the door hard in Daryl's face.

It took him a moment of heavy breathing to compose himself. He glanced back at Mrs. Jillian. She was standing, as were the two other parishioners who'd never left the church. They looked stunned—but it was what their shocked faces stared at that unnerved him the most. They were looking at his right hand, where he'd instinctively swung it, low and behind. He was clenching the long handle of the huge claw hammer.

He dropped the tool and backed away from it. So it was starting again. He had to get out of this place.

With deep breaths he waited about twenty minutes, leaving the main lights on inside, then led the three parishioners out the poorly lit side door, helping them to his truck, glancing nervously toward the front steps and street. Daryl was not in sight.

He started the engine and waited, still seeing no one. Eventually he pulled quietly into the street, turning left, to take the three to their homes. In the rear view mirror he saw what looked like a primer-red truck parked in the other direction across from the church, the tinted windows obscuring whether anyone was inside.

After driving Mrs. Jillian to her door and leaving her in the care of her daughter and grandchildren, Mick dropped off the other two and returned to the priest's residence. The street lamp a block away now illuminated the deserted road. To his relief the primer-red truck was gone. He exited the Landcruiser and began to head toward the residence door, but froze at the soft sound of feet on gravel behind him, across the street. He knew he was visible; there was no value in remaining motionless. He turned purposefully and strode back to the edge of the road, peering into the shadows there. Standing in the open was the very thin Indian man he'd seen staring at him his first day here. The man was motionless, and staring again.

Mick watched him for a moment. Could the man be trying to contact him? Curious that he should show up here now, he thought, immediately after the earlier incident with Daryl and Thad...and he seemed nervous. Mick decided to try to bridge the gap. He glanced around to make sure they were alone; seeing no one else, he stepped slowly onto the street and began to walk toward the thin man, smiling and raising his hand.

But the man shuffled off sideways up the sidewalk at Mick's same speed, neither losing nor gaining distance between them. They were still twenty yards apart; the keen stare continued. Unsure how to handle this, Mick opted for directness. He stopped and called out softly, "How can I help you sir?"

The man continued to shuffle, but replied in a soft, clear voice, "Their secrets are buried."

"I'm sorry? Secrets? Whose?"

But there were shadows, and the man was gone.

CHAPTER ELEVEN

Night finally put an end to the disturbing day. If nothing else had changed, Mick's simple, short-lived preoccupation with passing time doing carpentry repairs was forgotten. There was something very wrong with this place.

He straddled a backward chair in the kitchen, facing Elmer, who was stocking in food. "You eat more'n other priests," the old man grumbled out of nowhere.

The comment roused Mick from his silence, but failed to derail his troubled thoughts. "I'll tell you Elmer," he said, getting straight to what was on his mind, "I've about had it with these self-appointed constables, or whoever they are."

Elmer dumped potatoes from a burlap bag into a thin metal bin with a loud rumble and did not answer.

"I guess that's no big surprise," Mick tried again. "I see a lot of fear whenever those guys are around...I've only been here a little while but I've already witnessed more abuse of these townspeople by those thugs than would ever be tolerated in a normal community. Is there anyone in this town who thinks they serve some kind of purpose?"

"Their employer most likely—he's payin' 'em." Elmer moved to the stove top, where he began to scoop the contents of the skillet onto a plate.

"Knox, as I heard it. Never seen him yet. Is he worried about this guy...Wayne Aak, is it?...coming back and raising hell or something? I mean, else why the mercenaries?"

"That little shit is a fly to them people," Elmer spat out. He splashed hot oil on his finger and swore.

"You're certainly not shy around priests," Mick chuckled.

"Well then that shit is a gnat," Elmer rephrased, changing the wrong word, not to let his point be missed.

"So you're not a fan of the hell-raisers."

With his back still to Mick, Elmer answered. "I don't like the god-damn hell-raisers, nor the rest of the damn Indians, nor the damn outsiders who run this town, nor the damn cowards that live in it. I don't like nobody and I don't like questions." The fiercely independent, rough hewn, equal opportunity hater turned and placed before Mick a dainty dish of trout almandine.

Mick surveyed the plate before him and smiled a big, knowing smile at Elmer, who stared back self-consciously. "Well you seem to like cooking," the priest observed with a grin.

"I like fishin'," the old man growled reluctantly as he seated himself.

"That's enough for me, my friend," Mick replied eagerly, swiveling the chair around to face the table. He and Elmer dug in simultaneously. It was good. Mick noticed a peach pie waiting on the counter, and inclined his head toward it as he chewed. "That pie from the woman with the deep voice?"

"Mine!" defended Elmer. "That ol' biddy can't do right by a peach."

"And...you catch this trout yourself"?

"Took a Hair's Ear in an eddy behind a big ol' cedar stump," Elmer boasted. "Twenty inches, that one."

"Now I know where you go during the day! It's damn good...if I wasn't a priest and you weren't such a mean cuss I'd marry you."

It had taken him weeks, but he finally pulled a grin out of the old man.

*　　*　　*

They stood together on the gravel bank of a tumbling stream, tall conifers towering like perpetually dignified sentries on the steep slope behind them and opposite side. Not relishing the prospect of having little to think about except disturbing events, Mick had convinced Elmer to show him some favorite trout habitat. The clear cold water slid across a smooth glide upstream of them, then rolled over and around small rounded rocks and boulders as it passed the point where they stood.

They'd risen about four AM, yet even here, between the forested banks, it was already getting light. Elmer had chosen a creek only a half hour's drive west, down a once-graded gravel road he said no one else ever used. The caretaker had brought a spare fly rod for the priest—a seven-foot stiff glass number with an old single-action take-up reel that held size five floating line. The eight-foot tapered leader was already rigged, and ended in a light 4x tippet and a tiny austere fly Elmer had tied by hand the previous winter.

"Givin' you a little bitty imitation of a Granhom Caddis," he said. "Nymph. Let 'er swirl down low behind stuff. Can you do that?"

"What do you have there?"

"Mine'll look like a green drake, dry. I don't see nothing in the air, but we might fool 'em just the same. Been itchin' to try it out. Too early in the day probably, but right time o' year anyway."

"Drake? Looks like a tiny duck?"

"Mayfly! I thought you said you'd done this a'fore." The old man peered at him over the bent-up tackle-box spectacles he needed to tie leaders to lines.

Mick smiled and with a cough avoided reply; he'd already shown himself for the greenhorn he was.

They separated then, Elmer ambling upstream fifteen yards through the weeds, Mick staying where he stood. It had been more than a year since he'd gone back into the Adirondacks to tempt the wily trout. He stripped the leader from the rod's tip guide until it hung free, checked the space behind him, and tried a cast, promptly catching a stunted pine over his shoulder. Right, he thought, start by noting the length of the thing. Quickly he shook slack into the line and dropped the rod tip to ground level, lest

Elmer turn around and see him battling the sparsely needled branch. At least he hadn't snagged a loose twig and propelled it forward to smack down over the fish in front of him.

Upstream, his back to Mick, Elmer was already standing mid-current. His balance and strength were uncanny, the priest thought, considering the wooden leg. The old guy didn't let it slow him down. Mick watched him flip a strong wrist and execute a roll cast, avoiding the chance of fouling the line behind himself. He clearly had good control—could probably write his name on the water with the line.

Over the next hour Mick caught the same tree twice more, but managed to avoid losing the tiny fly. He kept things simple and stayed in one place, watching Elmer slowly work his way further upstream. Insects of various kinds flitted past, but as he had no other fly patterns anyway, he paid them little attention and concentrated on laying line to water. The trick was, he knew, to settle the fly on the water where it would sink and drift into the area of interest, keeping the thick, visible floating line from rippling across places a fish might hide. Watching the pale green line as it swept in lazy curves across currents swift and slow, he worked the nearer and more downstream spots first, then gradually angled his aim leftward, more upstream. The noisy little creek was not large and he didn't have to throw very hard.

He wondered whether the local tribal population ever fished this way. What he was doing had descended from European sporting technique...how did the Washokki normally catch fish? They'd likely be more interested in food gathering than in playing and losing half the fish they hooked. They could even be still fishing with traps, set lines or spears, he thought. He realized how ignorant he was of the locals' ways. Thinking about that, he took a few steps into the water, stopping when thigh-deep, sacrificing the leather of his shoes to improve his angle for the next few casts.

He realized he was not unlike Knox's men—he too was an outsider. He didn't belong, yet here he was, darkening local doorways, treading on local soil. It was something that still had to be remedied. When would the Bishop respond and extract him from the place?

A small bump on his line brought him back to the present. Something two or more feet deep had taken the fly, probably in the turbulated water behind that smooth black exposed rock. Mick raised the rod tip lightly and gave a delicate jerk, but there was no resistance, and he drew the fly in for another cast. Maybe he'd been too slow to react, or maybe it was nothing at all. That was the problem with nymph fishing, he recalled—one never knew whether one was getting a strike or just hanging up momentarily on a stone at the stream's bottom. It didn't pay to get distracted by the disturbing events of strange towns—not if the idea was to fill the creel.

A soft crunching of pebbles to his left made him turn his head; Elmer was walking in his direction through the ten-inch-deep water near the stream's edge.

"Sun's too high now," the old man said simply, signaling the end of the brief outing.

"Okay. How'd you do?"

The caretaker reached for the burlap bag trailing in the water behind him, opened it, and held up a sixteen-inch fish, its sides flashing a swath of varying color as he turned it artfully in the sun.

"Rainbow," Mick smiled.

"Yep, but Redband," Elmer corrected. "Local fish, these here parts only."

To Mick's surprise the old man then stooped, carefully placed the beautiful creature in the water at his feet, and cradled it upright until it figured out what to do. With barely a splash it was gone. Elmer smiled and nodded to himself, then stepped out of the water and turned back to Mick.

"You?" he asked.

"Oh...let's see...had one a fair bit bigger than that, and did the same thing with it."

"Uh huh. Redband, Cutthroat, or Bull Trout?"

"Oh, pure bull, no question."

The old man chuckled and moseyed back up the trail toward his car. Mick exited the cold water and followed him.

"Thanks for that," the priest offered as they headed up the gravel path. "Thanks for showing me your secret spot, too."

"Well it warn't my best one."

They both grinned, then fell silent. Mick chose not to tarnish the morning with more questions about the town's troubles. Within the half hour they were back at the residence; Elmer took the tackle into his own bedroom and Mick quickly readied himself for morning Mass.

Afterward, he made up for lost sleep with a nap, then busied himself realigning kitchen cabinet drawers that had long since come off the rails, doing his best to continue to stave off the constant tension he felt here. Elmer went out.

*   *   *

The following morning Mick decided to distract himself with another field trip. He gassed up his truck and took a leisurely drive out North Fork Road to Gabriella's farm. He stopped the vehicle in her driveway and stood for a few minutes beside it, gazing around him at the beauty of the small valley. The high treed ridge behind him seemed a silent sentry for this place, contrasting gradually with the more open pasture land to the immediate north.

Thirty yards away, Gabriella walked out of the barn cradling a partial bale of hay in both arms, a long-sleeved flannel shirt shielding her forearms from abrasion. Angelo tagged along behind her. She did not see his truck; she carried the hay a short distance to a wooden fence by which a small pony stood waiting. Mick watched her for a few minutes feeding the tan-colored animal while her little boy stroked its thick blonde mane and held small portions of hay between the fence rails so the pony could eat from his hand.

Eventually the dog gave Mick away, barking a welcome and darting out to announce him to all within earshot. Gabriella spotted him and took Angelo by the hand. Softly, gracefully, she walked her child back to the house, the friendly Border Collie darting to rejoin them. Smiling, she turned as she walked, and waved Mick in.

He walked to the porch, instinctively scraped his shoes against the sharp edge of the lowest step, then mounted the steps and waited by the screen door. A longish seed-studded bird feeder hung to his left between the screen door and the kitchen window, and he watched for a moment as a diminutive, grey-hued Mountain Chickadee crawled upward along it, tiny hooked beak searching out only certain seeds. Gabriella appeared behind the screen with a tall glass of lemonade, ice cubes clinking invitingly on the sides of the glass. She opened the door and handed the glass to him. "Hi," she said simply, with a smile. He accepted the glass and the implied invitation, and stepped inside.

They stood in the kitchen. In sharp contrast to his first visit, Gabriella was looking at him, smiling. He took a sip, smiled, nodded. "Good," he said. "Nice...on a...warm day."

She was still watching his face.

"What?" he finally asked.

"The rumor is you're becoming an outlaw."

"Oh, you mean...the...uh...those...goons. Well I guess outlaw status puts me in an elite group of thousands," he replied, grinning. "Anyway it seems word travels fast."

"In all directions I'm sure."

An easy silence reigned for a moment, and Mick took the opportunity to change the subject. He turned to Angelo. "So you have a pony! Wow."

The boy smiled but still hid behind his mother's leg.

"A pony, and a dog, and a turtle...he's a very lucky boy," Gabriella answered for him.

"Although I'll bet Mama does most of the feeding," Mick guessed.

"He's pretty good about wanting to help. We take care of them together, don't we?" she answered in the child's direction, tousling his hair. Then to Mick, "The 'break of dawn' duty does fall to me though."

Mick chuckled. "Do you...have any help here, Gabriella?" The question wasn't intended to sound as probing as it did. Embarrassed, he added quickly, "I just mean...it's a big place, especially to add to the full-time job of a child."

Gabriella paused an indecisive moment, then addressed Angelo. "Go wash your hands." The boy tottered off to a back room, and she turned back to Mick. He was afraid he'd opened the crate where pain was held captive.

"My husband...disappeared about a year ago. We'd been under a lot of pressure to give up this land."

"Pressure from who? Where?"

"Various directions, but Knox and his men. He's behind it."

"Behind what exactly?"

"Strange things," she confided, "like contracts to sell out appearing on our doorstep, harassment from the law, rumors designed to make us feel unwelcome.

116

He...just...." She paused to take a deep breath, and gestured toward Angelo in the back room. "Since then we've...my son and I...have been living off some savings, and I rent one pasture to a neighbor to graze their stock on. That gets us by."

"But...did you file a 'missing persons' report? I mean, is disappearing the kind of thing you might expect...from...." He trailed off and left the sensitive question hanging.

"Carlo...is a good man. He's maybe...not so...he's naive, like good people often are. They said they opened a file but I don't think anyone's really trying to locate or contact him. All I can do is wait."

"He's Mexican, I think you'd told me? Could he have gone back to stay with friends or family there?"

"Maybe...I think maybe...I don't have any way of finding out who or where."

Mick was silent for a moment. This story clearly went a lot deeper. He tried a different angle, redirecting the conversation back to Knox. "Is there something special about this chunk of land?"

"A mine needs water."

His mind always saw it in slow motion, although the sound of it never changed: A wooden railroad water tank lying on its side, gushing water into the mouth of a filthy mineshaft. He'd seen it many times—once when he was seven years old, and thereafter whenever it chose to replay itself. It was always out of order that way, in his memory—the broken gushing tank first, then the backward jump in time to the rusted old school bus coasting into a tall, stilted wooden water tank that stood by the train track, knocking it over.

He'd been gone into the past an instant, no more. Gabriella hadn't noticed. "...without sufficient year-around supply, he'd need to pipe or truck it in. Gasoline too, for all the generators he'd need if he can't get power from running water. He can't rely on some seasonal creek. Anyway, for this little stream here, we're the key."

Mick recovered his thoughts. "Key to what?"

"Knox needs to divert it. Carlo figured it out about the same time Knox did. Here, I'll show you." She called to the boy and together they led the priest through the door and out to the wooden fence, then ducked between the rails. They walked past the barn, where the dog joined them, and continued through increasingly taller grass. The little pony, out of curiosity or sensing some treat, joined the procession at a distance.

Mick noticed they were approaching a meandering stream hidden in the tall ground cover. Clear, shallow in some places, and several feet deep in its channel, it flowed over fist-sized mottled brown stones through the shaded meadow. Even at very close range it was partly concealed by the long overhanging grass. They stopped at a point overlooking a little gravel bar near a bend.

"It runs year-around," Gabriella explained, pointing upstream, then sweeping her hand out and toward the north. "Flows through here and down a narrow gap onto federal land, where it can't be touched. It's the elegant solution—if he can turn it here, where it bends naturally, he can get away with it."

Mick wasn't quite following yet. "Okay let's say he somehow got hold of this land. Now, if he did what you're suggesting—if he diverted your stream—which I guess would be his stream—couldn't anyone just inform the federal authorities? I mean, you can't just divert water like that. I'm sure of it. Water rights usually extend to landowners far downstream. You can't even extract more than your share. Couldn't that be pointed out to him—make him see he can't profit by grabbing your land?"

"The federal authority in these parts seems to default to the Bureau of Indian Affairs," she scoffed. "They're more intent on jailing drunks and showing a growing economy out here than on getting tangled in land or water issues. Land law has always been abused in remote places like this...and it's easy enough to change the course of a stream down a path it took centuries ago and simply say a cloudburst returned it to its original channel."

"So...his mine depends on this stream?"

"He needed power and road easements too...but he bought all those ranchers out for pennies, telling them they'd be flooded and worthless after he got hold of my property. Unless he wants to find another source of water, this little farm is the stone unturned."

They walked back to the house and ascended to the porch. Mick was trying to piece it all together. "Did he at least openly make you a legal offer? Or an offer to lease?"

"He knows a lease won't help, because diverting is illegal, as you say. He has to own it and keep his actions secret. And he knows it's not for sale. So, he uses harassment."

They sat again in the kitchen. Gabriella set out some sliced fruit in a small bowl, and a glass of water for Mick. Angelo went back to the other room before Mick spoke again. "You said Carlo figured it out."

"Yes...he'd gotten...in trouble with the law. Knox came out of nowhere and helped...so we trusted him—we didn't know him back then. That was maybe two years ago."

"Your husband was the 'marked man' you mentioned earlier. The one they tried to frame with this Wayne Aak fellow."

Gabriella nodded softly. "It turned out it was all staged to put us in Knox's debt. Knox needed Carlo; Carlo is educated. He got him out of jail, then hired him—researching old claims, the old technologies, mapping tunnels, acting as liaison to the Washokki community on Knox's behalf. But...our trust turned sour when Knox shifted the focus to sources of water and the answers weren't coming up like he wanted. Knox saw—and we saw—he had to own our land." She thought a moment. "Come to think of it, I believe he knew this all along, and that's why he cultivated Carlo's trust. He is a very calculating man."

Mick watched her face. It was clear she didn't find it easy to talk about.

"Of course we also lost face with the Washokki," Gabriella confided, "for Carlo's association with Knox. In the end almost no tribal members would even speak to us. And because of me we weren't in the white world. We were pretty much alone."

"People need friends," Mick murmured, realizing how empty the words were.

"We had a few. At the time, Carlo trusted the other priest. And one Washokki man...who...he never held anything against Carlo, even though everyone else believed the lies. And your caretaker Elmer has...asked about Angelo since Carlo...left."

Mick listened quietly.

"A boy needs a man, needs his father," she explained, "and Elmer knows that. I'm sure you must remember how you felt about yours."

"I...didn't have a chance to grow up with him," he whispered almost too softly to hear.

Both Mick and Gabriella faded back into their own memories. After a moment, Gabriella returned to her tale. "Anyway Carlo began to drink. He was under a lot of pressure—he and Father MacArthur. Carlo realized Knox was treacherous, and Father MacArthur knew how he had altered the community. They dreamed secretly of destroying him."

"Did they...do something?"

She described a surreal scene that seemed straight out of third world revolutionary fiction. The picture her memory painted was of her husband and the small, nervous, bespectacled Father MacArthur seated at the kitchen table on a hot summer night. In front of Carlo had stood a half-empty bottle of liquor. Voices in the dark outside, then the heavy sound of boots on the porch. Carlo had evidently expected them, and had risen quickly to open the door. Three rough Washokki men had entered; one bore an ugly scar across his face. Inaudible introductions, Gabriella said, although she'd recognized one of the men. Drinking, very low voices, suspicion and secrecy. They were violent men, she said, and they were armed, even that night.

"They finished the bottle. I watched through the bedroom door. They would not speak while I was in the room, and Carlo also didn't want me to hear. They acted like he was important to whatever they were discussing."

"Do you know what the meeting was about?"

She went on with her story; Mick wasn't sure if she was answering his question or not. "About a week later Carlo drove to Missoula and put our farm in Angelo's name without telling me...we'd never discussed that...and...left. It's been a year. More now."

Both of them fell silent, staring at the floor. He waited until she raised her head. "Are you still being harassed?"

"Pressure has increased over time—starting with the isolation, then hoping to make us afraid— gunshots in the middle of the night, a knife stuck in our door once...we had two sheep we found dead one morning—and then of course driving my husband off. They watch my every move; they're just waiting for me to give up."

He wondered how long she could hold out.

"Well we're not the only outcasts anyway," she consoled herself. "Knox is one himself. He's got no friends at all. Even the people he pays are only hovering around because they smell a payoff in that mine. And the tribes are against him in everything he does."

"Why do they oppose him?"

"Ask them. They're his enemy, but they're just as lunatic, and nearly as ruthless."

"I've tried to chat with some of them, but I never get very far, especially with the younger ones."

"And you won't."

"Not that I have any real reason to. I mean, this is all just idle curiosity. I'm...not involved."

She said nothing to that.

He sighed and diverted the discussion back to the common enemy. "Anyway, this Knox certainly keeps some poor company. I don't think much of that tall silent character, for one. I read him as a mean and dangerous man. I've heard him called Daryl."

Gabriella stiffened at his mention of the name, and abruptly interrupted him, by force of habit a measure of distrust creeping back into her voice. "I would think a priest should know there are demons everywhere and their names should not be spoken. Not in my home."

He'd eaten the sliced fruit; she reached abruptly for the empty bowl, but he rose and brought it to the sink, rinsed it and several other dishes sitting there, and placed them carefully in the drainer. The contrast between the people they'd been discussing and this strong gentle man surprised Gabriella. She watched with mild interest both his easy willingness to assist and the fact that he ignored the dish soap sitting right by the sink. He was a priest, but after all still a man.

Mick gazed out the window in front of him, watching a pair of small Grosbeaks feeding on the hanging seed post. "You must like birds, to keep such a buffet for them."

"It's for Angelo, so he can watch them. We sit out there sometimes, and they come if we stay still." Her expression softened again. "And for me too, I guess. I probably love them as much as he does."

"No doubt he gets it from you."

"I guess so. I've always envied birds."

"Envy...." He thought about that. "Not everyone would use that word. May I ask why?"

"I suppose because they are so free. They belong to the earth and the sky at the same time. They can choose...and they have the courage to choose. If they like, they don't give it a second thought—they just go up and play. In the sky."

He smiled, knowing. She caught the look and initially mistook it for disbelief. "No, it's true. They set an example for the rest of us." She was trying to gauge his reaction as she explained, now unsure whether he doubted or understood. "Like...Angels of the present world...."

"And you admire that."

She smiled and nodded, tentatively at first, then definitively.

Mick studied her face, looked back at the birds on the feeder, and thought for a few moments. He turned back to her, a decision made. "You can drive a truck?"

"Yes...of course...."

"I want you to come with me tomorrow. For the day."

"Where?"

"Just...don't give it a second thought. Come and play."

CHAPTER TWELVE

The sun had managed to extend only half its face from behind the high ridge into a clear blue sky. Cool air from the evening before still lingered wherever shadow hung on. The dirt road wound tightly against the rocky mountainside, the alluvial plain two thousand feet below their present position stretching from the steep right side drop-off to the next range roughly eighteen miles to the north.

The Landcruiser was up to the task. Mick worked the narrow, sometimes rutted track, aiming the front tires for the smoothest sections and between the sharpest rocks as they climbed, striking a balance between forward progress, safety, and steady transport for the long bagged object tied solidly to the roof rack. Gabriella, white knuckles clenching the cushion beneath her, sat on the front edge of the passenger's seat and kept constant vigil out her side window, to Mick's secret amusement regularly imploring him to stay away from the deadly naked edge on the right. Between them, Angelo rode with eyes wide. He held his mother's leg but stole glances at the man who was his mother's new friend.

The grade relaxed a bit and Mick took the truck from first to second, accidentally bumping Angelo's knee as he shifted gears. He turned and winked by way of apology. The boy reached forward and touched the shift knob when Mick's hand left it. Mick's face clouded involuntarily and he quickly moved the child's hand off the lever.

"This range we're on is where most of the smaller independent claims were filed, way back when," Gabriella commented. "They say it's riddled with holes in the ground where men tried to change their destinies."

"Why this particular range?"

"Carlo said the geology is similar to where the Slide Mine is—just a little further around the corner to the west. It's in the same range. People assumed they could find what the big money said was here."

"All I see is mountain. Amazing how people could get their equipment and provisions up into places like this. Pack animals, I suppose."

"And their own backs. This track we're driving started as a trail. They'd get mules up in here, and those without animals would make ascent after ascent carrying up to a hundred pounds at a time on their shoulders."

The dry rocky track steepened for a stretch, and they climbed close to another thousand feet in the next thirty five minutes, the air warming slightly as they went. Angelo began to transition from shyness to boredom. Watching Mick's feet working the pedals, he reached his tiny toe down to touch the top of Mick's shoe. Mick smiled and tousled the boy's hair. The open plain was now nearly three thousand feet below, and Mick knew that it would be more than enough.

"Let's try here," he said finally, stopping where the track widened. He pointed the truck down-slope, toward the direction from which they'd come. They got out, Gabriella quizzical, following blindly, holding tightly to Angelo's hand. They stayed a dozen feet behind Mick as he stepped to the edge of a firm promontory. A whisper of air flowed up to touch his face, and he smiled, raising an open hand to feel it. "It's coming," he said, satisfied, and walked back to the truck to untie and unload the long package from the rack.

"You still haven't told me what we're doing up here," Gabriella chided, "but even so I'm getting nervous about it."

"All shall be made clear," he replied mysteriously, hefting the long bag to the ground a half dozen strides from the truck and unzipping it lengthwise. "Best stand back for this."

Gabriella looked on, disbelieving. Like he'd done it a thousand times, he quickly assembled a thin metal frame with bolts and wing nuts. Then he lifted and inverted the mechanism, propping it up on the triangular frame he'd created. Unzipping the long bag the rest of the way, he carefully rolled it and placed it nearer the truck, then opened out the standing gear into a well-used but brightly colored hang glider.

Gabriella's jaw dropped. Despite the child's pulling to break free, her grip tightened on Angelo's wrist.

"Don't tell me you're...no. You're not going to do anything insane...?"

"Completely over the edge!"

"No, I mean really!"

"I'm going to show you that we too can be free like birds," he smiled, laying out a series of curved aluminum battens behind the limp sail.

"But...we're so high!"

"High is far away from low, and low is where all the sticker bushes are," he replied with a twinkle.

She moved around to the side of the glider away from the promontory's edge, and allowed Angelo to play in the dust at her feet. While she watched Mick, he stood at the back of the sail and stuffed the various-length battens one by one into thin fabric sleeves, moving from the metal keel outward toward one wingtip, then repeating the process for the other wing. The battens got smaller as he moved toward each wingtip. He flashed her another swashbuckling smile.

"Tell me you've done this before!" she demanded, still half refusing to accept.

"You mean, am I an imbecile?"

Speechless, she watched him prepare for the unthinkable. He sat on the ground behind the metal keel and grabbed a pair of thin steel cables hanging there. Taking a deep breath, he stretched them backward down the length of the keel, hooking them to a fitting. As he positioned the shackle, the lumpy, wrinkled sail tensioned into the taut, graceful shape of an elegant flying machine.

Mick noted Gabriella's continuing shock, but also observed how her expression softened after he'd tensioned the wing. Angelo too now took notice, and approached the sail to run his tiny fingers over the more colorful parts of the fabric sail.

The priest smiled in reassurance. "Been a few years, but I've seen a fair bit of New England terrain from this ol' bird. I think I still remember how." He hooked an identical pair of steel cables from the triangular control frame to the glider's nose, completing the setup; then he began a walk-around pre-flight check of wires, components, and the sail itself. "See how the triangular shape sweeps backward from the pointed nose to the wingtips? The wingtips double as the tail. The most important parts of this whole thing are those tips, and how they sweep upward in back. Those, and the rear edge of the sail all along its length. That's what keeps me from becoming a dart buried in the ground out there in the valley."

He continued his pre-flight check, walking around the glider until he returned to where he'd begun. Finding a grasshopper sitting on the leading edge, he flicked it off with a click of his finger, calling out, "No hitch-hikers!" It broke the tension; Gabriella laughed, and Angelo mimicked her mirth.

They stood in the flow of the air rolling up the mountain. "It's beginning to cycle," Mick explained, feeling the strength of the breeze fall off to nothing, then half a minute later blow nicely again. "What they call 'thermals'—columns of warm air heated by the sun in the valley down there—are banding together and rolling up the slope here. Bubbles of lift. A glider, just like those soaring birds over there, can use that lift to stay up, even gain altitude." He pointed out over the valley where a Cooper's Hawk was soaring, and to the east high over the ridge, where what was either an Eagle or an Osprey flew at higher altitude.

"You mean, go up?"

"Absolutely...if the lift is strong enough and easy enough to find. Depends on the day, but the goal is to make good guesses about where the rising air might be, based on terrain below and the wind strength, and spend the entire flight higher than where you began."

"How do you get back down?"

"Fail to find lift. And that's usually not a problem to accomplish."

He pointed out into the valley below. "You see those two marks, what look like thin lines in the dust of the valley?"

"Roads," she said.

"Roads, right. See the junction where they cross each other? Do you know how to drive out to there?"

"One will be the old road toward Drakk Lake. The other cuts across that plain and I don't think it has a name. Might be what some call Slide Mine Road. But there's only one that crosses, so yes, I can take the one I know and get there."

"Then let's pick that spot as the place where I'll land, if I can find enough lift to make it that far, which should be no problem on a day like today."

"Won't you get there first?"

"Oh sure, if I were to head right out," he confirmed. "But I'll stay up over these hills we're in now for as long as I can find rising air. Even so, if you stand and watch a little while from here, it's likely I'll beat you there. I'm not as young as I used to be, and if there's any turbulence, my arms will get tired eventually."

"But how will you land?" she asked, genuinely concerned.

"With dignity I hope," he smiled. "Either that or with a good coating of dust."

"So I'll know your skill by how clean you look later," she warned with a laugh.

He went back to the truck and pulled out the old cloth duffel that held his flying harness. He stepped each leg carefully through its own leg strap, and tightened the right one down until the tension matched for both. He slipped his body into the main portion and buckled it securely, taking care not to tangle the spider web of lines that would suspend him from the glider. He clipped the hefty carabiner to one of the steel cables attached to the nose, verifying that the suspension lines were not twisted on each other. Then he unclipped the 'biner from the cable and back onto his harness, dug a battered old helmet from out of the same duffel and donned it, added goggles to stave off the 25mph breeze he'd feel once airborne, and lifted the leg cocoon to a clip by his waist.

Gabriella and Angelo watched this transformation from man to pudgy google-eyed alien with amusement. As he waddled back to the glider, calling out, "keys are on the driver's seat," Angelo laughed outright. Mick shot him a comical salute, hooked and twist-locked the carabiner to the hang strap on the glider, lifted the airframe of the aircraft to his shoulders, and carried the 60-pound contraption to the edge of the promontory.

He stood there for several minutes. "Cycles are every ten to fifteen," he said aloud but mostly to himself. A gust lifted the right wing, taking the glider out of level, and he took a step backward to settle it again.

"Can I have your help, Gabriella? Just you; Angelo should stay back."

She stepped forward and he described how she should crouch under the left wing, ready to grab the load-bearing side wire in case the far wing acted up again. "Just keep this one from bottoming on the ground, but only if I yell."

"Okay."

"When I say 'Clear,' don't touch a thing."

"Okay."

She still didn't quite know what to expect. A moment's pause reigned, the breeze quickened, the level was maintained. He gave the word. She was aware of about two running steps, and a third that never touched the ground. And suddenly he was a bird, completely off the edge, rising dramatically in strong lift right in front of her. She gasped in disbelief and joy as he surged out over nothing, still climbing. He turned fifty yards out in a big clockwise arc, coming back around and over-flying her and the boy, flashing a broad smile and delivering another dashing salute.

Gabriella and Angelo waved in uncontainable excitement as the glider soared in graceful, ever-widening circles, climbing higher while they watched. The mother stood dazed, intoxicated, enthralled; she wept openly. The boy laughed aloud at this wonderful thing, his innocent face jubilant, his cheeks caressed by the warm late morning September breeze. Years later, he would recall snippets of the moment, and write, "That was the most wonderful thing I had ever seen. And it was the first time I ever remember seeing my mother cry. He didn't yet know what he would come to mean to us, but by showing us freedom, courage and the impossible, he had already begun to save us."

CHAPTER THIRTEEN

In 1928, a boy was born in Hartford Connecticut to an unmarried woman of dubious character. The father was an affluent man by the name of Todd Bernarde. Given the nature of the mother's profession and the illegal world in which she trafficked, Bernarde sought and was granted full custody of the child.

Bernarde was a highly successful Man of the Cloth—an independent promoter of the Christian faith, answering to no particular church or hierarchy. From a prosperous family and himself properly educated, he authored a number of books, which he marketed among congregations of churches throughout the Northeast. He was versed in Latin, Theology and other classical subjects, and managed to remain in relatively constant, lucrative demand among religious organizations in the northeastern states, for revivals, fund raising, lectures and the like.

When the boy was four years old, Bernarde married an Irish immigrant woman some years his junior, hoping to have more children. A daughter was born a year later, and she and the boy, now five, constituted the sum total of Bernarde's known offspring.

Bernarde was a brutal man when drunk, which was not infrequent; the children both endured severe beatings on a regular basis, as did the girl's mother. When sober, the minister was a strict disciplinarian and unquenchable adherent to the most rigorous tenets of education. The boy in particular was drilled in Latin, mathematics, classical literature, and of course religion. Bernarde knew he was himself a fraud; his hope was that, through unrelenting education and uncompromising punishment, his son would rise above fraudulent existences to become a man of true stature.

When the boy reached the age of six he was enrolled in a private, non-denominational boarding school in New Haven. The establishment reflected Bernarde's own style of militaristic discipline. The boy spent the next eight years living and studying there, including summers, as Bernarde had taken to European travel during the warm months, and child care was inconvenient to his profession, energies, and fascinations. After eight years the boy was transitioned to a similarly run school structured to shepherd students through the higher grades of nine through twelve.

The boy was not a model student; as he matured, he incurred more and more disciplinary action, for infractions ranging from theft of fellow students' possessions to insubordination to violations of the establishment's Victorian honor code. As his family had sufficient means, however, he was punished regularly but not compelled to leave. His was a not inactive mind; he consumed romanticized adventure literature voraciously, and being bright, absorbed sufficient knowledge of other academic pursuits to pass examinations and still be promoted, albeit without particular distinction, to each next academic level in turn. One particular emerging strength was the subject of Finance.

In 1946, triggering a particularly ugly public scandal, the Reverend Todd Bernarde was accused of and arrested for multiple counts of statutory rape. He immediately brought his significant wealth and influence to bear in his own defense, but as more and more victims and former victims came forward to add additional charges and testify, defense became an exercise akin to ejecting the raging sea from a collapsing ship with a small chalice. Recognizing the hopelessness of his legal and social predicament and intent on sparing himself the anguish of the public's retribution, Bernarde drugged and drank himself to death in a single sitting, on the evening before his son's seventeenth birthday.

The event constituted an obvious loss of social standing for the surviving family members; the daughter and mother disappeared over the next few months, possibly to Ireland, and were not heard from again. The son quickly established that he held legal claim to his father's money, but soon discovered that, save for tuition expenses and a modest living stipend, he could access none of it until he reached the age of twenty one. He continued in the traditional boarding school in which he was enrolled, but lost interest in most academic pursuits, and his performance showed a marked decline. His fall-off had provided the school a convenient excuse to avoid the embarrassment of an outcast's ongoing matriculation; he was expelled for "insufficient academic promise" at the first opportunity in less than a year.

In the many years that followed, it was the expulsion and the hint at his intellectual inferiority that he resented, rather than the loss of his family. He had been branded a person of poor breeding, and to him the truth of that implication was beside the point. He also secretly regretted providing the opening for such intellectual inferiors to discard him. He feared he had squandered the golden opportunity to be groomed for aristocracy, where lay wealth and, in particular, power.

The young man's resentment and private regret festered; he eventually fell to thoughts and then crimes of vengeance, and two years later was convicted of arson and involuntary manslaughter when the mansion belonging to his former school's Headmaster was destroyed by fire, in which happened to be an elderly caretaker when the blaze began. In fact the young man had hoped the Headmaster himself might have been there. He served the entire length of an eight year sentence at the state penitentiary in Danbury, Connecticut, and was released at the age of twenty eight, older, taller, more focused, more gaunt.

While in Danbury, he had made the association of two individuals who had previously spent some years in paid mercenary work in Central America and Colombia. The prospect of light danger and real money appealed to the gaunt man. He obtained introductions to key contacts from his prison associates prior to his release, and made arrangements to seek similar work for himself. After being released, in advance of travel he established a series of financial investment instruments in which he parked the money he had inherited from his father. He also effected a legal change of his surname.

Opportunity in Central America proved available. The gaunt man made the in-person association of the contacts to which he'd been referred, and became involved in transport and logistics for smuggling contraband in and out of Panama, and later drugs and weapons between Panama and Colombia. It was in the weapons trade that he met Daryl Lievestro, an individual seemingly with no ethical boundaries and no loyalties. This combination excited the gaunt man, and he courted Lievestro's association with talk of larger goals and the finances to launch them.

Drug and weapon smuggling occupied his energies for nine years, and, he discovered, if one was not averse to risk, provided opportunities for financial gain independent of one's employer. He met others whose skills leaned more toward the violent than did his own, and noted who was reliable and who could be bought.

In the course of taking those risks he made a mistake, and for his own immediate safety abruptly left the extended smuggling organization with which he was associated. He went south, into northern

Brasil and then Peru, in pursuit of gold reported to be discovered along the upper Amazon. For the next two years he worked with, helped finance, or initiated a number of small gold extraction operations in the region, all with limited or no success. He learned, observed, and began to shun mercury-spreading and sluice box techniques in search of something much more substantial.

At some point he fell in with a larger, more profitable operation run by a powerful Venezuelan-Colombian named Rojas, and the gaunt man hired on to assist with logistics and supervision of operations. He sent word to Lievestro, still in Panama, who joined him in Brasil as a security contractor for the Rojas operation. The two worked for Rojas over the next four years. Although the money was very good, they continued to look for a way to participate in the extraction of wealth beyond just salary, but were unable to identify an opportunity and unwilling to repeat the risks taken in the smuggling operation in Panama.

One of the other security contractors Rojas had hired was a kindred product of the American penitentiary system. He had also originally been a member of an Indian tribe in some area of southern Alberta, before running afoul of United States law. Under the influence of whiskey the Indian once spoke of a mine that was said to have been demolished by landslide and abandoned at the turn of the century. The gaunt man befriended the Alberta man over a period of months, then introduced him to Daryl Lievestro. At a point soon after, the Indian's mutilated body was discovered in the rain forest by locals, pinned to a tree with iron spikes.

The gaunt man returned to the northeastern United States in 1972 and repositioned his finances, which he was already aware had grown considerably in his absence. He engaged in some targeted research, including geology and historical records of estates and deeds, and also effected some travel to the western states. Soon afterward, he purchased land in Montana.

CHAPTER FOURTEEN

The late morning air was cool at altitude. A good sign, Mick knew—lift would top out higher than the mountain range from which he'd launched. He'd climbed to a point level with the top of the ridge, and sighted across the half mile or so to where its rocky jagged spine scratched the belly of the sky.

At first he had tried to hug the air right up against the steep terrain, knowing that rising thermals often contour-climb a mountainside, rolling up gullies and aggregating with other lift at the tops of fluted ridges. Today that wasn't producing much in the way of sustained climb, and he had lost several hundred feet trying to make it work. So he took another look at the positions of the soaring birds he'd seen earlier and decided to put some distance between himself and the slope. He found the lift band further out, over the mountain's base. It was triggering at the seam between flatlands and highlands, rising vertically with strength, and within a minute he'd gained past his launch point to an altitude roughly even with the ridge top.

As he passed the promontory he saw the tiny figures of Gabriella and Angelo still standing, still watching. Angelo had apparently been waving non-stop since Mick had first become airborne, and was waving still. Mick guessed they wouldn't be able to see his outstretched arm, but he returned the wave anyway, then made another circle, this time counter-clockwise, staying in the core of the lift.

Gabriella had evidently been waiting until he was even with her position, for he saw her and the boy walking back to the truck to begin the drive down. He focused again on working lift. When he got to ridge top level, as expected the lift became less vertical. The ambient north wind was inclining the column thermals southward, slanted over the ridge. He estimated the drift and stayed with the core he was in; he had no variometer but knew his climb rate had increased to probably eight hundred feet per minute, maybe more. At about a thousand feet over the ridge top, and now directly above it, the thermal broke up and he topped out.

He looked around. The range to the north looked like a high school relief map project, its seismic force origins and erosions over time all too evident by its shape. It would likely take him several hours and a few dozen good thermals if he were to try to fly to it. Eastward, the land stretched into bluish haze, and slowly flattened over many miles. He scanned across to the south, where the next range was so far away it blended visually with a line of clouds setting up on that horizon.

He stumbled into another thermal then, which angled his drift more east than south; he had reached the altitude where microclimatic conditions in individual valleys gave way to the famed and ubiquitous Westerlies.

He climbed again to about the same altitude as before, possibly gaining a few hundred more feet this time, before encountering the same ratty, broken, rock-and-roll air that had caused him to fall out of the last core. Top of lift was receding upward as the day heated up, and the stronger thermals were beginning to collide with and try to punch through the thermocline barrier. This time he fought against losing the core, staying with fractured elements of it despite the more violent air at that altitude. He found a fragment of the column and climbed through to smoother air again, immediately noting the even stronger Westerly flow and the markedly colder temperature of the air mass. He was probably at about fourteen thousand feet now, give or take, and knew he'd soon be shivering uncontrollably if he stayed up here. He also knew the capacity for thin, oxygen-depleted air to inspire foolish decisions from otherwise sane men, and decided to opt for comfort and safety by shedding some altitude. He left the thermal and meandered around, indifferent to the availability of lift, slowly losing height until he was under twelve thousand.

Floating westward into the wind and pulling the glider's nose down slightly to increase his sink rate, he spotted a large bare slope of loose boulders and talus, and saw a tiny building in a clearing scratched bare by human hands. The mine, he realized. Detail was indistinguishable from this distance, so he was not surprised that he saw no shaft openings, vehicles, or human activity. There was only the slope, the dot of a building, and the evidence of the huge slide that nature had wrought.

He slightly repositioned one shoulder strap of his harness, thinking as he did so how the terrain generally became higher, more rugged, and less accessible as it faded into Idaho in the west. If the wind had been pushing him in that direction, he thought, there might even come a point where he would be hard pressed to find a level place to land. Far better to boat around over this ridge and the valley it flanked, where he was always able to stay within a one-to-one glide of the flatlands.

He relaxed his mind then, knowing he was in smooth, relatively plentiful lift, thousands of feet in every direction from anything with which he could collide, sharing the air only with birds and the occasional bit of thin grass or dust borne randomly aloft by the thermals as they rose.

He'd flown in less serene ways, in his past life. Sitting with other soldiers in austere military transport planes was a different experience altogether, tension building in the mind and heart as each second passed. It was the kind of inescapable tension inspired by this strange and troubled town. Events began to replay in his head, seeking to sort themselves into some overall meaningful picture—the fallen woman on the church steps...the sport made of townspeople by Knox's men...the tribal element waiting with anticipation for this Aak to return...the thin man seeking him out, yet saying almost nothing.

He guided the glider's control bar a few inches to his left, tipping the wings in a right slipping turn, then eased the nose up to coordinate the lazy arc into a nicely carved circle. Why was he sent here? Why him? His skills were not a match for a parish spiritual guidance role, that should have been clear. What had the Archbishop said that day, in his office? "Scholars have their place. We all have our place. And you have yours. I think your past experiences, mistakes, triumphs, might be of value now."

Mick recalled his response to that, his attempt to talk sense: "I can work with my hands...I can build things. I...can't...take any more conflict in my life, Excellency. I came here hoping this would be a haven, and I could...end my days struggling with myself instead of others."

But the Bishop had been undeterred: "Don't worry too much about whether you are worthy to serve, when a time like this comes. Your best may be as good as any man can muster, and as much as any God could ask."

He'd protested from his soul...almost a confession. "But I came here because I don't want to be what I was anymore. I want to leave what I was behind." It had not been easy to say.

"You came to us," the Archbishop had intoned in terms of simple wisdom, "and that is all we know. Why is not for you to say. Everything happens for a reason, my son. It may be ...what you were...is what I thank God I can now send to these people in their time of need."

And that had been the end of the discussion.

He shook off the collage of disturbing recollections and refocused on the flight. It had been quite awhile since he was last airborne; he was glad of the impromptu decision he'd made back in Boston to tie the glider on the truck.

Boston...seemed so long ago. But then, it didn't have mountains like this one, nor such valleys either—big, flat, beautiful valleys to land in, clear enough to put down a Boeing.

He'd been up for an hour and decided he should start thinking about heading out toward the crossroads where they'd agreed he would land. Gabriella might make better time than they had on the way up, and he didn't want to keep her waiting. He considered for a moment, then decided to head out over the alluvial plain in the direction of the chosen spot, and see along the way if there was any lift rising off the flats. If not, no harm done, as he ought to land soon anyway. He had enough altitude to make it all the way out even if he encountered mostly sinking air along the way. And it would be good to find out if the soil of this valley kicked off midday lift, for future flights when he might have trouble staying up.

He pointed north and kept level, watching the clearance between his belly and the terrain directly below quintuple from 800 feet to 4000 feet in a matter of a few minutes. He was working no lift, but he didn't encounter massive sink either, and arrived roughly over the area where he'd land high enough that a normal sink rate would mean another quarter hour in the air—maybe more. He looked south and noticed a thin wisp of dust on the road where it left the timber. That could be Gabriella. She probably couldn't see him from this distance, but he'd enjoyed some wonderful soaring and would now have a little fun with the descent.

Shifting his weight to the right, he stood the glider on a wingtip and pushed the nose out hard. The graceful spiral he'd been holding transformed into a clockwise corkscrew dive earthward, shedding altitude at close to seven hundred feet per minute. Mick let out a whoop, then gauged his clearance. He'd already decided on a right-hand pattern, and the movement of the grass told him the air was drifting southeastward at this particular spot. He pulled out of the spiral into a gentle arc several hundred feet from the ground.

Leveling, he executed a downwind leg to about 70 feet over the turf, then threw the glider into a fast turn back into the wind, again leveling and sliding smoothly into ground effect. A blur of sage brush and bare dirt slid by just below his feet. He raised the nose slowly enough to keep the glider the same height off the ground, decelerating progressively. When he felt the energy was about gone, he raised the nose high with outstretched arms in a well-timed flare and took two steps, executing an elegant landing just short of the junction of the two dirt roads.

The silence always thrilled him after the relentless brisk wind of a long flight. He paused a moment to enjoy the contrast before setting the glider down and turning to unhook his harness from the hang strap. He took a deep, satisfied breath, stepped out from beneath the glider's sail, and tripped on the thin steel cable that connects the control frame to the left wing. He got up caked with dust.

Chuckling but disappointed in his clumsiness, he stopped to remove his helmet and lay it on a small tuft of sage. A half-hearted attempt to rescue his honor by dusting off his harness and jeans proved to be wasted energy, and he gave up in defeat. He removed the harness and draped it over a large sage bush, returning to the glider to disconnect the nose wires, de-tension the rear cables, and remove battens from one wing.

Crouching to pull the opposite wingtip batten, he heard a vehicle pull up amid the sagebrush on the other side of the glider. That would be Gabriella. Beaming, he waved as he rose.

But it was a dirty tan pickup truck. Exiting the cab and approaching him were two unfamiliar men, the thick dust kicked up by their vehicle's tires still drifting away on the breeze.

"What was you lookin' at?" one of them asked him humorlessly. They continued to approach slowly, splitting up, flanking him on two sides.

"I don't follow you," Mick replied. "Looking at?" He extended his hand to the nearer of the two men, thinking to begin the meeting again on more cordial terms. "I'm Father Mick, new in town." He took a half-step in the man's direction, but the man froze and pointed at him, a posture that halted Mick as well.

"What did you see from up there?" the man repeated in the same menacing tone. "What was you tryin' to see?"

"I'm still not following you. See? What did I see? I guess I saw everything. I saw the whole valley. I saw the next one too, beyond that range there. I probably saw 200 miles in all directions."

"Why?"

"Why? It's fun. It's magnificent. Haven't you ever looked at something because it was magnificent? So...what's this all about?"

"What was you tryin' to see?" the other one echoed.

"Where is this headed, guys? I think I've answered your question." Mick was beginning to feel annoyed.

"Mebbe you need to steer clear of what don't concern you."

"Maybe that's a piece of advice I'd suggest to you."

The near one bristled at that, but came no closer, as Mick had shown no hesitation in delivering the warning.

The one who'd spoken least, who had circled around to his far left, addressed him again. "Heard you was seen fraternizin' with some Indian punk friend of Wayne Aak earlier in the week. You better tell yer friend Wayne we're waitin' on him."

"Wha...what?" It was hard to know how to reply to this kind of paranoia. "What's wrong with everyone around here?" he demanded at last. "What has any...." But he trailed off as the noise from another engine interrupted them. Gabriella has arrived in his truck.

Mick knew she should stay in the vehicle, but she was too far from him and, off balance from the aggravating accusations, he reacted too slowly. Gabriella got out, pulling Angelo behind her, and approached the glider. The two men leered at her as she walked.

"Lordy, lookit what dangles itself in front of priests these days!"

"Amen brother! Heh heh...got a feelin' there's somethin' besides soul-savin' goin' on!"

"He try the old 'holy water rub-down' line on ya, girlie?"

"Yew done it on the altar yet? Haw!"

Gabriella walked as though they weren't there, and Mick felt suddenly proud to watch her. She was elegant; she exuded dignity. Smiling, she lightly touched the leading edge of the glider, Angelo copying her, and looking over at Mick, raised an eyebrow in comic inquiry at the heavy dust covering his clothing. He was too alarmed by the intruders' presence to respond.

Having run dry of cleverness and failed to inspire indignation, the two men tired of their vulgar sport. They pointed at Mick in soundless warning and returned to their truck, faces once again threatening as the driver started the engine and put the beat-up machine in gear. Before Mick saw it coming or could act, the man gunned the engine and backed over the glider's right wing tip, crushing the still-in-place battens and the leading edge tubing, spinning the wheel on the fragile sail cloth as they peeled away.

A thick cloud of dust enveloped Mick, Gabriella, and the child, taking several seconds to blow by. Angelo, unaware whose leg he was clutching, dug the fingers of both tiny hands into Mick's knee and clung in fear. Gabriella, feeling a sudden rage at the attack on her friend, picked up a rock and flung it where the tan truck had been, not waiting for the dust cloud to pass.

But the two men had not yet gone. Their vehicle was stopped thirty yards away, idling menacingly in the dusty air. Mick didn't know if the rock had hit anything or whether it had even been seen. But he assumed the intruders were debating further harassment. He quickly shepherded Gabriella and Angelo behind the glider, where they were at least out of immediate sight. The tan truck continued to idle for what seemed an eternity, but then slowly crept back onto the dirt road and headed the way it had come.

The valley returned to how a valley should sound. Mick swallowed his anger while Gabriella fumed. He couldn't get drawn in, he told himself. That's what they wanted. He had to remain above this. Grumbling, he inspected the damage to the glider. Without new airframe sections it would not fly again.

Together they packed the broken wing into the long glider bag as best they could, and tied it tightly back onto Mick's truck. Mick drove; Angelo slept stretched out between them, his little feet on Mick's knee. Both Gabriella and Mick were silent. Late afternoon shadows lengthened as they went, as did Mick's brooding struggle between conflicting impulses.

Gabriella eventually regained her calm. "Where are you?" she asked softly, respectfully.

He replied almost unconsciously. "I can't get...it's not me...anymore, it's not...for me."

She regarded him in silence.

He tried again to explain, and to grasp. "I'm an outsider. I haven't a clue what's even...I lack the...."

Suddenly she knew he was addressing her and no longer himself. "I'm not a holy man," he confessed. "I'm just a guy who swings a hammer."

She said nothing, but continued to watch him without his knowing it.

CHAPTER FIFTEEN

While Gabriella opened the door, Mick carried Angelo up the porch steps. The boy was awake now, though still rubbing his eyes. Evening was beginning to settle in.

Gabriella turned and took her son. "Dinner on a farm doesn't make itself," she said. "I've got a lot of chores to do before the evening is over." Mick nodded and took a step backward, assuming he'd been dismissed, but she continued. "And you're not going to enjoy the potatoes if they're burned."

He accepted gladly with another nod. "Can I help in some way? Do you have...I don't know, wood to chop or something?" They both chuckled at the cliché, but the spirit of his offer stood. "Anyway," he added, "I doubt you know how burned potatoes can be unless you've had mine."

"Ah, skilled with fire too!" she chided.

"Not to mention brimstone!"

Gabriella turned to her now alert son. "Why don't you take Father Mick out to feed the pony and Zeke?"

The little boy took the priest by the hand and led him off the porch toward the barn.

As they went, Mick called to Gabriella over his shoulder, "I'm not going to like it if Zeke turns out to be a big pet rattlesnake."

"No? And after all those paintings of you guys standing so bravely on serpents' heads." She laughed and went into the kitchen.

The pony was waiting at the fence, as much for the child's company, Mick thought, as for the food it was about to receive. The boy showed his new friend how to grab alfalfa hay in one's bare hand, which the priest then discovered must be fed to a pony one sprig at a time. There was also a wooden bin of feed, mostly shelled corn, doled out a small scoop daily. Zeke turned out to be the Border Collie, who accompanied them and who was clearly a favored playmate of the small pony, who teased the dog by nibbling the hair tufts on its ears until Zeke let out a playful bark and gave the pony's chin an affectionate lick.

In the soft golden evening light, Angelo proudly led Mick to other points of interest around the yard, including a partially hollow tree and a place where reputedly lived a ladybug.

Gabriella called through the kitchen window that dinner was ready. They raced each other to the door and, if not for Zeke cheating, Angelo's home court advantage would have carried the day. Mick removed his boots and left them on the porch.

Dinner was balanced and simple; the day's troubles, dwarfed by the greater powers of wonder and friendship, were forgotten. Gabriella produced a half bottle of wine from somewhere, which she offered to Mick. When he accepted, with a twinkle she poured just a few drops into his glass, in ritualistic style. He laughed and motioned for more, and yet more. Angelo mimicked in his own glass with apple juice, and they laughed again.

After dinner they retired to the next room, near a small hearth. A few books, a lamp, and toys lay scattered here and there on the floor. Mick stepped outside and returned with a few pieces of sap-covered pine from a stack behind the house and built a tiny fire, more for the aroma and to hear the crackle than for any other reason, and they settled into nearby chairs. There was contentment here, the priest thought. By force of habit Gabriella reached for a partly mended child's shirt sitting on the lamp table and continued work she'd started previously on the buttons near the collar.

"Why don't you read something to Angelo, Father Mick?" she prompted. "He loves to learn."

Mick leaned over to survey the small collection of children's books on the floor beneath the table, wondering what he could offer a little boy. Fitting, he thought, that the book on top of the stack, easiest for him to reach, was a small child's picture bible. He chose it without thinking, for once without contaminating his impulse with self doubt. Angelo leaned against him to get a close look at the pages as they were turned, and Mick hefted the tiny child up to his knee. Gabriella glanced up momentarily from her mending to see them, and a warm feeling crept over her, which she allowed to linger.

Mick began by turning pages and waiting for the child's finger to point to some portion of a picture. "Oh, that's a cup," he would say, or "that could be a handkerchief; I think that lady is going to sneeze."

Gabriella smiled and interjected, "He can absorb the stories too. Maybe you can tell us some."

Yes, he could do that. He turned a handful of pages, where began the story of Saint Michael the Archangel. The priest explained in non-zealous, fable-like style how it was told to have happened, how the Archangel was said to have cast down Lucifer. The boy lingered long on the pictures.

"Then they say Michael the Archangel pushed that bad guy Lucifer out of heaven, and told him...never to come back." Mick watched while Angelo ran his tiny finger over the drawing of the triumphant Archangel, and how he followed the image downward, hesitating but finally touching the drawn image of the defeated Lucifer sprawled beneath Michael's feet, disgraced eyes bulging in fear, cowardice, and regret.

Thinking the child might benefit from a little extra clarification, Gabriella chimed in. "And what is an Archangel?"

Mick wasn't sure who was asking, so he sought to give an answer appropriate for them both. "An Archangel is a Defender. A sword of Good. The angels are God's personal warriors, and Michael the Archangel was a captain of that army." He was doing alright; he knew this stuff.

"So, Lucifer was an angel too, at one time."

"Yes, that's true. And...he was equal in rank to Michael, more or less. He was a captain too."

"And he was bad and God punished him," Gabriella prompted again for the boy.

"He was, yes. He was greedy, and tried to become the...boss, over the world, and Heaven."

Gabriella thought for a moment, and then asked a question of her own: "Why didn't God cast him out personally?"

Mick considered the question; it was a perceptive one, and not one that normally came up. In fact he wasn't formally prepared for it. To offer an explanation, he shifted to personal experience, personal interpretation. "Well...this is the pure style of a Master. A Master will let his best loyal officer, or his number one student, eject a disobedient student from his school, or throw a disrespectful guest out of his house. This story of Michael the Archangel is told in that way too."

"Why does a Master need to let someone else defend him?"

"Because...the Master knows that a fight diminishes the combatant. If you lose, of course you're killed or hurt, and thus diminished. But even if you win, even if you're the righteous Master and you can't fail to win, entering into a fight diminishes you. You're put into a situation where you injure or destroy another being...."

His memory cut in again, only for a split instant, flashing him another indelible image. He saw himself, long ago, standing, holding something, in a deserted clearing near a crude wall. It was night, but he was aware of a low, weak floodlight on or near that wall. He was standing over the crumpled body of a soldier.

He had dropped the thing he was holding, and was reaching, stretching out his hand, for something else.

Gabriella watched his face and the secret that fluttered across it like a shroud. Her voice brought him back. "Where are you right now?"

He jolted back and tried to finish what he'd been saying earlier, but to both their surprise his words had already turned far more personal. "...You're put in a situation where no matter what you do, you are diminished. You either hurt or you get hurt....you become a lesser human being either way." His voice trailed off softly to nothing.

Gabriella knew she had to retrieve him. "And God would rather let his Captain be placed in that position?"

Still disturbed by his recollections, Mick again clawed his way back to the present to answer. "Well the, uh, Captain...is glad to spare the Master the indignity of combat. He offers himself in his Master's place. He considers it an honor."

"But...Michael was greater than Lucifer...."

"Yes, he was greater...not because he was larger, and not because he had more skill or power...but because his arm and his sword drew strength from his motives. He didn't fight for his own interests, as did Lucifer. He fought in service to his Master, and out of love."

Gabriella gazed at Mick for a little bit, and he noticed. Embarrassed, he tried to get back to the simplistic story for the boy, and cleared his throat. "So this picture shows Michael the Archangel defeating Lucifer."

But Gabriella wouldn't let it rest. "But then why wasn't Michael 'diminished,' as you say?"

At a loss, Mick looked up from the little Bible. "Well...uh...he...it's his duty, and...." A realization slowly dawned on him. "It's his...duty. His Mission."

She let him go on.

"What saves a warrior from being diminished, when he strikes down another, is that...he...does it not to save himself, but to protect. He sacrifices his spirit to keep another's spirit undiminished. He...that's the difference. That's the difference."

A long quiet pause set in. Gabriella had stopped mending the tiny shirt. She was looking at Mick with pleading eyes, and with trust, and hope. Mick did not notice; he was deep in thought. But for the first time since he'd arrived in Montana, his face took on something of a resolute quality.

CHAPTER SIXTEEN

It can be said that a man is committed to his deeds if he acts in broad daylight. The sheriff's office looked as it always did, with the single exception that this time it appeared to be unlocked. Mick strode to the door and opened it in a way that suggested a heavy iron deadbolt might have done little good.

A desk in the corner of the room was flanked by one four-drawer file cabinet, two of its drawers hanging open and empty, and a bookcase, also empty except for a jacket hooked over one corner and an empty leather holster sitting on the second shelf. Behind the desk, in a listing wooden office chair, sat a portly Caucasian man leaning over a lesser section of a week-old Missoula newspaper, guiding his finger below the words he was trying to read. His head jerked nervously when Mick burst in, but he attempted to cover the twitch by lifting the paper higher in front of himself and leaning back in his chair.

Mick ignored the discourtesy and addressed the newspaper in front of the man's face, stepping to the near edge of the desk. "I want to know who those men are who act like they own this town, what real authority they have, if any, and why nobody does anything about them."

The sheriff lowered the paper enough to peer at Mick over the top edge, but otherwise did not stir. He raised the page to completely obscure his face again before answering. "Why, them boys is a private peace-keepin' force. Somethin' like...like a neighborhood watch."

"What the hell are they watching?"

The indifferent voice continued to come from behind the paper. "This fine community sleeps easier for their efforts, reverend. You can feel safe knowin' them boys' vigilance is on duty."

"Against what?" Mick challenged, reaching out to swat the newspaper down with his open hand. The sheriff was torn between indignation and apprehension, but made no sound. "They threatened me," Mick continued, "they vandalized private property...and they scared a little boy and his mother half out of their wits! And this wasn't by accident or out of some...misunderstanding."

The sheriff began to chuckle but didn't manage more than a half smile before Mick cut him off. "It was out of meanness, lawman. I want their names, all of them."

"Now padre, meanness is what they're out there protectin' against. No, you must have been hangin' with the wrong people, and maybe been somewhere you shouldn't a'been."

"Shouldn't have...?! Sheriff, I'll 'hang' with who and where I...and I was on Federal land, out in the damn tundra, for Chrissake!"

The sheriff continued his condescending tone. "Tck tck...you'll set a poor example to be swearin', reverend. Besides, around here we call it Open Range. I don't reckon a New Yorker like you would know much about these parts though. No, if I was you I'd maybe go back where I belong...yeah...either that or stick to what I know, from now on. Like the inside of that ol' church. That's your place, reverend, not stirrin' up trouble with the natives and snoopin' around where you got no business." He picked up and straightened the crumpled section of newspaper, and leaned back again in his chair.

"Are you going to do something about this or not?" Mick was beginning to lose his temper. "Do the guys I'm looking for work for this man Lucius Knox? What about the damage they did to my gear? Are you going to take my complaint?"

"I don't know nothin' about no gear, an' you got no proof. And you of all people should know, reverend, that if the Good Lord meant for Man to fly, he woulda given us wings." The lawman chuckled and went back to pretending to read his paper.

"Or some guts," Mick shot back. He left without further acknowledgment of the sheriff and without bothering to close the door.

Sheriff Andrew Silo scowled at the parting shot, but he was intimidated by the priest and elected to keep his mouth shut. Fighting one's own battles was not his way. He'd make sure the insult was paid for. As soon as Mick had gone, he hurriedly locked the door and exited via the back door. He slid two and a half blocks up-street to an alley, cut through, and slipped into the back door of the Inferno saloon.

*   *   *

Legal authority was going to be a useless avenue, Mick could see. And it wasn't clear what other options there might be—there didn't seem to be any center of community action or government. Maybe the best thing he could do was to simply provide moral support for the residents, in hopes that over time they would come to establish their own voice here. It was the priestly thing to do; maybe that's what his Bishop had intended. One thing was clear: He was in no frame of mind to want anything to do personally with the other camp.

The following evening, he posted a notice on the small outdoor bulletin board left of the church front door, announcing the theme of the next Sunday's sermon: "No Man Is Your Master." He had yet to write it, but was at least locked onto the topic. As usual it was a quiet night, and he heard them coming. He'd been expecting them since the incident with the glider. He continued to affix the note to the board and let them make their chosen approach.

A black van with darkened glass pulled slowly to the curb at the base of the steps. His back turned, Mick tracked them by sound. Two men got out of the vehicle. One waited for the other and they ascended the steps together; he noticed they were always careful to outnumber him. The two stomped with slow scraping strides up the steps, making plenty of noise, like self-proclaimed great hunters do when in the territory of a beast they fear.

He made his own statement; despite their noisy approach, he didn't turn to greet them. One of them, unaccustomed to being discounted, stared at the back of his head with silent resentment. The other looked past him into the church, spat on the top step, and instructed, "You been invited to dinner."

"I decline," Mick replied over his shoulder without any consideration. "Prior plans, better offer. But splendid of you to ask." Only then did he turn to confront them. He kept his expression blank, and raised his head in silent inquiry as to whether there would be anything else they might need from him.

The taller one now spoke, finding it difficult to do it politely. "Mr. Knox...requests the...presence of yer company at dinner." With face-saving mockery he swept his hand outward toward the van, paused a moment, then added, "Attire is coincidentally what ye got on now." There was little humor in his tone.

For a moment Mick considered giving free reign to his anger. It would be easy to do. But he knew he'd lose any capacity for perceptiveness, and also they'd sense the crack in his armor. And he, of all people, dared not lose control. He glanced at the van. The sheriff's office was such a joke that this might be the only recourse—fraternity with the enemy.

And he was curious, he had to admit. It took him another moment to weigh his thoughts and decide. "Sure, why not. Saves me the trouble of opening the pork and beans." He descended the church steps first and waited like royalty for the taller of the two men to step past him and open the van's side door, then entered the vehicle. The tall man followed him in, sitting by his right side. The other man entered on the opposite side of the van and sat in a rear-facing seat in front of Mick.

Elmer, peering through the curtains from the residence window, watched them drive away.

The passenger compartment was opulently furnished; upholstery was plush and exquisite. A dark padded barrier isolated them from the front seat area, where an unseen driver put the vehicle in motion. They took side streets and drove slowly, almost soundlessly.

Unsure how far they would need to go, Mick put the time to good use, probing to see what questions got a rise. "Are you two on Lucius Knox's payroll?" he asked first.

The two men didn't look at him, acknowledge him, or answer. One picked his teeth with a small stick. Mick wondered if they were under orders to stay to some script. He might have to push an extra button or two.

"What exactly is your job?" he tried again. "A skilled role...or not?"

Silence.

"Where is the one named Daryl, the one who showed up on my church steps a few days ago?"

The two men still gave no answer. The van rounded a bend, giving Mick a moment to think of a better catalyst. He thought he had one. "What do you guys think of this Wayne Aak character?"

Pay dirt. Again they didn't look at him, but the one facing him addressed the taller one to Mick's right. "You know, Stu, they say Prison Injun is due here any hour. Could even be here now."

"Yep," replied the large fleshy one called Stu, "like waitin' to squash a bug." The one facing Mick finally glared at the priest momentarily, but turned to regard the window again and said no more.

The van stopped and Mick glanced out. They had arrived at what looked like a gate outside the strange dark mansion he'd spotted the previous week. The driver, his face still unseen, exited the cab and fumbled with the chain and lock of a rusted wrought iron gate out of Mick's field of view; the priest could tell what was happening by the sound of jingling steel links and keys, the rattle of the gate bolt, and occasional swearing. Eventually the man succeeded and swung one of the two squeaking gate halves inward, then re-entered the van and swerved it to pass through that portion of the opening.

The van crossed the austere grounds and slid with locked brakes to a stop twenty yards from the house itself. The tall man to Mick's right opened the side door and stepped out. He stood there saying nothing, disdainful eyes straight ahead, until Mick understood he was to disembark. He stepped out and returned the discourtesy, ignoring the men in favor of turning toward the old house and studying it in detail. It was a fascinating old structure. He didn't hear the vehicle's doors close, but at some point the van and the three men were simply gone, as if evaporated into shadow.

The compound—and that's what it was, by all outward appearances—had a decidedly gothic feel. The full-circle view from where he stood reminded him of what he'd seen from the road. The property was a large block long in both dimensions—maybe as much as four acres. The grounds were bare except for fallen limbs and denuded cedar trees, inundated by some kind of blight. One large oak in the center of the lot, alive but sparsely foliaged, stood shrouding the mansion in twisted, writhing, tormented branches, as though trying to hold out the sun. Gopher burrows, or possibly snake holes, riddled the dirt.

A wall made originally of local stone surrounded the perimeter on all sides. Covered with decayed mosses, it stood out by the roads; where it had crumbled, it had been patched more recently, with some kind of urban rubble brought in from elsewhere and dumped.

The ground floor of the mansion seemed to have a clear view to the stone wall; some upper story windows did as well. Gables glared down on him balefully as though the structure itself was alive. The house had been dark the first time Mick had seen it, and was still, with the exception that small torches were affixed to its dark stone walls near a front entrance.

He took a deep breath and approached the massive door. There was no knocker or doorbell that he could see. He considered just waiting to be discovered, but decided he should use his bare knuckles for what they were intended. Before he could act, however, the door opened.

He saw no one; evidently this was the ritual associated with a summons such as he'd received. He stepped into an entryway of warm earth colors—umbers, coppers, oranges, reds. Tasteful, he decided, except for the absence of the host.

From the dimly lit foyer's far end he became aware of the soft sound of breathing, and with a start made out the side-lit silhouette of a man. The man was around Mick's own age. He was taller than the priest, with sharp features. Almost gaunt. His mostly silver hair was impeccably groomed. He wore a costly-looking jacket, Spanish gentry style. Pale floor-level lighting deliberately added extra drama to a first impression.

"Welcome, priest, welcome," the man said warmly, suddenly striding toward Mick with an outstretched hand. "Allow me to introduce myself: Lucius Knox, master of this simple abode, and your humble servant."

Mick nodded and grasped the hand as confidently as it had been offered. "Father Mick Calahan," he announced himself simply, choosing to use his title as well as his name. They exchanged a moment of awkward silence, and then without further words the host's long-fingered hand grasped Mick gently by the upper arm and led him gracefully through an arched passage entrance and down a short winding stairway, to a sizeable partly-below-ground-level hall.

"My semi-inner sanctum, shall we say," Lucius beamed with a sweep of his hand. "I like to eat meals here on special occasions...although I can count them annually on half a hand." He smiled and accompanied Mick to the near end of a long stone table already set with fine tableware and a lavish spread. With a well bred wave of his hand he bade Mick sit, holding the chair back while his guest complied. "I'm so glad an educated man like yourself has shown up," he added genuinely.

Lucius glided to the opposite end of the table a dozen feet from Mick, pulled out his chair with the gusto of a nobleman, and sat. With another hearty gesture he encouraged Mick to dig in. Then he waited, again demonstrating impeccable breeding by allowing Mick the right of first conversation.

"Thank you for the unexpected invitation," Mick began, privately noticing the well-bred man had forgotten to offer his ordained guest the customary moment to speak religious words of thanks. "The fare looks great."

"I'll tell my cook the beatings were premature," Lucius joked. "Anyway, welcome to our town! I almost feel I'm late in making your acquaintance, although I've heard something about you of course."

"I must say I've heard a lot about you," Mick ventured in return.

"Ahhh, let's see, not all bad I hope...and I'm probably the one man in recent history with an honest right to use that worn-out line." He smiled, and Mick did as well. Lucius Knox was charming—not at all like he'd been led to believe. "Oh yes," Knox added, "I know more or less what's on the streets. Nobody likes a man who doesn't have to punch a clock. It's...lonely at the top."

"There goes another old one," Mick pointed out with a mild grin.

"Can't stop myself!" Again they both chuckled.

They relaxed as they sampled the food. Mick noticed the roast beef was very rare. He helped himself to some sautéed mushrooms and dug in, searching simultaneously for a gracious opening. "So...you mentioned freedom from the time clock, but I notice you didn't exactly imply that you're a stranger to work."

"A distinction the common man wouldn't catch, but I knew you would," Lucius replied in a pleased tone. "Yes, I work—we all work in one fashion or another, if we're good men. I'm...something of a philanthropist I guess, so my energies are directed more at projects that can benefit a whole town, rather than simply putting gruel in the mouths of some runny-nosed progeny in a trailer somewhere." He paused comfortably to chew. "I do have big visions for Terradise Valley, and I'm pretty tireless at making those visions a reality. People here don't see or know it yet, but when it takes shape I'll be godfathering all their babies, you watch."

"Always the way, isn't it? Sports teams talk about the fickle fans. Guess it's the same kind of thing."

"Human nature," Lucius agreed with a broad grin. "Can't let it get to you. I try to keep it in perspective—not let the small view break my resolve, you see."

"So...grand visions, you say. Sounds intriguing."

"And it is. I'm talking about some real prosperity here. Not the kind of short-lived boost a politician might promote, but something with a real foundation and real results. I see this place growing, becoming a Mecca of the West. I see its inhabitants basking in that prosperity. Opportunity, teamwork, and common benefit will make undesirables a thing of the past. I see culture. Finery. Taste."

"You drink excellent wine," Mick observed, holding a goblet to his lips.

This was not exactly the ambush and knife fight he'd been led to expect. It was pleasant. Lucius Knox seemed...perhaps rugged at his core, but also polished. He had education and complexity. He gave off a trustworthy vibe. Mick realized he could sum up his initial impression by saying Knox was interesting. Could it be that the town was wrong about him? Maybe the man himself could be separated from his thugs; maybe his reclusive nature kept him from knowing what his hired help was up to. People who are themselves above cruelty can be genuinely blind to it, the priest knew. And maybe Knox's habit of being invisible had people judging him by the actions of those other men. Mick sensed the man's intellectual uniqueness, felt his straightforward sincerity, and had to admit it was contagious.

"You know," Knox confided, "men are different, priest. I confess I intended to size you up this evening. But I'm happy to say I find a kindred spirit. You're an outsider here, but you know, that's the contact I crave." He raised his glass with a broad grin, also appearing to enjoy the dinner.

Mick raised his own again to match his host, and they drank. "Well we all know that many people—most, in fact—are afraid of change," he offered. "Historically it has often brought with it other evolutions or adjustments never wanted, and there's never any going back. People find themselves in a situation where they have to adapt, and they may not be able to. The social evolution process itself thrives, but individuals are the casualties. Tell me, would this prosperity you speak of affect the flavor of life here?"

"Oh, yes!" Knox beamed. "Schools, for one! There's no formal learning opportunity here past the garden-grade elementary school, and even that could use a big boost. They could use a high school too. What about a real library? How about putting this remote little place on the map—drawing visitors, building a tourist industry to take advantage of and share the natural beauty...the setting aside of parks and reserves...you name it. What about the local inhabitants' ability to launch environmentally friendly businesses? What about a real town hall, and a recreation commission, and property values? All these add to the picture, priest, and more. It doesn't have to cost us the quaint local flavor. It depends on how it's managed."

It wasn't hard to be enthralled by the man's vision. Mick found himself nodding. "Sounds pretty appealing, I have to admit. And...what will bring this prosperity?" he asked politely. It was a leading question and he was sure he knew how it would be answered.

"The Lord!" Knox prophesied, surprising Mick yet again. "He's already provided. It's been part of his Master Plan from the start!"

The slant caught Mick off-guard. "I...don't...."

"Mining!" Okay, there it was. "This is the Promised Land, priest! I feel I've been chosen to recognize this, and to develop the potential of this God's Gift of a valley. I know you of all people can see the power in following the will of God."

This was a mildly uncomfortable remark; it was unclear whether it was disingenuous or sincere. Knox had chosen to describe these practical matters within a framework of religion. Was it truly how the man looked at his work, or had he slanted the dialog that way because of Mick's profession? Mick had known politically wired individuals in the past who chose their words differently depending on their company. On the other hand, Knox might be someone far more religiously zealous than Mick himself. He took a drink of water, giving the comment an opportunity to explain itself.

"I mean, you're a priest, aren't you?" Knox continued. "And a white man—an educated man. You are yourself a product of the best thrust of all God's experiments."

The hint at supremacist dogma was unmistakable, but Mick knew real people could rarely be labeled along such well drawn lines. After all, Knox's words danced just as equally with virtue. And it could be that some of these sentiments—of both types—were simply bait, to gauge the priest's reaction. He decided to respond in a different way.

"I would hope we're each more than experimental," he commented off-hand. "In species, just like in structures, I think diversity is strength. Every kind of person equally contributes to the beauty and survivability of the system. Master Plan and all."

"Yes of course," the host replied in a slightly absent tone.

They ate in silence for a few minutes. With his mouth full of a new gulp of wine, Lucius went on. "Still, at the risk of sounding like I'm building a case for greed, because I'm not...I have to say there's no denying that you...and I...are the 'cream' of this world. It remains a savage world, despite the rise of superior intellects over the animal kingdom. But even in savagery, even in nature, the fittest survive, and flourish. The best man wins. You and I, priest, we are that Best Man."

"Best, how?"

"It's not merely by virtue of resources, of course, but because we are men of letters, men of intellect. We are those truly intended to inherit the Earth...or maybe that sounds a little egotistical...call us Guardians perhaps. Or Stewards. God made Man in his own image, but some of us are perhaps able to reflect that image better than others. Not everyone is cut out to be a Steward, nor does the world need more than a small number." Lucius smiled. Mick wondered if he was being sized up after all. He knew already that Lucius was a highly intelligent man. Gabriella had described him as calculating; how accurate was that assessment?

"No doubt," Mick smiled, partly to cover his thoughts. "Still..." he paused while sipping his wine to think of an appropriately priestly reply, "isn't it the Meek they say'll end up with it all?"

Lucius pierced him with his gaze, then broke slowly into a hearty laugh. "They do indeed. Come with me, priest, let me show you something."

Dinner, it seemed, was abruptly over; the real portion of the agenda was now to begin. Lucius wiped his mouth with a sweep of a fine linen napkin, raised himself up to his full noble height, and stalked away from the table toward an empty wall. He turned and waited gracefully for Mick to get up, take one last drink of cool water, and follow him.

Mick's builder's eye saw that the wall appeared to have been added sometime after the rest of the house was built. Lucius abruptly raised his arm and pressed his hand against it, then added a bit of shear pressure. The wall began to slide laterally to the right on unseen rollers, revealing a hidden door. Pleased with his drama and proud of his castle, Lucius opened the door, saying, "My secret lair, known only to a few...and now you."

The door revealed a circular stone staircase that descended into the blackness of an even lower level. Knox threw a wall switch to ignite dim yellowed lights that barely illuminated the upper portion of the descent. He navigated the steps to the bottom, into a cavernous room dominated by a huge stone fireplace at one end, with logs already ablaze. By turns incredulous and delighted, Mick followed.

The air was damp down here; Mick knew they were now fully below ground level. Condensation glistened lightly on the masonry walls, especially low near the floor; the place smelled faintly, although not overpoweringly, like mold. Books and old documents were piled everywhere in the room's corners and on small boxes. Those documents were the reason the fire was lit, Mick reasoned; this was a research room—a work room—and the fire probably burned day and night to drive out the moisture.

Mounted on the end wall furthest from the stairwell was a small collection of old armor and ancient weapons, Spanish mostly, but also perhaps some English. Candles burned in elaborate old-world-style holders also mounted on the same wall. On the side bulkhead at the same end of the chamber, a nondescript floor-length tapestry hung as a backdrop for an old shovel and pick-axe, which were crossed and mounted on that wall overtop the tapestry cloth as display pieces. They were significant to Knox's dreams and progress, Mick assumed; there were still bits of old dirt clinging to them.

Under a pair of floodlights attached to the ceiling, a long drawing table in the center of the chamber held two items of particular interest: a large topographical map, and an impressive three-dimensional model of a hillside, including a rugged grade with tunnels bored into it. Even boulder fields were represented in lifelike detail. "I'm told you've seen this already," Lucius commented pragmatically, gesturing toward the model, "so there's no sense in pretending it's not out there. Here is the future of this Valley."

Mick stared at the intricate model of the mine, whistling softly at the work that must have gone into it. It wasn't very different from what he had seen from the air.

"This mine is what initially created this town," Knox said, repeating what Mick had heard from others. "It's said to have had a strong growth heyday, even with the old hand-worked techniques, but then was abruptly and prematurely forsaken when bad luck struck. Now I'm resurrecting it, and with it the dreams and futures of the God-fearing people who live in this place. I'll make it the success it could have been. I'll manage it personally. And the people here will finally reap the fruits God had intended for them."

Again ignoring the sermon, Mick gazed courteously at the detail. "It's an impressive model," he admitted.

"And believe me, it doesn't do the real thing justice."

Shifting his gaze to the topographical map, Mick pointed to a specific area. "Is this the place here?"

"No, you're too far east still. Here. At the head of this large alluvial plain."

"I see. Yes, makes sense. I would have gotten only as far west as...about here...the other day." He again placed his finger on the map. "So I possibly could have been able to spot the hillside...if I'd cared, and known where to look, and wasn't so bleary-eyed from wind and cold. But the truth is, this model is the first time I've seen it." He knew it was technically a misrepresentation, but wanted to disarm any concerns his host might have.

Knox ignored the denial and walked to the other side of the table, where he flicked a bit of dust off the clay hillside.

Glancing over the topographical map, Mick saw an opportunity to learn a bit about the local area apart from the mine. Privately he noted relative elevation of Gabriella's valley with respect to the town and the mine, verifying how the water would naturally flow. Her story rang true, at least geographically. He estimated sizes of nearby open plains and took mental stock of primary obstructing ridges.

"What's this little road here?" he asked with genuine curiosity.

"An old route eastward. Better highways have come along since those days, out there. It winds through and over this set of mountains." Lucius put his finger on the map absently.

"I like those old ones," Mick smiled. "The kind of road that would make a nice little getaway."

He slid his finger further west on the same map. "Here's an area up here marked on the map as 'probable historical site.' I'm guessing that would be referring to local tribal history?"

Knox did not respond, so Mick went on.

"By your 3-D model it almost looks like the mine shafts could tunnel partly under that area. Does this pose complications for you? What does the law in this state say about ownership below the surface? Will you be buying mineral rights or sharing the prosperity plan in some other way with those folks?"

Lucius' demeanor remained pleasant, but Mick noted that his message sharpened substantially.

"This is my land, priest. I bought it, I unified this site, much like Garibaldi did Italy, or Genghis Khan the whole of Asia. I am the 'prince' here, if you will." He paused, obviously considering how to answer the question more directly. "I would say the operative word on that map is 'probable.' I haven't extended any shafts further than what they were originally...yet. And I won't extend them past where they should go." He began to pace, making two passes across the head of the table before continuing. "A lot of those people are more brother to the coyote than they are to you or I or the hard-working inhabitants of this town. They're opportunists. Scavengers. Rumors of old burial grounds can spring from anywhere—who knows who starts a rumor? Just because it finds its way into a cartographer's notes and onto a map doesn't mean it was even researched. Fables never substantiated vs. industrious, constructive development? I think I'm in the legal right, never fear...and the future won't be stopped by guesses about the past. Hell, none of my critics had a clue what was really under there until I found it and started to shore it up, and now suddenly they're all infallible students of their heritage?" He smiled skeptically, but the amiability had returned.

"So...you found it? I thought..."

For a moment Knox looked as though he'd let a secret slip, but recovered himself almost instantly. "You thought...that the mine had existed for many decades? Oh, it had. But nobody knew exactly where anymore—underground that is. Out of fear of claim-jumpers its features had never been marked accurately, or not the prime shaft locations on any public maps or documents anyway. What ended the mine's days was a huge slide, and nobody knew whether their digging had destabilized the slope or whether a small rogue quake did it—believe it or not, they do occur in these parts. But the entrances were all buried, completely obliterated, from then till recently, and all the money went away and those days were forgotten. I came here three quarters of a century later—I'd already bought the whole damn mountainside—and I used low frequency sonar, guesswork...and divine guidance...and after two long, tenacious years, years during which we had only faith and hope to sustain us, we found a part of a shaft. From then on it was like peeling an onion."

"Went more quickly I guess."

"Well, you have to understand that most shafts had names, from the old days. When I bought the slope I spent thousands of hours piecing together unsubstantiated accounts, hearsay, tall tales...and building more versions of this model you see here than I'd like to think. Nobody else did that work, you know. Ever. I mean, perseverance does pay off sometimes, and there's nothing more fair than that."

Mick nodded his acknowledgment; there was no arguing with it. Entrepreneurialism does lay valid claim to its own fruits.

"Anyway," Lucius continued, "based on nothing more than gut instinct, a few of my guesses about shaft locations were surprisingly not far off, although many key ones had still eluded me. When we found part of one, badly crushed in both directions of course, the real guess-work began. Which one was it? Shafts had been dug at different times in this mine's brief history, with different crews and different materials. A close associate of mine, an educated man, figured it out by the kind of wood that had been used to shore that section...."

He paused a moment in almost reverent reflection. It was probable he was referring to Carlo.

Knox returned to the present. "Anyway, it eventually unraveled. And now we're gearing up for the next phase...as you'll soon see. Very soon the real work begins. The shoring crews almost have the main shafts stable and we'll then start moving some serious dirt. I have initial gear lined up already. Been arranging the financials and special equipment for some time now."

It was hard not to acknowledge the dedication and intelligence the man had applied to the project, Mick realized. Most of the residents of the town would likely not be able to appreciate that kind of analysis, that creative level of problem-solving, that degree of business management. The admirable qualities of industrialists and developers had been under-appreciated for centuries, yet they were indispensable if history was to unfold.

"All I can say," Mick smiled, "is that you must be a very motivated man."

Lucius pursed his lips self-consciously, evidently pleased at the compliment.

"Not for another to ask, of course," Mick added, "but a driven man should always be clear on what it is that drives him."

Lucius averted his eyes, for the first time not in charge of the moment.

"Well if you don't mind my asking," Mick continued with the tone of innocent curiosity, "where do you get your means? I mean, nice house...."

"This is very old—built by the original operations partner of the mine. It seemed fitting, and proved readily achievable that I should acquire it when I purchased the mine itself. Of course I modified it extensively for my own needs."

"Classic...reflects the personality of its occupant I think."

Again Knox appeared silently pleased.

"But beyond that...the big plans, the power to 'unify' large tracts of land as you say...how can one individual find the resources to do it?"

Lucius recovered his air of leadership and paced dramatically to the fireplace mantle, where he poured himself another goblet of wine. "Back East, long ago, I was blessed with a very greedy old man who didn't have the sense to avoid drinking and snorting and defiling himself into an early grave." He chuckled at something.

The priest considered that for a moment. He had thought he might gain some insight into Knox, but the man added nothing more. Mick tried to prompt. "So...you were from an industrialist background?"

"Worse! Evangelist!" Lucius beamed. "Yes, oh yes. Classical household. There was a time I even aspired to speaking in tongues! I actually still believe I have the gift." He chuckled. "Anyway, 'the Guv'nuh' found not only the chance for hypocrisy in his trade, but money too, plenty of that." He shook his head free of the topic and did not return to it.

There were other details Mick wanted to piece together, and he changed the subject. "I'm thinking the thick necks all around town must be your boys."

"A fair description, too, I admit," Lucius replied. "Brought those people in to help out with things here and there. A few came to us from up and down the line...but most of them I knew from, shall we say, a previous life. Did some...work...in Central America and points south, years ago. Various...technical...and yes, I'll admit lucrative...work. Nothing as uplifting as my plans here. But while there, I saw this very thing work for someone down there, priest! Amazon Basin, actually. Gold mine. He milked—that is, uh, developed—a whole region, and let me tell you it was a recipe for success. I participated too, and did well I have to admit, although not to the degree I wanted. When I recognized the same potential for this town, I brought in some experience to help organize the place a bit. I pay them; it's all above board, I assure you."

"Do they expect to share in the rewards?"

"Oh...probably."

It didn't sound like the strongest commitment to his staff. If he didn't intend to reward them, Mick wondered, why would he seek to make the townspeople—folks who Knox felt would have no appreciation for what he was accomplishing until it was done—participants in the benefits? What was his opinion of the naysayers? He decided to probe the point.

"You know, some would say you've got your own little army keeping peace and order the way you see it, and probably that fat Sheriff and maybe the Bureau of Indian Affairs in your pocket, and they're all hoping to get rich or have free reign off of this...prosperity plan." He gestured to the model of the mine. "You mentioned critics. Is that about the gist of what they say? How do you handle them?"

Lucius regarded Mick with a degree of pause, but his response remained civil. "'Not the critic who counts, nor the man who points out how the strong man stumbles....' I believe those were the insights of Theodore Roosevelt." He paused, then recounted more town history. "There was a riot here some time back—an uprising, you might call it. Quite amazing, really, little town like this; I mean it's hardly an inner city ghetto. Copycat insanity of unrestful times, I suppose. We...put it down. Folks were scared of that happening again." Lucius strolled to the back wall, to the hanging armor, old weapons, and coats of arms, lit by candles in their gothic holders.

The sight of implements of human mutilation always seemed to bring that scene back. Mick's unwelcome memory played momentarily again in his head—the floodlit clearing, a body prone before him. There were civilians there—a woman and an old man. They were...standing behind the body. Mick was holding a weapon, although not a sword. It had been blunt. A length of pipe. He had destroyed the armed guard with nothing more than a piece of rusted pipe. And then he had leaned forward, reaching toward the body, when he'd heard a noise behind him.

Stay with the here and now; try to focus on Lucius' voice, he thought. His host was still speaking.

"...the town was scared of its own shadow. I'm their guardian angel, if you will. I saw a need..."

'Opportunity' was the word Mick would have chosen. Or...could it be that Lucius was in fact unaware that the town feared and hated him? A wealthy philanthropic hermit lost in his own dream of the perfect society? Maybe this was the disconnect Mick was tasked with repairing, to bring this community back from the edge.

"...and I brought my superior mind and skills—and yes, my will—to bear. I'm what saved this town. They look to me."

There was some of that, Mick decided—some oblivion. But it was mixed with an ego and an ambition that was causing the dream to fail to take hold. In any event, a man is accountable for the results of what he has put into motion, and Mick knew it was time to address that obligation. It almost didn't matter where and how to begin. He chose a place. "Well if we're to look to you," he said frankly, "then you're the one who owes me a new glider."

Lucius continued to face the wall of weapons, his back to Mick. He reached up to caress the handle of a sword with one finger. "A priest ought to know his place," he observed generically, then sharpened it. "Civic leaders don't come spying in your church. Still...perhaps my people were a little heavy-handed. They're trained to protect my mine from unwelcome eyes...and...actions." He turned suddenly, flashing benevolence. "Sure, send me the bill."

"And you can start by apologizing to a little boy."

Lucius ignored the comment and turned back to the wall.

Mick pressed. "And what of this other fellow, this Wayne Aak, Mr. Knox? Your boys run him out on a rail? Was he somebody who didn't sit down for them? Did he really do whatever they said he did?"

"Throughout history there have been the rebellious few who threaten the order of a kingdom. The disgruntled always rally around such a vagrant...but when a good man gets killed—my man—well the law caught up to that boy as it always does. Sent him up to the State Pen a couple of years ago, and that's the end of that story." He paused, then added, "No matter. He's a flea."

"They say that flea has gotten an appeal to stick and will be back. Looking for a little retribution. Could be strolling into town as we speak. Surely you know this; I know your men do."

Suddenly the curious charm was gone. The haughty control, the overlord façade, the tone of kindredship, had all evaporated, leaving self indulgence and tumult in their place. Knox lifted the sword from the wall and sliced the air in slow motion, then faster, and faster still, slowly approaching Mick at the fireplace end of the room as he slashed. His voice had changed, and Mick knew he'd pierced the carefully constructed persona his host had created. The real Knox was beginning to seethe.

"Aak will meet with swift justice if he shows his face in Terradise Valley!" the angered host predicted. "We have our avenging angels. And a priest would do well to consider carefully the side he takes in such things."

He approached Mick with the outstretched sword, waving its tip in a small circle at face level not quite menacingly. Mick stood still. Knox turned his back momentarily as if to step away, but then with a victor's grin, whirled dramatically and slashed the blade wildly through the air along an arc very close to Mick's face. It never got there; the sword's cut rang sickeningly against cold steel, crashing with deafening suddenness in mid-air. It had collided with the raised wrought iron fireplace poker Mick had pulled unseen from the hearth.

Their gazes locked; Knox saw the priest was neither chilled nor impressed.

"Let's put down the steel, Lucius."

"Ahhh. Lord let thy Blade of Retribution be raised only against Thine enemies?"

"Or perhaps just leave decorative toys on walls?"

"Ha ha! Very good, priest, very good. Well met!" Lucius lowered his weapon, inspecting the antique's metal edge and glowering momentarily at the nasty dent it had sustained, but softened his expression by degrees, determined to re-clothe himself in the persona of well bred host.

Mick lowered and returned the implement to its holder by the hearth. "Uh...I should get going," he apologized. "Early Mass, and all that. Really, Mr. Knox, thank you for a wonderful meal, the tour...and a fascinating evening." He moved toward the stairs, hoping doing so would add finality to his decision to leave.

Lucius nodded and smiled, then once again took him physically by the upper arm, to guide him as they ascended. "My man will drive you."

They reached the top of the hidden stairs. "Actually it's not far," Mick said. "I think I'd like to walk."

Knox did not immediately reply. They ascended the upper stairs and came to the dramatic fire-colored entryway, and the outer door. Lucius released Mick's arm. A primer-red pickup truck sat idling just outside, illuminated dimly by the outer wall torches, which were burning down but still alight.

"My man will drive you." The heavy door closed behind him, and Knox was gone.

Mick stood a moment, looking at the austere grounds and the wall beyond, breathing the darkness, trying to absorb the many turns the evening had taken, and the many faces of the man called Lucius Knox. The priest had seen no one else in the house— no kitchen help, no sign of friends, family, or visitors. He wondered what kind of man had no contact with anyone he did not pay, and what such an existence does to the balance in a man's mind.

One thing was clear: A corner had been turned. He and Lucius Knox were no longer strangers. The master of this house seemed enigmatic to a fault—as obscure as he was transparent, perhaps more so. It was difficult to know what to think—how to balance the obvious aspirations of dignity and strength Mick had detected with the underlying habitual focus on what seemed to be...baser motives. What was Knox capable of? He was a large spark here; how could the powder keg be defused?

Above all, Mick could not allow a man of his own nature to be drawn in.

He started to walk as he pondered. There would be no getting into any truck; he thought it best to simply move past the idling vehicle and cut behind, without a glance. He made it partway before the vehicle's engine revved and the truck lurched backward to block his path, dust kicking up from the rear tires as they dug into the dirt. Mick abruptly changed direction and strode across in front of its front bumper. He peered in through the windshield as he did, but the dark window tint and the glare from the torches obscured the driver from his view. He rounded the front corner and approached the driver's door, staring coldly through, inches from the glass, but could not pierce the dark tint to touch the unseen driver inside.

The priest turned and disappeared into the night. The truck continued to idle, but did not move. A dim yellow point of light from a lit cigarette escaped the darkness of its glass. The bare gable windows of the mansion showed no movement.

CHAPTER SEVENTEEN

Intention and reality are two different things, often kept apart by the agendas of others; Mick's hopes of wandering home and discussing the strangely informative evening with Elmer at the kitchen table never made it to action. He did make it to the sidewalk in front of the church—at least he'd gotten in sight of the day's finish line.

A young teenage Washokki boy was waiting silently in the shadow of a tree and the church; he initially startled Mick because he didn't move until the priest was almost upon him. He was very thin, with long arms; he looked about twelve or thirteen years old, although Mick knew he was not good at guessing the ages of the tribal people. The boy wore jeans, tennis shoes that had seen better days, and a mostly clean collared shirt.

"What do you...are you looking for me?" Mick asked him.

The youth did not speak, but nodded. He pointed down the street. Mick stared, initially not understanding. The boy pointed at Mick, and again down the street, then began to walk, motioning for Mick to follow.

They walked poorly lit side streets and alleys, skirting the main sections of town, gliding more quickly across stretches that provided no shadow cover. Mick wasn't sure whether that was by habit, or whether there was a particular and immediate reason for stealth. The boy looked around them carefully but did not listen for sounds, and Mick decided he must be deaf. At one point Mick heard what seemed like footsteps on a street to their right. Assuming their caution had a reason, he touched the boy's shoulder and signaled that he'd heard something. The child thanked him with an imperceptible nod and smile, and waited patiently until Mick let him know it sounded okay to continue.

They arrived at a small home on a quiet street near the northwest edge of town. The boy approached the residence from the back, entering the fenced backyard through a waist-high chain link gate, and taking care to close the gate behind them. Then, with a noticeably reduced sense of caution now that they were at this address, he led Mick across the small grass yard toward the back door of the house.

The house was a single story wood structure with one chimney and tan, well-weathered clapboard siding. There was no back porch; a small window looked out onto the yard from what was probably the kitchen. The house and grounds were simple but reasonably well kept.

Crossing the yard, Mick noticed several young tribal men loitering in the shadows to his left. They were talking in tones low enough that a dozen feet away he heard no sound as he passed. The young men looked at Mick suspiciously, pausing momentarily in their conversation to stare as he moved on. Three were burly, angry-looking men, wearing dirty clothing and perpetual scowls. One middle-aged man with thick matted black hair and a disheveled, transient look also turned to gaze absently at Mick through bloodshot eyes. The priest was aware of one or two other people elsewhere in the corners of the yard.

The boy had reached the steps in front of the back door, and now turned, waiting for Mick to catch up. They mounted the few steps and entered the house. As they stepped inside, Mick saw more silent, strong-looking men standing just inboard of the door. Sentries, he knew. They stood expressionless, in contrast to the men outside, and Mick got the distinct impression they were veterans at guard duty. The deaf boy nodded to one of them, who gave the barest hint of acknowledgment in return. Mick followed the boy past these men, who noted him but did not glare.

Still led by the deaf boy, he went through a short hall, passing a very small room on his left where an older boy sat operating an amateur radio transmitter. He was listening to someone speaking a local tribal tongue, and responding in like manner. Mick presumed it was one of the Kalispell dialects and that the older boy was connecting with some distant tribal gathering similar to what was clearly happening in this house.

The deaf boy tapped Mick on the shoulder and beckoned him to stay focused and follow as asked. He nodded and was led into the small living room, where assembled on the sofa, chairs and floor were roughly a dozen Washokki and Tissoma elders.

The crowded room was silent. All eyes were watching him. He may have been an intruder in their affairs and their home, but as they had obviously summoned him, he felt no compulsion for apology. He remained standing, and waited a full minute for them to finish studying him and get to their point.

A middle-aged man by the name of Reuben Bitterroot eventually did so. "We don't want your religion or your friendship," he addressed Mick aggressively, dispensing with any lead-in. "And we don't need your approval."

"You're the...influential members of the Washokki and Tissoma tribal communities," Mick guessed aloud, avoiding the word 'elders' because some were far older than others.

They responded with silence.

"Okay," he tried again, "what is it you would like from me?"

Bitterroot opened his mouth again, but an older woman overrode him quietly, and he deferred to her. "We want you to keep the white folk out of this," she said simply. "This is between us and Mr. Knox."

"What is?"

"What's going to happen," Bitterroot cut back in. Then as an afterthought he added, "You're not on his side I hope."

"I can't condone violence from anyone, if that's what you're asking."

"Nobody cares what you condone," Bitterroot reminded him. "Nobody cares who you befriend, as long as it's not him. What we want is for you to keep all your kind out of whatever happens."

It was an odd demand, Mick thought, aimed as it was at a newcomer. "What makes you think I can do that?"

"You...."

A very old man on the right end of the sofa suddenly addressed Bitterroot, and as he did so the room became quiet. "I will speak with this man, Reuben," he intervened. Then he turned to Mick, pausing before speaking to ensure he had the priest's full attention. "You are new here, young man. To you, we are an unknown. You do not understand our language, and how we have been shaped for generations by the mountains, and the winters. You imagine that you do not understand our ways.

"And to most people here, even in this room, you are also an unknown. In the town, they stare at you without speaking. They hold secret fear. But also they carry secret hope. They want to know if you are part of the disease that lives among them, or if not, then what you will do about this sickness."

He paused, looking only at Mick; the others in the room remained still, knowing he had not finished. "But some of us in this gathering," he went on, "know what people are made of, and so we know something about you. You are a priest, and ...how did you say it? ... an 'influential member of the white community.' It was a good way to say it."

Mick listened intently. He knew that this man's message, rather than that of the younger one they'd called Reuben, was why he had been brought to the gathering.

"I have watched you," the old man added. "I think maybe you are fighting too, inside your heart. And I have a feeling you have seen trouble before. And so you know it can be very bad. We don't want to hurt those who are not part of this."

Mick nodded, acknowledging the old man's perception, but still returning to the pragmatic question. "If I may ask, sir...part of what?"

The bolder Bitterroot jumped in one more time. "That land, that mine, it's ours. It was our land before, when we ran them out, it was ours when we died for it—and in it—and it's still our land. Anything in it belongs to us."

A different old man, sitting cross-legged on the floor and quiet until now, interrupted, admonishing Bitterroot. "Reuben, you do not speak for the elders." There was an uneasy silence. Bitterroot scowled and stalked out.

The elders sat silent and stone-faced, looking at Mick. He was getting some of this message, but still needed context. "You are...supporters of the young man named Wayne Aak?"

Those in the room murmured to each other in their native tongue; but Mick gathered that what he'd feared might be an idiotic question was more complex than that. The old woman who had spoken earlier finally provided an answer. "Young man, that boy is a fool and a brush fire...but he's our brush fire. Some want to use the chaos he's created to take back what they say is ours."

Mick nodded in silence, and the very old man on the sofa added to her answer.

"And some do not want that. You see that we too are divided in some ways. This is why tomorrow is so important for us. Tomorrow we will have a celebration of the long-ago unifying of the Washokki and Tissoma peoples."

"Yes...I saw the posters."

"This has been planned for a long time. There will be many councils. We are coordinating with our people over the whole region," the old man explained, gesturing with a slow hand toward the small hall and the side room in which Mick had seen the radio transmitter.

"Many have arrived already from other towns and reservations. More are coming. We will meet and make plans, and will honor our ancestors openly, and I think there will be trouble. I think you would be wise to prepare for that, and to try to shield innocent people from getting hurt."

"The notice is a bit late."

"We were...watching you."

So they'd been on the fence up to now whether to approach him, to trust him, or not. Mick wondered what had moved them from indecision. Simply the impending arrival of the Unification Day and the need to lean one way or the other? Or was it his dinner earlier that very evening with Knox? Surely they knew of it...and surely knew how he'd been invited. As the old man had said, they had been watching him.

A long silence prevailed, while they observed his reaction, watched him think. Then he spoke again. "Gabriella Cielo says you're fools like the rest of the town—like Lucius Knox. She says you all have the same fever—the fever of greed. Is she right?" Straightforwardness and the decision to trust worked both ways.

"She's not one of us," the woman replied.

The elders were silent from that point on, and Mick realized he was dismissed. He thanked them with a wordless nod and left through the short hallway as he had come, his path again intersected by the deaf boy, who had evidently been waiting in the kitchen for him to pass. The boy followed Mick to the back door, but not past the men standing guard.

Mick crossed the back yard solo, toward the gate at the rear. The same group of younger tribal men he'd seen before still loitered there, this time talking with Bitterroot in earnest tones. They again suspended their talk as Mick passed by, glaring anew. There were agendas here not in line with those inside. The middle-aged transient man with thick matted black hair and bloodshot eyes bummed a cigarette from one of the others, smirking.

Mick closed the gate behind him and, although he wasn't sure why, elected to exercise the same caution as the boy had when they'd come here. The streets were deserted, and he made it back to the road on which the church stood without incident. He began to relax. He certainly had a string of stories to share with Elmer, and needed the caretaker's opinion of this strange long day.

He passed a street lamp and kept moving; best not to linger under the light. A half-block from the residence, he stopped to listen. Was he being followed? Turning quickly to look back, he saw only the small trees lining this side of the street, their shadows lined up and stretched out to one side. Only...it seemed that...one narrow shadow resembled the shape of a man.

Mick took slow steps back toward the spot. He was sure someone was there; whoever it was would have to make themselves known—either face him or cut and run; with the path he was taking they would not be able to melt away. He closed the distance and no one bolted. A spot behind a tall bush came visible now, and as he walked a man's thin, still figure slid into view. Mick recognized him as the small Indian man who had almost approached him before. He slowed and stopped his approach for fear of spooking the man. Instead he said quietly, "Hello my friend."

The thin man did not reply, but neither did he run. Was he connected with the tribal meeting Mick had just left? Not likely; his methods and nervousness said he was acting alone.

"You're not sent to watch me by the elders, are you," Mick commented quietly. It was more a statement than a question. Then, guessing, "Are you...a friend of the Cielo family?"

The man did as he came to do, going straight to his point in a soft, clear voice: "The secrets are buried." He had his own brand of courage, and this time he did not disappear.

"What secrets? Whose secrets are buried, sir?"

"They are...buried." The man seemed to emphasize the last word.

"...Whose are they?"

"They will belong to who finds them."

Mick paused to absorb this new riddle, gazing for a moment into the jet black night sky. Then he returned his eyes to earth and replied, half to himself. "You mean me."

But the thin man had disappeared somewhere in the line of small trees, soundlessly, as they say only an Indian can.

CHAPTER EIGHTEEN

Sleep was not so easily coaxed, despite the long, draining day. Now in addition to his Bishop, there was another faction expecting some kind of action from him...and yet in both cases he didn't know quite what. Or did he know? Was he simply afraid to act? It wasn't like he had no good reason.

He paced the living room, kitchen, hall. He sat on the corner of his bed and got up to recount the length of the hall again. He stepped onto the porch without knowing why, and returned, to pace again. He needed information...and support.

On an impulse he picked up the phone, dialed the operator, and asked for a connection. "Yes, it's in Missoula," he confirmed. Waiting, he began to pace absently again, pulling the phone off the table. Out of long discarded habit he almost swore at himself, but listened instead, relieved that the connection was not lost. A voice on the other end prompted his hastily prepared introduction.

"Hi, my name is Mick Calahan. I'd like to speak with whomever is in charge there. Yes...no, the main guy. Uh...Greene, Vernon Greene you say? Okay sure, sounds good ma'am. Yes, I'll be glad to wait."

A full minute passed before another voice greeted him. The earnest calm of the conversation lasted nearly a quarter hour. "No, sir, that's correct, it is not a good situation," Mick agreed near the end of the discussion. "Yes sir. Yes, I will do that at the first sign of anything. I'll keep you apprised. I appreciate your time. Yes, we'll talk again Mr. Greene. Thank you; 'bye now."

He hung up the phone and stood another ten minutes without moving. He had to put some pieces together. The day had taken its toll on him, and he stretched out on the bed. But he rose again a moment later, to pick up the phone once more and redial the operator. "I wonder," he asked, "if you could connect me to a state facility in Deer Lodge...."

*   *   *

In the grey, even light just prior to dawn, two huge diesel mining trucks eased off the highway west of town. They negotiated the hairpin turn and started their slow roll up the long grade toward Terradise Valley. At 170,000 pounds each, the Unit Rig Electra Hauls represented the state of heavy mining equipment art. Each one capable of carrying close to a hundred tons of dirt, they stood seventeen feet tall, not counting the additional eight-foot height of the spare excavator boom being transported in the bucket of the first.   Wider than they were high, the behemoths spanned the entire road.   This morning they traveled one behind the other and translated to a combined seventy-foot train of power, diesel fumes, and noise.

Two men in a small white pickup truck met the trucks before they got near the town. The little utility vehicle sat sideways, blocking the road, forcing the professional heavy equipment drivers to slow their machines to a stop. The white pickup then pulled alongside the first diesel. A tall man named Rowe with an untrustworthy face and a perpetual scowl leaned out the little cab's driver-side window and addressed the diesel's driver without bothering to get out.   Over the din of the large idling engines, instructions were given. Rowe pointed up the road toward town, and repeatedly waved his hand like a knife edge, indicating a straight path.

The Electra Hauls were put in gear; their huge eight-foot-tall tires started to turn.   The monsters picked up speed and rolled on, nearing the town's edge. The small white utility truck followed them.

Joel addressed Rowe with a comical look.   "You sent 'em right up the goddamn main street!"

"So?" Rowe was always cool—even when he was lying, which at the moment he was not.

"Mebbe they can sneak through without bein' noticed."

"Ain't likely. It's four fuckin' somethin' in the AM."

"If we gotta be up, I guess the Injuns can too," Joel gloated. "Gonna rattle Grandma's teeth!"

"Yep, and they're still in the fuckin' jar."

"This is sure to be the biggest show this dump of a town has seen in years," Joel said, lighting a cigarette.

Rowe sneered. "Well it better rattle some action into that damn mine. I'm not hangin' out in moose-shit country just to smell ol' weird Knox's farts."

The pickup truck decelerated, putting a little distance between it and the diesels, which had reached the edge of the town. The big machines slowed again to a stop. Cursing, Rowe exited the white truck and walked up to stand beneath the driver's window of the lead truck.

"What the devil you stoppin' fer?" he demanded.

The diesel driver leaned out and looked down at him. "What about them wires and traffic lights and such? Some of them's gonna come the hell down, if'n we go any further," he shouted above the engine noise.

"Them wires has all been disconnected," Rowe replied coolly. "All gotta come down anyways. Don't worry about them wires, just drive."

"Yer the boss, mister." The diesel driver waved for the second truck to follow him; his head and shoulders disappeared back into his cab, and the two machines were put back in gear.

Rowe returned to the small utility truck snickering. "I told the fucker all them wires was disconnected."

"Well," Joel observed, "I don't think that's gonna be a lie!"

The huge Electra Hauls began their slow creep through the Terradise Valley commercial district, waking dogs and rattling residents into consciousness as they came. As tall as buildings and rumbling like diesel thunder, they spanned the street from boardwalk to boardwalk, their huge wheels dwarfing houses and trees.

Residents began to lean out windows and stagger into the pre-morning air, cursing the noise, the exhaust, and the sheer size of the machinery. Afraid of damage to windows and roofs, shopkeepers threw on clothing and ran down to their businesses. The trucks rolled slowly, almost defiantly, up the main street, headed for the far side of town, where their drivers assumed they would intersect a road out to the mine. As the diesel engines revved, exhaust belched into the dark sky. Behind the huge beasts, the small white pickup truck followed at the same creeping pace, its occupants smirking and smoking.

Scattered groups of Indians and Caucasians stood now along the street, gaping, holding half-awake children or restraining dogs by leather collars. "What the hell," an elderly tribal man remarked to his wife.

"Tell me they need to move this much dirt on this day," she replied. "This is our day and they know it." She grabbed her husband's elbow and drew his attention to a handful of younger Indian men across the street who were moving quickly, knocking on doors, mobilizing others. The streets began to be lined with frantic onlookers.

The engine noise woke Mick. Groggy but no longer surprised by anything, he arose and staggered onto the porch, peering in the direction of the main street two blocks away. Elmer, evidently shaken to unwelcome consciousness by the din as well, stepped out with him, and the two listened. "Big ol' Cummins engines," Elmer said with concentration.

The Unit Rig trucks continued their relentless crawl. So far they had carefully managed to avoid tearing down wires. Near the old hotel where the main street slightly altered its eastward angle, they began to navigate the 20-degree change of direction. The drivers took it very slowly. The first truck narrowly missed dislodging an overhang, but slid by and was through. The second machine then began to attempt the same feat.

When it was halfway into its turn, a small, low, beat-up dark brown pickup truck suddenly lurched out from a side street in front of the lead truck. The intruding vehicle ground its gears and slid to a stop. Behind the wheel sat a bleary-eyed middle-aged tribal man with thick matted black hair, already handcuffed to his own steering wheel. The lead Unit Rig slammed on its brakes, nearly being rammed by the one behind, whose driver had not reacted immediately and so had to swerve somewhat to avoid a collision. The lead diesel's monstrous front wheels had stopped only a few feet from the tiny brown truck.

Rowe and Joel, still following the procession in the white pickup and unclear as to what had happened, jumped infuriated from their cab and ran cursing to the front. The handcuffed tribal driver, having ground to a stop, locked the doors of his decrepit vehicle. A large number of teenage tribal boys and young men leapt ecstatic into the street behind him, chanting. "Jimmy Leake! Jimmy Leake! Jimmy! Jimmy!" Within half a minute they numbered more than fifty, blocking all approach to the reeking, bloodshot little man.

Coming within sight of the makeshift blockade, Rowe sized up the situation instantly and sought to effect an immediate solution. He shouted up to the lead diesel's driver, above the din of the idling engines. "Keep rolling, damn you! Push this fuck out of the way!"

Ten feet above Rowe, the driver leaned out his window with a scowl. "What are you, nuts?! Get him the hell out of there or find us a way around!"

"There ain't no way around! Do what I tell you!"

The driver shook his head in refusal, and pulled back into his cab. Both Cummins engines revved, belching fumes into the thickening sky, as if trying to scare the drunken Leake out of their path.

"Fuuuuuck!" screamed Joel. His bosses would not be pleased. He turned back toward the white pickup; Rowe caught up with him. Taking the risky path straight up the main street had been Rowe's own joke, and Rowe knew Daryl and Knox would task him with undoing the mess one way or another. He and Joel had to get the fiasco under control. And he wasn't about to wade into a few dozen Indians alone, or with his back covered only by this fuck-up to his right. Amid shouts and taunts from shopkeepers and tribal onlookers, the two men quickly approached the driver of the second diesel.

"Go back, damn you!" Rowe cursed at the driver, waving his arms. "Back up! We'll find you another way!"

"I can't back this thing up in town, you idiot! It ain't like that toy you drive! Maneuverin' forward is tough enough, for Christ's sake! I'd tear the place apart!"

"Do it!" Rowe screamed in a fit of rage.

Mick arrived on the street in time to see the rear diesel's driver reluctantly put his machine in reverse. The priest witnessed the giant front tires cutting hard and the truck beginning to roll backward slowly through the bend it had previously almost completed. Attempting to straighten out, the driver gunned the engine too hard; the right rear corner of the rock bucket caught the edge of a wooden transformer pole, splintering it instantly. With a sickening crash, the pole and transformer tottered and fell across the truck, dragging power lines from other poles across a nearby metal shed roof. The transformer shorted against the truck. Ranting and hooting could be heard from the growing mob of young men surrounding Leake's vehicle.

Cursing and fearful of electrocution, the driver immediately cut his engine and leapt down from the cab. The driver of the first truck followed suit. In the unexpected sudden quiet, they stood as close as they dared to the downed wires, assessing the damage, the danger posed by the wreckage, and what it would take to extricate the giant trucks.

The driver of the lead truck spat on the pavement. "This ain't good," he said in frustration.

Joel and Rowe approached them from behind. "What the fuck did you do?!" Joel began.

Rowe was more authoritative. "Back these damn things out!" he commanded.

The lead diesel driver took a step toward him and stood menacingly close. "Let me tell you somethin', bud," he breathed emphatically. "I don't know what yer problem is, but we got no intention of flattenin' citizens, damagin' property, torchin' this town or gettin' injured ourself. These trucks don't move unless I say they move. Now you tell yer man Mr. Knox he'd better solve this. You got wires—live wires, so don't give me that shit about them bein' dead—and poles down and who knows what the hell else. We'll give you...we'll give him... till Friday—that's two days—or we're outa here and the keys come with us. And the meter is still runnin' on these goddamn machines."

Rowe backed down with a scowl, muttering a threat the driver either ignored or didn't hear. In front of the lead truck, Leake's supporters were removing the wheels from the small brown pickup truck. Within three minutes it sat axles-to-pavement, unable to be towed from its blocking position, with Leake still inside, nodding and playing the role of proud hero for the first time in his useless, bleary life.

"This'll bring the whole damn town to a standstill!" a man near Mick grumbled in disgust. "I got a business to run!"

A woman next to him chimed in. "Damn ridiculous, paradin' this show right up the middle! What the hell were they thinkin'?"

"Where did the heavy equipment come from?" Mick asked.

"Gotta be Knox behind it," said the woman. "And the damned tribe tried to stop him. Whyn't they just let him do his thing?"

"Goddamn standstill! This bullshit is their fault." The shop owner spat in disgust.

Elmer surprised Mick by stepping up behind him; despite his wooden leg he was risking the jostling of the agitated crowd to talk to the priest. The caretaker spoke in a low tone. "I seen that one around, that one up there in the dark brown truck," he murmured. "A drunk and a damn bum. Somebody loaned him that ol' junk truck and sent him out there, sure as I'm standin' here. He don't own no damn truck, that much I know."

"Them that's behind it is the damn loudmouth friends of the punk who went to prison," the woman interjected.

Mick turned back to Elmer. "See how this kind of thing polarizes a town, when it should be bringing these people together to solve a common problem," he said quietly. "The Indians are out there going door-to-door and putting their contingency plans into action, and somehow they saw all this coming. And the whites are standing here blaming them. Truth is, this is none of their fault."

Elmer said nothing, but his scowl did not lessen.

"Anyway," Mick added, "I'm going up where I can get a better look at that chocolate-colored piece of junk and the guy you're talking about."

"You watch yerself."

Mick nodded, put his hand on the old man's shoulder, and made his way through the onlookers to a point where he could see Leake's truck. He spotted Joel and Rowe standing on the opposite side of the street, twenty yards from Leake's position, yelling. Thad, Ofstedder and several other Knox men were with them. They were keeping together for their own safety, Mick knew; it was likely the first time they were not in abusive control. And they'd not forget— men of their kind would find a way to punish.

Enraged by the makeshift uprising, Ofstedder sought to bully an immediate solution. He walked closer to the crowd surrounding Leake, his voice rising above the din. "Get your asses out of there!" Thad, following him, pulled from his belt a revolver and brandished it in the air. Ofstedder got within range of a tribal teenager and attacked him, shoving him hard. To his surprise, an older, larger Washokki man stepped in without hesitation and took a swing at him, catching him on the side of the head with a punishing blow, knocking him back but not down. Thad moved in immediately and leveled the gun at the Washokki man's teeth, forcing him to back off. The crowd around Leake was stamping and yelling now, as were many onlookers lining both sides of the street. Ofstedder and Thad backed up.

Loud, vulgar threats from Knox's men proved empty; Leake didn't move. The Unit Rig drivers, knowing it was best to get out of sight, disappeared through the hotel door directly in front of their machines. Ofstedder, Rowe and Thad cursed, loitered, cursed more, and finally stalked off to inform Lucius Knox of the unforeseen development.

The sizeable crowd of onlookers lining the street remained for almost an hour more, cheering, complaining, and watching. The commotion gradually abated as the minutes passed. The young Washokki men settled in around Leake's immobile vehicle, some sitting on the pavement, others on the little truck's fenders, preparing for a long vigil.

Mick watched the events with growing unease. Others could convince themselves the worst was over and that the delicate stalemate would eventually and quietly resolve. But Mick knew it for what it was—a keg of black powder bloating larger and more explosive with every minute it was not defused. He knew egos on all sides now ran far too rich for this to blow over. Where was the sheriff through all this? No one appeared surprised that there was no sign of the law.

Torn between investigation and detachment, he watched, started to step into the street, turned away, paused, turned back. He knew he'd never been one who could remain true to discretion when action was called for. Whether it was a decision or just caving in didn't really matter; he clenched his fists, lowered his head, and stepped with conviction off the boardwalk, slowly approaching the tiny brown truck.

To his amazement the tribal guards didn't impede his approach. They didn't even seem overly surprised by it. As he closed the distance, they slowly and deliberately made a very narrow path between themselves through which he could move. He felt their breath as he passed through, but they laid no hand on him. He walked the way they had cleared for him to the truck's fender, and peered into the cab, seeing Jimmy Leake, recognizing him from the back yard at the house where the elders had met. He noted the chains binding the man's wrists to the steering wheel. Leake met his gaze with the blank look of a martyr who'd spent the night drinking. No words passed.

Caucasian townsfolk saw the priest's approach too, marveling secretly. They themselves kept their distance, and gradually evaporated with the strengthening rays of the dawn.

CHAPTER NINETEEN

The sun climbed, and hovered. The Unit Rig trucks sat where they'd been left at dawn, clogging the main business artery like a log jam in a narrow river. Fearful of violence erupting or of being linked with the stalemate, Caucasian and tribal residents alike avoided the main street, except to peer surreptitiously from a distance at the machines, the downed utility pole and wires, and the small dark brown truck surrounded by its entourage of tribal guards.

By the point in the road where it had occurred and the timing with which it had been executed, Mick knew the blockade had been planned with a certain amount of military precision. It was the kind of thing he'd have expected from Knox, but that the tribes had managed it implied they knew the timetable of the trucks' arrival and the approximate route the machines were likely to take. Evidently Knox's men had leaked their plans through boasting or other carelessness, and clearly they'd been caught unaware. He knew it did not sit well with them. They had underestimated their enemies and it was costing them now, in time, probably money, and most importantly in the perception of their power. Knox must have planned the arrival of these machines as an undeniable demonstration of his dominance and the overriding priority of the town—his mine. He had meant to squash notions of tribal solidarity with pure noise and diesel exhaust. But that dominance was now in question; it was a joke hanging in the air, for which Knox's men were likely to pay.

So Washokki and Tissoma reactionaries had tossed together a plan to bring Knox's progress to a standstill. There were people in these tribes with some military background, that much was clear—and people who were probably students of Lakota/Nakota military history, something Knox wouldn't have foreseen. Mick recalled the muffled, urgent tones with which Reuben Bitterroot had conferred with the men in the yard the night before. He remembered how Gabriella had described the radical men who had met her husband and the former pastor at the kitchen table a year before. They had been men of violence, she had said.

The morning bored itself into stagnant afternoon. There was no wind to break the soundlessness, and no movement on the main street beyond the occasional stirring of those protecting Leake. About midday, a black-tinted van paused at a corner a block to the east, unseen eyes surveying the situation from within. The young men guarding the small truck watched the van as it paused, and several minutes later watched it slowly ooze away. An hour later the same van returned, this time following another truck from which the sheriff emerged, accompanied by Ofstedder, Raam, Rowe and Thad. The five men approached the crowd in the street. The sheriff demanded the extrication of the handcuffed man, one shaking hand on his holster, the other holding his badge before him as he walked. Thad rested a hand on a revolver in his belt. The unseen eyes in the van watched from a distance.

The young men surrounding Leake rose and tightened their ranks, shouting and brandishing blunt weapons. A number of other tribal men, evidently remaining vigilant, ran from nearby streets and houses to join their compatriots, a few of them carrying shotguns. The sheriff faltered in his demands and took a backward step, and the shouting from the center of the street gained strength. The black van pulled away then, momentarily spinning tires and spraying loose dust as it accelerated. Ofstedder, Rowe, Thad and Raam backed up to their truck and followed in the direction the van had gone, leaving the sheriff to walk down the same side street and disappear.

In the minds of onlookers, tension mounted throughout the day. Caucasian business owners kept shops locked. The street remained mostly clear of people. Late afternoon crept with lethargic apprehension toward the advancement of dusk. A snapdragon jerked its noisy, jagged flight along the edge of the boardwalk. Just before the sun dipped behind the taller roofs, a last rogue dust devil, ignited by the stagnant heat, ripped up the main street from the clear eastern end, partly circling the guards seated around the little brown truck. The men followed its path with their eyes, watching it suddenly dissipate at the base of a wooden power pole and realizing with a jolt of surprise that they were being watched at close range. How long Daryl and Rowe had been leaning against the pole they didn't know; the two were simply waiting, watching, smoking. They stood motionless, indifferent to the passing of time; the glow of their cigarettes remained brazenly visible as their features and identities faded in the failing light.

Mick kept vigil too, listening intently and now and then walking to the main street to see what, if anything, had changed. As darkness set in he wondered if they might get through this day after all. His phone was no longer working, and he assumed the electrical mayhem on the main street was the reason. He ate a late and hurried dinner alone, and spent his time in thought, and in foreboding.

Streets overall remained empty. The Unit Rig drivers had kept out of sight all day. A black sky now displayed the wonders of deep space. Daryl and Rowe had vanished as silently as they had appeared, a half dozen cigarette butts on the road the only testament of their earlier presence.

Jimmy Leake, still chained and smelling of urine, slept uncomfortably in his brown truck, aided in unconsciousness by the former contents of an empty whiskey bottle that now lay on the truck's floor at his feet. A smaller number of complacent, burly tribal men sat by the axles, cradling shotguns across their knees, their backs to the small truck's fenders and bumpers. A few empty bottles lay among them as well. An owl screeched twice near a tree to the south.

Unseen, a pair of boots appeared silently on the step of the forward diesel's cab. Hands soundlessly opened the door, then a moment later closed it. Undetected, the glow from a tiny flashlight very dimly illuminated the fogging cab windows, as curses were muttered and fingers faltered with a knife and wires under the instrument board. It was taking far too long.

Twenty minutes later the uneasy peace was interrupted by the diesel engine's starter turning over. The tribal guards sprang to their feet, looking this way and that, trying to get a handle on what was going down. Belching a black cloud into a black sky, the big Cummins engine roared to life at deafening RPM. An anonymous hand jammed the Unit Rig's gearshift lever into first, and the truck lurched violently toward Leake's crippled vehicle.

There was no time; nobody had expected mechanized lethal force. Shouting, the guards rolled and jumped out of the way to avoid being crushed themselves. On the far side of the stranded truck, two of them pounded for a brief instant on Leake's locked door, but the eight-foot tire of the Electra Haul rammed the little vehicle, sliding it on the pavement, instantly forcing them to abandon the rescue and save themselves. They stood helplessly as the giant tire rode up onto and collapsed the little cab with the awful screech of rending, tearing metal and a shower of exploding glass, crushing it slowly, grinding the small chassis underneath. Leake awoke in time to let out a gurgled scream, his horrible wail just as suddenly stifled as the huge truck crept overtop and compacted him in the wreckage.

Mick was still awake. Slouching at the kitchen table like a schoolboy in front of his homework, he'd been alternately jotting down notes for a report to his Bishop and toying with thoughts for a Sunday sermon, using the quiet of the night. It wasn't going well; he'd gotten nowhere in the last hour, and knew it was more because of his own doubts than due to any lack of material. The paper in front of him bore the words "People who put themselves above the rest— above morality," followed by another line that read "above humanity," ending in no punctuation and a sea of blank paper. In frustration he had scratched the line out and was tapping the pencil on the side of an empty mug, struggling through fractured images, subconsciously hoping the cadence he drummed would somehow lead to inspiration. The roar of the big Cummins engine two blocks away brought him to his feet, the pencil clattering to the floor.

Had the two drivers decided to return the machines to their employers? Had the transformer and wires been isolated and untangled? In the middle of the night neither was likely, he knew. He dashed from the house and ran to the main street, hearing Leake's extinguished scream as he went, dreading what he would find. He approached in time to see the professional driver, shirtless and swearing, leaping into the street from the hotel and sprinting to the driver's side of his big machine. Mick saw him spring to the foot step and haul open the truck's door. With a single angry hand the driver took hold of the man inside the cab, casting him headlong out the door and down onto the street below. The man who fell out was Rowe.

In an instant the professional driver swung like a cat into the cab, jammed the gearshift lever into reverse, and backed the big wheel off the tiny wreckage of Leake's truck, indifferent to whether Rowe lay in the path of the reversing tire or not. Tribal supporters of Leake, loathe to glimpse his condition, still hung back from the dark brown wreckage; some of the younger ones instead pounced on Rowe, kicking and beating him while he screamed denials and pleas. Thad emerged from the Inferno and, again relying on his firearm, backed them away at gunpoint.

Arriving at the edge of the street, Mick lost no more than a running step and made it to Leake's truck first. Panicked, the driver of the lead diesel shut down the engine and swung down, still cursing, and joined Mick to assess Leake's condition. The second diesel's driver leapt from the hotel boardwalk and approached as well, until both of them were shouldered aside by tribal militants trying to do the same thing.

Unable to assist, the outraged driver of the lead diesel began to shout. "This damn town better get itself straightened out! You all better think twice about any lawsuits!" He turned and whispered something hoarsely to his compatriot, and then without ceremony they both climbed back into their machines, fired up the engines, and with a deafening belch of fumes and a grinding of metal gears they backed both trucks out, indifferent to the trail of smashed roof overhangs, poles, and wires as they went. At the edge of town where they had entered that morning, they came about and returned to forward gears, picking up speed and losing the train of dragged poles and wires on the pavement behind them. The townsfolk, many of which were by now reassembled along the main street, en masse tracked the trucks' progress by sound, hearing them roar westward until they had regained the highway and were gone.

Unable to see Leake clearly in the twisted metal and the crowd of heads and arms, Mick looked around for a plan. Would Hawkins have tools to cut the roof off? It was unclear whether there was any urgency—no one had yet seen movement in the crushed vehicle.

Several large tribal men produced a crowbar and managed to pry the roof upward on the driver's side. The door fell apart at the hinge, but remained crimped to the rest of the chassis; they hauled on it and managed to get it mostly dislodged. Leake's body, slumped somewhere between seated and prone, was now visible. Mick saw Lucius' black van appear silently at the corner a block away. This time the door opened and Lucius himself, tall, commanding, gaunt, stepped out.

Knox made no inquiry, but fearlessly approached the crowd of tribal militants surrounding the victim. Mick saw tears in the tall man's eyes...but also a hint of something far less rational. Amazingly, the Washokki did nothing to resist his approach. Knox took one quick, wild, commanding look into the cab, wrestled a twelve-gauge shotgun from one of the tribal men standing near him, and stuck the barrel into the compressed truck's mangled door where Leake's body sat. Only Mick gasped. Knox fired a single, sickening round. The crowd along the entire street flinched. The handcuff chain parted. "Take that man to my vehicle!" the tall gaunt man barked.

A crowd will always defer to the note of authority when a moment calls for action and normal experience comes up short. Leake's crumpled body was yanked out feet first and carried by three Washokki men to Lucius' black van. Lucius followed a dozen feet behind, walking alone, his path clearing for him as he went. He looked beyond the victim to the driver of his van and barked another order. "And fetch my personal doctor," he said. The driver nodded and keyed a hand-held radio as he climbed back into the van, ready to drive as soon as Leake was loaded.

Mick shouldered his way out of the crowd surrounding the wrecked truck and followed Knox to the van. He got there as Leake was stretched out on the back seat. The tribal men did not move to accompany the crushed man; the door was closing and the van was preparing to roll. Lucius remained standing on the street, his still wild eyes now locked with Mick's silent, intent, questioning gaze.

Seeing the confrontation and mistaking it for a threat, Thad appeared from the side and started to put his revolver in Mick's face. In half an instant Mick had the gun, tossing it on the ground behind him, stepping through Thad as though he were a child, never taking his eyes off Lucius. Mick knew cowards like Thad, men who derived their strength from guns, and that they didn't matter; he needed an answer from Knox. Lucius maintained his wild look, but he had understood the wordless question. His face suddenly softened and he nodded unspoken agreement. Mick climbed into the van with Leake. Lucius murmured to the driver and the vehicle raced off.

No sooner was the black van gone than a second truck—Daryl's primer-red pickup—pulled up to the same corner as if choreographed. Lucius was already standing on the passenger's side; Daryl leaned across and pulled the latch on the door, and Knox entered the vehicle as soon as its forward motion was stopped. Daryl waited for a word from his boss, then turned to breathe an order out his rolled-down window to Thad, now standing with Ofstedder where Knox had left him: "Get every man up here to deal with this shit," Daryl commanded. "Every one." The truck lurched through the turn and Lucius Knox was driven from the scene.

The Washokki and Tissoma men were still surrounding the mangled brown pickup, but were fast losing their militant resolve. A short youth holding one of the crowbars said to two of his older compatriots, "See that? The gun? That priest didn't back down from those bastards. Why the hell do we?! I'm not taking this."

Another agreed. "It was exactly what Wayne would do."

The tribal men milled around the wreckage in frustration for awhile longer, eventually dispersing in smaller agitated groups, some hoping to find ways of inciting retaliation. Thad and Ofstedder stood in the shadows for several minutes and then slid quietly over to the Inferno, disappearing inside. A moment later the sheriff appeared from its door; he remained on the side of the street until Hawkins, driving a small four-wheeled tractor, arrived to meet him. Together they chained Leake's brown truck, now unguarded, to the tractor's three-point hitch and dragged it very slowly down to the empty lot beside the garage, two bent steel wheels screeching on the pavement like some torturous sound from hell.

Although councils had convened, the day-long incident had usurped any unification celebrations the tribes had planned, fortifying a dangerous breed of solidarity in a way none could have predicted. It left a wake of snapped utility poles, damaged rooftops, downed electrical and telephone wires, angry, polarized, confused citizens, and percussive silence.

CHAPTER TWENTY

Mick avoided inspecting Leake's crumpled body as the van drove, telling himself there was little he could discern in the darkness. He guessed they were being taken to Lucius' house, both because he'd never found a community doctor's office in Terradise Valley and because he knew Lucius would need to control any news of Leake's condition.

When the van stopped he got out. As expected they had pulled up to the rear of the mansion. A dirty yellow station wagon, hood still warm, was already there. Daryl's truck arrived right behind them; Knox exited nearly before it stopped. He spoke an inaudible word and two men emerged from the side of the building, tucking small revolvers into their belts, and together with the van driver hauled Leake out onto the dirt, then into an open door of the house. Daryl remained in his truck, smoking, staring expressionless at nothing.

Mick followed them in and up a flight of stairs. With Knox leading, they carried Leake to a small but comfortable guest room overlooking the side of the house at which they had parked. A chubby man of about 70 years with thick spectacles and a pronounced limp took over, instructing them to place him on the bed, which had already been covered with a plastic tarp over which a plain white sheet had been laid. A dim table lamp sat by the bedside, and the old doctor switched it to full brightness to get a good look at the victim.

Amazingly Leake was alive, but was in bad condition. Lacerations and deep dark bruises, indicating bleeding under the skin, were everywhere. His right shoulder had suffered a yawning puncture wound, with a piece of something still in it, which Mick knew might explain why it wasn't bleeding as much as it should have been. The man's head flopped around in a sickening way; the neck was probably broken. At least one leg was fractured, the femur just beginning to protrude through the skin. He was struggling to breathe as well. The man was lucky to be unconscious, Mick thought.

The van driver and the other two men left. The old doctor prepared a heavy syringe of morphine and administered it immediately, then began a dispassionate, methodical audit of the obvious injuries, starting at the head as was taught to interns, reacting to major and minor concerns with equal mechanical torpor.

Mick watched unimpressed for several minutes before realizing that Lucius had not followed them into the room. He found him in the hall outside the door.

"We need to get him to a hospital now. There's very little that old man can do for him."

Knox did not look at him or respond.

"Lucius?"

"I was relying on those trucks. It's a setback now." He was somewhere else, but then returned. "And of course they dragged down so many poles and lines that communication to the outside isn't an option."

"This guy will fare no worse in a car than in that bed. That old quack of yours isn't cutting it. Let's drive the man out. Get some help."

"My physician is good. We have oxygen here. He'll stay here."

"Where no word can leak out? Come on Lucius! We have to do something!"

Lucius appeared simultaneously distracted and disturbed, and Mick knew he was witnessing the unraveling of the first few threads of the fabric. "He'll stay," Knox replied with a hint of irrational aggression. "Can I have some quiet, please." He stalked further up the hall to a wide west-facing window and peered out, his back to the hallway where the priest still stood.

Frustrated, Mick returned to the patient's room. The old doctor was still noting the litany of injuries, pursing his lips occasionally but otherwise monotonously going through the exercise. He wrote nothing down. He had straightened the patient's legs and arms, but Leake's head still sagged too far to the side on the pillow. Mick carefully propped it into a more natural position; the doctor said nothing.

The doctor left abruptly and Mick heard the door of the yellow car open below. In a minute he returned carrying a small bottle of compressed oxygen, strapping a mask to Leake's face and cracking the valve open a very small amount. Then he sat in a chair in the corner to wait.

The night wore on, punctuated only by the sound of Leake's labored breathing and Mick's own pounding pulse. The crushed man hung on, and Mick persevered alone, monitoring him, standing by the bed, listening for choking and interrupted breath. Leake's heart rate varied between weak and fast, but Mick knew the trend was downward.

The sound of soft snoring from the corner armchair told the priest he was the only one who held out any hope. On an impulse he picked up the receiver of the phone on the nightstand. The line was as dead as Lucius had predicted. He awakened the old doctor.

"I want to take him out of here. He's getting worse."

The doctor yawned. "Wouldn't be a good idea," he mumbled in presumed veto, turning away to go back to sleep.

Mick thought. "Look, I can maybe drive out and get some help then, but someone has to stay alert here. He gags a lot, and you have to keep repositioning his head to let him breathe."

Awake now and annoyed, the doctor turned back toward Mick. "Where d'you intend to go?" he challenged. "He ain't goin' to let this out. There's one road out to the highway and I'm sure our host has it blocked. Even if you could sneak past, nearest hospital is over two hours. Kalispell. That's five hours round trip, even if you get an ambulance to come back here. Then what? What gear they going to bring that we don't have? An iron lung? Get serious, Reverend. No, he'll stay here. You best focus on whatever rituals you do in such cases." The doctor turned away once more, hoping now that explanations were made to return to sleep.

"Can't you stay awake long enough to watch this man and let me try?!"

There was no answer from the doctor, save a shift of his weight to his other hip. Leake began to gag, and Mick had no choice but to turn back to him and try to keep his air passage open. He watched the injured man another hour, seething but unable to do more. Clearly the others had accepted that this man was going to die. And just as clearly it rested in Knox's hands.

He continued to keep ineffective vigil. A half hour later he awakened the doctor again. "Does this man have any family we should be contacting?"

By now resigned to be interrupted, the doctor replied in a civil tone. "His name is Leake. Jimmy Leake. I've treated him before, when I was practicing."

"You're no longer a doctor?"

"Retired, sir. It is the eternal paradox of the medical profession that we can maintain the health of everyone but ourselves. To the point about the patient: He spends most of his time drinking...and in gutters. I don't know of any family who'd claim him. Hell, they all saw him out there; if there was any family they'd have stopped him or talked him off that street. They'd certainly be at our door now."

"Then what about friends?"

"My guess is none."

"Your guess? How can you say that? I mean, what makes you assume so? He's connected to someone. Why would a lone drunk care enough to put himself at risk like that?"

"Who else would a bunch of trouble-makers pick to do it? They pumped him up and sent him out. He's a pawn—got no friends who care what happens to him."

Thinking about that, Mick looked back at Leake and said nothing.

*　*　*

Bleak dawn had already begun to break. Despondent, defeated, Mick wandered up the hall and found Lucius where he'd left him hours before. It was as though the man had been fixed to the same place the entire time, staring reflectively out the window, westward, into the receding darkness of night. He was standing quietly, a nearly untouched mixed drink sitting on the sill before him, his back to Mick as before. Mick stopped a few feet behind him.

"He died, Lucius."

Lucius did not respond, did not move.

"Did you hear me?"

"I didn't plan this of course," Knox replied just above a whisper, his back still turned. "I didn't make this happen."

"You didn't...? For God's sake, a man is dead! A direct result of your strong-arm bullshit! I mean...didn't plan it? How could the town not come to something like this? That huge truck stunt on their day...all your mercenary scum running wild...it's inevitable!"

A minute of waiting in doubtful silence made it clear he wasn't going to get an answer. Mick looked disgustedly around himself, taking in the enigmatic sullenness of the gaunt frame in front of him, the austere grounds spread out below them, the empty house with its secret staircase leading down to the mansion's bowels, to a secret map room with a meticulously accurate scale model of a mine and a crude tapestry behind a shovel and pick with dirt still clinging to them. He remembered Reuben Bitterroot's words laying rival claim to the uncertain prize. He remembered Gabriella's limbo, and the thin Indian man, who'd twice murmured of secrets buried.

Knox spoke aloud only after he knew Mick had left. "Anyway, it's only death. A necessary element of the greater cycle. And of course, we have all killed before."

CHAPTER TWENTY ONE

Up for nearly thirty two hours, Mick indulged a troubled sleep for sixteen. He awoke and rose around three thirty AM, well before pre-dawn light. He dressed in clothing suitable for physical labor, dispensed with shaving, grabbed Elmer's flashlight as he silently left the house, stuck a note on the church board cancelling the morning service, and eased the Landcruiser to the edge of town. He ran near idle until he was out of earshot of houses, then traveled northwest, choosing roads as he went, eventually selecting one that showed ample sign of heavy machinery having passed through over the months. As he'd hoped, it led toward the opposite side of the dry mountain range bordering the valley where he'd flown his glider.

Knowing he needed to get off the main approach, and trying smaller gravel roads at random, he struck out twice—once on a path that evaporated amid stunted sagebrush, another time angling too far eastward. Eventually he found a narrow dirt track that led up over two low rises, then down into a hollow between them. He knew the mounds were not formed by nature; he was among huge piles of tailings, and so getting closer. When he spotted the rusting, discarded blade of a bulldozer, he stopped. From here he would continue on foot.

It was still very dark, with no sound save the faintest breath of chilly catabatic wind in his ears, still rolling down-slope off the mountain. Deciding the truck was sufficiently hidden where it sat close against the tailings, he grabbed the flashlight and hooked it to the back of his belt without switching it on, then walked around the end of the near mound of tailings. The level ground disappeared a hundred yards further on, and he scrambled up and over the lowest tailing ridge, stopping with a cautious smile at the top, roughly sixty feet higher than the ridge's base. The famous hillside stretched before him, with a well developed main shaft entrance in sight a quarter mile ahead. He had found the Slide Mine.

He crouched for several minutes surveying what was visible, getting his bearings. Through deduced reckoning he'd evidently stumbled onto this spot from too far southeast, although just barely—anyway he'd managed to find it. Knox's crews would undoubtedly approach that shaft on the wide dirt road that now lay before him. That this was a main shaft—possibly the primary shaft at this point in time—was not in doubt. It was big, and shoring was high and elaborate—large equipment could get in and out. The entrance was lit by floodlights and barred by heavy wooden doors that probably slid on roller tracks.

A floodlit clearing in Mick's distant past flashed momentarily into his mind—people and a body in front of him, a noise behind. He put it forcibly out of his mind. There was work to do, for deserving people; this was not about him, or his ghosts.

On the right in his field of view, a bulldozer and two old backhoes sat against a pile of fresh tailings; it was unclear at this distance whether they were service-worthy or junk. A small beat-up house trailer sat another fifty yards beyond the tunnel entrance, no doubt used as an office for crew foremen. A very dim light glowed through the trailer window, and Mick knew there could be—probably was—at least one armed guard inside. Several makeshift long wood buildings sat behind the office trailer—work crew barracks, all quiet in the pre-dawn light. A wisp of steam rose from a ventilation duct of the smaller one.

There was no sign of a guard at the tunnel itself, and leaving the flashlight off, Mick eased closer, down the grade of loose rubble and slowly along the tailing ridge, to get a better look. Within forty yards he made out that the door was corrugated metal rather than wood, and secured with chains and a large padlock.

It was too quiet. Work crews would still be asleep, he knew, but as paranoid as Lucius Knox appeared to be about this mine, why no guard? He recalled one of the mansion guards repeating Daryl's command the night Leake had been crushed, that all Knox's men be summoned up-town.

He needed to take the risk. Entry through the locked shaft door was unlikely, and he began to sweep his eyes carefully around the surrounding grades.

Mines need water, Gabriella had said, but the native Appalachian knew they needed air too.

Beyond the tailing pile closest to the shaft door, the main slope of the hillside rambled left-to-right, relentlessly downward, at the angle of repose of loose shale. Whether Lucius had had time to establish forced-air ventilation yet was unclear, but the original miners seventy five years prior would have used natural convection. It was a vent Mick now sought, hoping the slide of the hillside had exposed some while it was obliterating others.

Where the slope curved due east, some older vegetation was evident, including a tree that had seen some years. The slide could have skipped this area, Mick thought. His eyes followed the grade higher, noting rough rock outcroppings that also indicated this terrain had been largely unburied. A small dark rectangle caught his attention.

It was not easy to scramble the roughly three hundred feet up the loose shale without dislodging small rock slides, but he stayed left, finding little areas of solid rock that further convinced him this portion of the hillside had been spared the brunt of the famous landslide. It took fifteen minutes to get even with his target, but he did it without attracting attention, then climbed an extra fifty feet higher, traversed across to a point uphill of the dark spot, and eased himself quietly down onto it from above.

It was another piece of rusted corrugated metal, similar to the door sealing the mouth of the main shaft below. Loose dirt had been piled in recent times over the metal, making the opening hard to see from below, probably even in bright sunlight; it was only because Mick had been higher than the road when he'd spotted it that he'd noticed it at all. Carefully he crouched and surveyed the road, shaft entrance, trailer and crew barracks below. No movement. He inspected the corrugated metal sheet and found that with a lot of force he could pry it out and up. He thought it was enough to squeeze under.

The sky was beginning to display a hint of pre-dawn luminescence. He took several deep breaths of the night air and disappeared into the hole.

He found firm footing and knew enough not to move more until he could see; as soon as the metal had dropped flush over him, he switched on the flashlight. As he'd hoped, the opening through which he'd crawled went deeper than the surface. An old air vent, most likely, by the vertical nature of the hole. And by the haphazard manner in which it had been sealed, it was probably not useful to the mine in its modern state. There were no doubt dozens of these old openings across the hillside, although how many went all the way to the surface anymore was questionable. He slid down a short forty-five degree slope, one hand still clutching the light, and found himself bottomed out in a small tunnel very poorly shored with old, pitted, rough-hewn logs. Swinging the arc of light systematically in a full circle, he mapped out the old excavated system in which he knelt. The passage tended downward ahead, up toward the surface behind and on his right. Given its proximity, he thought this vent should be able to intersect the main shaft whose opening he'd seen outside. He followed the passage downward, crawling and shuffling in a painful crouch at first, gratefully rising with a groan to a stooped position and then upright as the tunnel became tall and wide enough for a man to stand.

The hole momentarily morphed into a filthy alcove where a human being had once lived. Empty, rusted food tins, an array of shattered turn-of-the-century glass bottles, an old broken-handled shovel, a crushed carbide headlamp, and a wooden box littered the ground, entombed until Mick's narrow beam of light had bade them rise and dance. Still reposing on a dry level bit of dirt were the remains of a dilapidated bedroll and a broken piece of an old brass candle holder. This was where some laborer had slept and rested while digging and shoring the air vent, or possibly where a lone claim jumper had secretly dug for his fortune, out of sight of surface perils, secreted right there in the air system of the larger mine.

Mick continued down the long-abandoned shaft. A thin, dim point of light high above let him know another small hole pushed through to the surface, and that the sky was preparing for its master the sun. At one point he came upon a blockage where a cave-in sealed his further progress, but found an old piece of shoring plank sticking out of the dirt wall, wrestled it loose, and used it to scratch and scoop the collapsed dirt enough to squeeze through on hands and knees and continue on. Progress seemed ever northwesterly and generally ever downward, and at last the old air shaft fell through the corner of the ceiling of a main tunnel with much improved reinforcement and evidence of recent foot traffic. Noting a rock hand-hold that would let him climb back up if needed, Mick switched off the light, listened carefully, then let himself drop down into the larger shaft. He had reached the portion of the mine restored by Knox's crew.

He heard nothing, and flicked the light on in very short bursts in both directions. All seemed clear. Selecting first what appeared to be the slightly ascending route, he came to what he knew must be the entrance he'd seen from the outside. From within the tunnel he could make out at least two sets of padlocked chain link gates a dozen yards apart, inboard of the main opening. Roughly twenty five yards from where the first gate stopped him, he discerned the mouth of the shaft barred by corrugated metal, light from the exterior floodlights leaking in around its edges.

So far he'd seen no sign of people inside the mine this morning. A crudely wired light switch hung on a shoring timber on his side of the chain link barrier. Taking a chance, he tried it. Immediately a long string of very dim bulbs glowed along the wall at shoulder height, back down the tunnel from where he'd come. Intent on getting to the business at hand, he flicked off the flashlight and worked his way down the tunnel again, into the mountain, here and there inspecting the rock and dirt, smelling it, tasting it, noting the fragments embedded in the walls, ceiling, and floor. He pocketed some small crystalline fragments.

Up ahead the shaft bent right and increased the rate of its descent. Rounding the corner as he inspected fragments along the sides, Mick noticed a depression in one wall of the shaft. Thinking it may be another ventilation system and turning on the flashlight to verify, he saw it was instead a tiny tunnel that vectored horizontally off from the main. It could still be an air passage, he decided, and could possibly be an easier or at least a secondary way out. Always good to have multiple options, he knew.

Like where he'd entered, the little tunnel was shored with crumbling wood. He stuck his head and shoulders into the opening, sprayed light inside, and realized that it opened into a passage tall enough for a man to stand. It was blocked several feet inside his position; strangely, someone had gone to the trouble of stacking rocks and adding mortar, and the work had a sloppy but somewhat recent look. He eased himself closer and tried to pry parts of the wall loose, but without success. Hefting a loose rock the size of a cantaloupe from the floor, he bashed it against the blockage in several places until he found an area of mortar that made a dead sound.

He listened behind him; nothing. He repeated his attack of the mortared blockage and bashed out a small section about a foot off the floor. More rocks followed the first, and in half an hour he had made a hole large enough to let himself squeeze past on his belly.

Out of reach of the dim bulbs of the main shaft, he needed the flashlight again, and switched it on. He rose from prone to a crouching position and continued onward. As before, this tunnel increased gradually in height until he could stoop and then stand, and he slid between narrow walls walking upright. Here and there he swung the beam of light up and down the walls. On the floor he noticed many footprints in the dust. It was no colder than before, but he felt himself shudder. There was a bad feel to this place.

He knew before he saw it that the narrow passage would open into a larger chamber. Something about the way the air moved, and how the sound echoed. And there had been all those footprints, and the mortar. His flashlight beam led the way, tantalizing him with the room before he could get to it, filling him with a strange dread. The transition from narrow tunnel to oval-shaped chamber was sudden. He cast his eyes overhead first, noting that the place was dimly lit by an air shaft high above. The effect was almost cathedral-like. It was nearly mid-morning now and the sky was bright outside; the light would be enough to see by. Much better than focusing on only one bright point at a time, he decided, and switched off the flashlight to conserve the batteries. He stopped, listened, and allowed his eyes to grow accustomed to the chamber's low, even light.

He almost vomited. The human corpse was nailed to a cross-wise shoring timber at the far end of the chamber, in ritualistic crucifixion style. Where its sunken, desiccated eyes had once bulged in vulgar agony, now there was mostly a haunting void. Fighting back revulsion, the priest approached slowly, alternating his eyes between the horrific, imploring face of the body and the highly uneven chamber floor.

He saw the frail arms pinned to the timber with heavy iron nails, the open, distorted mouth, the dried skin still partly covering the cheekbones. He stopped approaching then, and took a deep breath, because he realized the body wore, under a ragged jacket, a priest's Roman collar.

The breed of malice that would allow a human being to subject another to this form of death is a difficult thing to fathom. There is mortality caused by carelessness, then murders perpetrated of convenience, pragmatically performed for selfish or practical reasons, and as base as they are a man can almost grasp such motives. What Mick saw here was something else again. He had descended into a place where evil had once held sway.

He took a half-step backward and nearly tripped on a new horror. Switching the flashlight on again and looking carefully, he became aware of another corpse between ankle-high piles of stones, propped with sharpened sticks in an awkward kneeling posture somewhat in front of the priest's crucified body. A rusted kerosene lantern lay nearby. The corpse on the ground, also a man, was more decomposed. Its hands were tied with wire in front, fingers intertwined as if in prayer. The skull had a small hole in the back, and no nose or jaw. The man had either been executed where he knelt, or, less likely, killed and propped there as part of some macabre ritual. Mick assumed the crucified priest— without doubt the former pastor—had been forced to witness this ground execution from where he hung, and had then been left to die on the timber. The crumbling skeletons had been here ever since, ravaged by exposure, subterranean scavengers, and a year's time.

He recovered his composure. Knowing that proof of identity would ultimately be important, he knelt alongside the firearm victim and carefully inspected the body. There was no wallet and no shoes. He then checked for rings or other jewelry, and again found nothing. Thinking for a moment, he located and recovered the metal buckle of the man's belt, parting it easily from the remains of the leather and pocketing it. Then he gently laid the body on its side, trying in vain to keep the bones from coming apart at the joints as he did so. He untied the wire from the hands and allowed the arms to rest alongside the body.

Rising, he began to attend to the remains of the priest. He was able to loosen one spike by striking it sideways repeatedly with a stone, to allow that arm to hang. The weight of the skeleton and tattered bits of clothing parted the wrist joint of the other arm, and Mick caught the priest's body in his arms as it fell. Gently he placed it beside the first man, then recovered the bones of the other hand from the spike still embedded in the shoring timber, and set them near.

He stood for a long, knotted moment staring at a bare dirt wall, trying to think of some other immediate task he could perform—anything to keep from thinking about the anguish his discovery would bring, and about the pain these two good men had known. Then in quiet resignation he nodded and lowered himself slowly to the ground, sitting on the dirt beside the victims, joining in their silence.

No one of substance deserves to die alone; no one should make the journey into the unknown companionless, or forgotten. How long he kept the two men company he did not know, did not count. He only knew he was the last companion with whom they would ever share moments on earth. He sat for a long time on the soil that would embrace their corporeal bodies forever, listening, honoring, feeling. The high cathedral ceiling they had glimpsed he now shared with them; the breath of the cavern they had felt on their flesh he now felt on his. Their silent peace he absorbed...and that they had tried to do what was right. Struggle for these men was now over, even though the task they'd set out to do was not yet complete. What must have been their final thoughts, of their dedication and of the safety and love of those they cherished, came into his mind, and heart. He was their last companion, and for a long, long time he very quietly kept them company.

It was afternoon when he finally rose, nodding one more time. The light through the high small opening, brighter before, had already started to soften. He looked about the chamber briefly, then made his way back the route he had come. He crawled through and regained the main shaft, listening for activity. The tunnel was momentarily clear but the distant, mechanized noise of an engine told him there was work being done far down the shaft. Continuing, he found the original air vent shaft through which he had entered the mine, and hoisted himself up and into it, making his way up to the spot where he had seen articles lying about.

He retrieved the broken shovel, dropped once more into the main shaft, and retraced his steps toward the chamber of the two men's death. At one point in the electrically illuminated portion he encountered two workmen walking in the direction of the tunnel's mouth, but they were arguing about the condition of a drill chuck, and took no notice of Mick as he knelt, keeping his bare head in the shadows, pretending to tie his shoe. After they had passed, he located the crawl-through, pushed the shovel in ahead of himself, and slid inside. He made his way to the chamber and quietly began to dig two shallow graves.

Later, filthy and exhausted, he climbed out from beneath the small rusted sheet of corrugated metal, in grateful relief drinking in the fresh mountain air. The late afternoon sun came across the slope now, leaving the mouth of the main shaft below in shadow. The door to the shaft was open and a handful of miners stood conversing there. Quietly, carefully, he picked his way down the scree slope, making the level and then the ridge of tailings without being detected. He retraced his steps of early morning, rounding the last mound of tailings in sight of his truck. Two men were leaning against its front fender, smoking.

On another day Mick's first reaction might have been to slow his stride. Now he went forward with abandon. The men, who he recognized as the two who had destroyed his glider, saw his fearless approach and came off the fender to intercept.

When he was within thirty feet of the driver's door, the larger man stepped in front of him. Without hesitation, without breaking his stride, and without bothering to look at the man's face, Mick hit him in the chest with a massive blow of his left fist. The big man crumpled soundlessly to the dirt. The other man hesitated, one hand reaching toward his belt. Mick gave him a single silent glare, and the hand froze in mid-reach. The priest turned to the truck, opened the door, got in, and left, squandering no further attention on either of them.

The fallen man did not get up.

*　　*　　*

It was full-on night before Mick coasted quietly into the gravel driveway at Gabriella's house. It had taken him some time to make the drive—twice he'd stopped and turned around, with intent to leave now, to distance himself from this town and especially from this small family. It wouldn't have mattered where he went; his own welfare had never been the point. If he stayed he'd only bring more anguish to heap upon what they'd already seen. He always had; he'd always been a conduit for evil, a lightning rod for the kinds of events that crush the lives of those who can take no more crushing. Why had he been so irresponsible as to stay this long?

But he'd pulled himself together and gotten this far; he'd pushed back the emotional storm his horrific find had stirred and told himself he'd still flee before it was too late. Now light streamed cheerfully out the little farm's kitchen window. He sat for a long time in his truck, knowing he had no right to delay this, but dreading it nonetheless. The inevitable question of whether the knowledge would accomplish anything positive allied itself with the convenient notion that she would be happier never knowing, and together they grappled anew with his duty to honor her right to know. For one more instant he was weak, and reached for the ignition key; but his shaking hand embarrassed him, and he steeled his nerves and opened the truck door. To hide his newfound knowledge would be to disrespect her capacity for strength.

A small family in Korea many years before flashed briefly into his mind, and he had to pound his fist into his forehead to blot them out.

Even the sound of boots on porch steps can foretell the weight of a moment. She heard his approach and let him in. He hadn't rehearsed, and never really recalled later what it was he had said; he remembered only standing in front of her, fumbling, and her eyes searching his fatigued, dirty face, then going vacant as she sat. He recalled digging clumsily into three pockets before finding the corroded belt buckle, offering it in the wan hope it might prove some other impossible conclusion, and he remembered that she didn't reach for it. In fact she barely looked at it, and Mick knew that in her heart she had known all along.

He set the artifact on the table near her, and knelt before her on the floor. She sat stoically; regally. In the loudness of her sudden strength he went silent. He thought to embrace her in consolation, but didn't know how, and finally managed only a brief, inept grasp of her shoulder with a firm masculine hand.

Angelo approached her then, mimicking the priest by stroking his mother's arm, his other hand reaching out to touch a finger upon the old buckle sitting on the table, and Mick softly ruffled the child's hair. Gabriella suddenly took the boy to her, clutching him tightly against her breast; it was the first and only reaction she had shown.

The privacy of the moment left Mick an outsider, and after several minutes he rose soundlessly and melted toward the door. Neither Gabriella nor Angelo moved from where they held each other in silence. Mick stepped out onto the porch and down the steps. Tears flowed freely and silently across his strong face and tightly clenched jaw.

CHAPTER TWENTY TWO

The priest's residence seemed as peaceful as always, despite some unusual commotion audible from uptown. Mick paused briefly on the front step to listen; the high-pitched sound of glass breaking and deep-voiced yelling on an adjacent block told him that others took recent events and the probable rumors of Leake's death no better than he'd feared. Further to the west and most likely on a side street, what sounded like a gunshot rang out—not exactly the productive council activity the elders had envisioned for the week. He gritted his teeth but knew he had more immediate, more pressing work, before he left town to avoid becoming caught up in—and drawn to— the brewing storm.

He burst into the residence. "Elmer!" he called out, before the door had stopped swinging.

No answer.

"Elmer!"

A noise of something clattering to the floor in the back room betrayed Elmer's presence. "I'm asleep, damn you!" the caretaker growled. Rubbing the back of his neck, he appeared in the short hallway, one leg of the old pajamas hanging empty. "What the hell...."

Mick cut him off: "Where are those old newspapers of yours from when the town was built? I need them now. I'm sorry, my friend, but I need your help. Get them for me now."

"The hell I will. My eyes was closed and I'm closin' 'em again. When I do that twiced it means goodbye." The old man turned, scratching his butt. "Them papers can sure as hell wait...."

"Father MacArthur never left, Elmer. He was murdered. I found his body."

Elmer stopped scratching and walking. He turned slowly to look at Mick. "Fou...?"

Mick held out his fist and opened it to reveal a small pile of stones he'd taken from the mine. Elmer blinked and stepped lethargically toward the priest, staring from the stones to Mick's face, at first not comprehending. Very slowly his old jaw dropped.

"I need those old papers, Elmer."

Together, far into the night, they pored over old documents. Mick was dead on his feet, and Elmer slid a chair around the end of the table for him. They studied articles describing early claims, hand-drawn maps, the few boom years, vague descriptions of the geology of the nearby ranges, and the eventual bust and population exodus experienced by the town.

Mick leaned back and rubbed his eyes. "I can't stop wondering why he needed those big trucks so early in his game," he said, interrupting the research. "I mean, I saw very little activity, real technical activity

I mean, when I was in there. It's clear they're still probing, still shoring. Probably still working on extending the few main shafts they have at present."

"That shit takes time. Damn crews have gone and come and gone again more times'n I can count."

"So why would there be such a need for trucks that can move hundreds of tons of earth? At this phase? Seems too early."

"Big diesels like that gotta be lined up a long time ahead."

"So...he accelerated the delivery."

"Upstage the tribes, and them councils."

"Maybe."

Elmer pulled out an old scrap of newspaper from the small heap. "Can't read this one anymore," he said. "All these old pages are fadin', gettin' too old."

"You don't seem to have anything from the last few years."

"Warn't no paper in this town. But I kin tell you what happened. Town nearly exploded when he first showed up. Tribe figgered since he was loaded he musta found somethin' worth somethin' in the old records. They started sayin' the whole damn hillside—or whole damn mountain, I ferget which—was sacred and always had been."

"How did they explain the mine being there already?"

"Claimed that bein' sacred was ignored from the start. Sayin' so didn't seem to slow Knox down much though, and so a bunch of 'em got pissed off and tried to get in there and take it."

"The riot Knox mentioned," Mick nodded.

"O'course he kicked their asses. That's when he brought all them bastards in here. To do that fer him."

"None of that ever got out? Like, to a state investigation or anything?"

"Hard to find people who knew what the hell happened. Bunch of 'em never come back. Their families was all scared to stir it up again fer fear of gettin' kilt theirself."

Mick began to understand the paranoia with which Knox's men protected the mine from prying eyes. "He's getting closer to bringing in bigger crews," he said. "He needs those big trucks to move or obliterate mass graves back in the tailings."

"I don't doubt it."

"So...just to get the whole picture here...coming out of all that turmoil, the riots and all, he had pretty much established his dominance."

"Warn't no doubt. He kept that peace-keepin' force around permanent. Warn't gonna be any new shit happenin,' not if he could help it. Except...then them boys messed with that idiot hothead."

"Wayne Aak. And he came out on top, and the notion of challenging Knox's authority got revived."

"Yep."

As Elmer saw it, Knox could not afford—could not accept—renewed opposition from the local tribal factions. Aak, the victim of a spontaneous moment of harassment at the hands of Knox's men, had been too tough or too lucky, and had beaten up his tormentors, one of them fatally. But it had happened without any planning; Knox's men would not have been able to prove to state investigators that Aak had been the one.

"Why didn't they just kill him and dump him with the others?" Mick asked.

"I can't tell you what a man like Knox thinks," Elmer replied, shaking his head. "My guess is he figgered he'd use the punk as an example—let the tribes see he could rig the law too, not just stack up bodies."

"So they framed him and got him sent up. All neatly packaged."

"Was supposed to be. Little Tissoma tribe boy found murdered, ton of evidence pointing to Aak, and they was just goin' to pin it on him."

Mick was silent.

"Trouble was," Elmer added, and his voice softened just a little, "things almost didn't go that smooth. That boy was stolen earlier. By white men. And somebody seen 'em do it."

"Who?"

"Me."

Mick listened as the old man recounted how the child had been wrestled from a back yard two days before his mutilated body was found. Elmer had never seen the abductors before or since, but they had been white, and that didn't fit well with the plan to convict Aak.

"Tried to step in," he added in a low voice. "A man's gotta, ain't no choice there." He slapped the stump of his leg.

"They injured you."

"Shot from behind. From the house. Damnedest thing."

"The kid's parent?"

"Made a mistake, I don't hold him no grudge fer it. Sheriff left me in a cell fer couple o' days. Soften me up, he said. Him I blame."

"And gangrene did the rest." Mick knew it was a tribute to the old man's toughness that he'd survived at all.

The caretaker looked away for a full minute, nostrils flaring, one eye glistening more than before. Mick let him take his time. When he looked back at the priest his mind had already returned to the less personal details of Aak's arrest.

"Anyways," he continued, "they was able to send him up. And they didn't stop there, neither. That Knox, he's a man who can see opportunity. While they was framin' Aak, they went ahead and put together some story about somebody else involved."

Mick's knitted brow posed his question for him.

"Mrs. Cielo's Carlo," Elmer clarified.

Ahh, the masterful stroke, Mick thought—the unlikely accomplice nevertheless damned by a volume of circumstantial evidence. Carlo Cielo—outsider, historical researcher, educated man—strangely linked to the murder.

"Carlo was useful to Knox," the priest guessed.

Elmer nodded, relating how Cielo's fate through the impending legal gauntlet was smoothed to the point that his involvement was doubted and charges against him were dropped. His benefactor through this synthetic process had of course been Knox himself.

"Carlo was a smart dumb-ass," the old man said, "if you catch my drift. He trusted that man. Grateful to him."

So Carlo Cielo had thus begun his association with Lucius Knox as indebted friend, then employee, and a year later as suspicious associate, estranged enemy, saboteur, and ultimate victim.

It was another bleak, promiseless dawn when Mick finally succumbed to a dire need for sleep. He made it as far as the living room floor and stretched out there for what he said would be but a moment, but sunk immediately into a deep, troubled slumber. Elmer let him rest; neither of them could have known that while they'd been studying the old documents, just after midnight the Inferno saloon was still alive with the movements of the wicked.

A larger number than usual of Knox's men were gathered inside the saloon, sitting at tables or leaning against the bar. As usual there was no music. The rotund prostitute, tied together with buckles and restraining straps poorly disguised with dirty lace, danced in a stiflingly entwined clench with Raam. They bumped now and then into the dilapidated billiards table, to the consternation of Ofstedder, who was drunk but still trying to win twenty dollars back from Joel.

"Get the fuck away from the table, fuck head! I told you twice now. Take that elephant with you."

"Fuck off."

Sheba stood against the bar, pressed between the sheriff and another chubby man. They pushed cheap shots of whiskey at her, then downed the poison themselves when she declined to do more than sip. At one point she excused herself and made for the toilet in back.

The teenage Washokki girl, dressed in the same dirty negligee as always, flashed drugged, dilated pupils and a sunken expression on Jaycoxx, who propped her up and offered her another hit from his tiny, spit-soaked reefer of weed.

Thad got up from a cracked, red vinyl sofa, downed the remaining swallow of his beer, and obtained a fresh can from the bar. He stepped to the center of the floor and cupped his hands like a catcher's mitt. "Send 'er here, Jaycoxx!"

Grinning at the prospect of some sporting fun, Jaycoxx returned the weed to his lips and spun the young girl to face Thad. He gave her a shove and she stumbled the ten feet until Thad's hands caught her by her breasts. He pulled her face to his and sucked roughly on her upper lip, then grinned, spun her again, and sent her staggering back to Jaycoxx, turning attention momentarily to his beer after she was launched.

Jaycoxx caught her by the crotch and the nape of her neck, bent her head backward, and ran his tongue from her collarbone to her ear, laughing at the same time. The girl giggled absently. "Back at ya!" he called to Thad, and spun her yet again. Both men could tell she was getting the hang of the game. Thad caught her, dumped beer into her open, gurgling mouth, bit her hard on the cheek, and kept the volley in motion.

A sound next to the swinging saloon door caused all three to glance up. Daryl leaned just inside the doorframe. He stood where a man would nearly have to brush him to leave. He was playing carelessly, absently, with a Colombian-made switchblade, pausing in his inspection of the steel to stare at and through the two men passing the young prostitute between them. There was no humor in his face.

Thad spilled a mouthful of beer. Jaycoxx, whom Thad had always boasted was not as smart as himself, chose to engage the big man directly. "Lighten up, Daryl!" Jaycoxx called, still grinning from his game. "Yew want a taste o' sweet red meat?"

Jaycoxx spun the girl several times, dizzying her, and then shoved her toward Daryl. Thad laughed nervously. The prostitute drifted toward her new target, colliding into him and leaning against his pelvis and chest. She turned her eyes slowly upward and gazed at Daryl with the same vacant expression of abandon she had turned on the two other men.

Daryl's face grew no less cruel. He fingered the knife and brought it up to touch its point on the soft flesh of her throat, drawing a fine, linear caress with the blade down to a point between her breasts. Then he put his open left hand over her face, raised his head to glare at Jaycoxx, and shoved her head violently away from him. Her neck snapped toward her spine and she flew backward and down, slamming her head on the dirty wood floor and skidding to a stop at the feet of Sheba, who had returned from the toilet.

The Inferno, quiet before, went deathly still. Jaycoxx and Thad each took an imperceptible step back. Only Sheba was seen to move; she stooped to help the young girl, who appeared dazed but conscious.

Daryl looked at no one. He licked the flat of his knife blade, turned, and exited the swinging saloon doors, the sound of his boots evaporating as he stepped off the boardwalk outside.

*　　*　　*

The hour before dawn is pale; anemic. Itself underdeveloped, it cares not for the welfare of high-born beings created in the image of deities. It is in this hour that cowardly deeds are performed—deeds contemplated, or savored, all night before they are committed.

Gabriella was awakened by the sound of boots scraping up her porch steps. She felt dimly aware that Zeke had been barking momentarily, but had stopped; still, she lay for a long time trying to decide whether she'd heard anything at all. It took nearly ten minutes before heavy knocking dispelled her doubt.

Quickly she sat up, reached for a long shirt, and pulled it on. She tossed back the blanket and stepped quietly into the kitchen, leaving the light off, keeping to the shadows away from the door. She peered into Angelo's room; he was still asleep. She half considered answering the door, but could think of very few visitors welcome at this hour—certainly no one who would have waited so long to knock. And Mick would surely have no more bad news so soon. The rough, militant Washokki men who had visited Carlo and Father MacArthur over a year before came to mind.

She realized in sudden alarm that she could hear someone breathing outside. Slipping into Angelo's bedroom, she peered out through a crack in the curtains, and froze in fear. Daryl Lievestro's primer red truck sat outside. Stifling a gasp, she ran through the scenarios in her mind, coming up with nothing good. One thing she understood—Carlo had made Angelo the legal owner of this land, and on the chance Knox knew that, the boy would be in danger and she couldn't let him out of her sight.

She backed away from the window quietly, making sure any shadow she had cast did not move side-to-side, as it would be easily spotted. Her only thought was that she might hope to trick the visitor into believing she wasn't home. Those hopes were dashed when the knocking commenced again, and Daryl's stone-cold voice pierced the darkness.

"Open up bitch, this shack ain't but made o' splinters anyway."

Fighting back tears, Gabriella roused the child and carried him quickly around the doorframe into her bedroom, holding her hand over his mouth for fear he'd cry. She set him on the floor.

"It's a game, bambino," she said, trying to act happy despite her inner terror. "Now, you hide under the bed...that's it, oh you're so good at it! ...and be very silent...don't come out, even if you hear a sound, until I say the game is over!"

The child, sleepy but trusting, crawled under the low springs and peeked out.

"No, sweetie, you have to go all the way to the wall if you want to win!"

His head disappeared and she whirled toward the closet to her right, digging frenetically for the little .22 rifle. She dragged it out as the fractured sound of splintering wood erupted in the kitchen. She tried to keep her head, scrambling on hands and knees for the small box of rifle shells she knew was in there, fingers shaking uncontrollably, her mind screaming in terror inside. In the next moment, the large, vulgar frame of Daryl loomed in the doorway of the little bedroom.

Gabriella abandoned the futile attempt to find the shells. She picked up the gun and rose, shaking, opening her mouth to defy him but unable to utter a sound.

Daryl chuckled at the tiny firearm. "I know yer all alone out here...in danger an' all...nobody around fer miles...figgered I oughta come on out an'...uh...lend a hand." He ended the sentence in a sneer.

Gabriella took a step backward, her legs stopping against the bed frame. He closed the small gap between them with a single stride. "Come on, half-breed," he muttered, "you know how this plays out."

He grabbed for her then, kicking the useless rifle from her grasp as he stepped, and with both hands she tried to go for his eyes, knowing it was her only chance, angling sideways in hopes of drawing him away from where Angelo hid. He clubbed her back toward the bed with his fist, and she collapsed heavily to the floor, the back of her head crashing against the edge of the metal bed frame. Daryl stooped and grabbed her under the arms, heaving her up onto the mattress. He tore off her underwear, loosened his own filthy jeans, and brutalized her without caring that she was dazed. Inches below the crime, the small boy remained silent, listening to the heavy grunting above him, watching the dirty boots sliding on the floorboards a short distance from his face, trying not to whimper, and hoping his mother would soon happily peek under to tell him he had won the game.

*　　*　　*

Mick awoke with a stiff back; it took him a moment to realize he was still on the living room floor. He'd only gotten a few hours' sleep, and it was late. He yawned and quickly lumbered into his room, pulled a rumpled cassock over his head, and rush over to the church to make apologies to anyone who hadn't given up on him yet, then started the obligatory morning Mass a half hour later than scheduled. He knew he was going through the motions; the dire events of the last few days were enough to distract anyone. All he could think of was the convoluted, sometimes naive, sometimes dubiously motivated interplay between the mine and those who had fought—and sometimes died—to own or destroy it. And the disruption promised by the impending arrival of Wayne Aak was a wildcard that boded no good. Most of all, he feared the growing inevitability of a personal involvement too unthinkable to face, and he prayed that it would not come to that.

As usual Elmer was in the house preparing a breakfast for Mick. He set out a plate and was breaking eggs into a skillet when there was a furtive knocking on the residence door. Grumbling, he set the skillet to the side, ambled out across the small living room, and opened the door. The prostitute Sheba stood nervously before him. She was still dressed in the trashy, provocative attire she had worn at the Inferno the night before, but had wrapped a faded blanket partly around herself, both because of the coolness of the overcast day and in an attempt to cover up.

"Is...Father in?"

Elmer inclined his head. "Church."

She looked over her shoulder in the direction Elmer had indicated, then cast a concerned glance in the other direction. Finally she got to why she had come.

"It's just that I overheard one of the guys...one of the men, you know...the outsiders."

"Sayin'?"

"They was...they was braggin' about...one of 'em abusin' some woman last night. It's all I know, I don't know nothin', and I just heard it this mornin'. But I just thought...someone should know." She gave another look in both directions over her shoulders. "Someone who would...you know...do somethin'."

Elmer knew her seeking out Mick meant that, despite this woman's nonexistent connection to the pastor, she still had more faith in the priest than in the law. And he knew something else Mick himself did not—that the sentiment ran deep in this town. It took an outsider to gain the respect of whites and tribals both. Even Knox had sensed it—he'd sought Mick out not only to size him up, but to "turn" him. It had been another of Knox's intended masterful strokes, for he'd known immediately that this newcomer was, other than the lowly hoodlum Wayne Aak, his only threat, and the only one who could coalesce the town.

Sheba glanced over toward the church, then turned back to Elmer, pulling the edge of the worn blanket higher on her shoulder and giving the old man a long, shameful look. "Tell...him...I...." She faltered then, stopping short of asking for appreciation or absolution. She turned quickly to leave, stepping off the porch and walking briskly out to the street, glancing back at the residence and church only once, with nervous eyes.

Elmer turned his mind to the message she had brought, and he feared his first and only guess. Grabbing a scrap of paper, he scribbled a note for Mick, left it on the kitchen table, then grabbed his old jacket and made for his car. He got in as quickly as the wood plank leg would allow and left hurriedly, heading on North Fork Road out of town.

*　　*　　*

The dull, dirty primer red truck sat idling. It had idled for hours, immobile, at the mouth of the lane. Daryl had been sitting behind the wheel, reclining, now and then smoking absently, playing with his knife. He didn't see why Knox had to have this shitty little farm. Just blast the damn stream bed, make the two half breeds disappear, and be done with it. He didn't see the value in the delicate little schemes in which his paymaster took such pride.

He'd done the squaw-Mexican, anyway; now maybe she'd leave and they could get on with it. It had been decent. Not the meat...the rush of power, of crushing someone just because he chose to. She'd been unconscious, which maybe ruined it a bit, but he had to believe her brain knew what was up. She did by now, most likely. He drew hot smoke from the cigarette into his lungs.

Broad daylight wasn't that far off, but he had no reason to care. He thought about how he could have killed her if he'd wanted to, but then she'd never have known he'd had his way—she'd be unaware he'd jammed his big filth into her. It's better when the rabbit knows it's being torn to pieces. It screams. The scream echoes.

He knew the snot-nosed little runt had probably been in the house somewhere, but he hadn't bothered to look. It could wait. Let her imagine that for awhile, and then when Knox let him come back for them he'd do the kid in front of her first.

He thought back to other kills. A mess of tribal punks a couple of years ago, now 'dozed over and rotting back in a maze of huge rubble piles west of the shaft entrances. When he was fifteen he'd killed a man on purpose—probably something Knox didn't even know. He'd grasped a co-worker's hand on a 200-foot ladder, a forty-year-old bald fuck who'd hired him to help repair a water tower—told the guy he had him, then let go to see whether a body would bounce or splatter from that high up. What else...some rival scum back in the Panama days....

He remembered back a year or more before, how the half breed bitch's husband and the other priest, the skinny little one, had thought they could sabotage the mine. They'd figured their dumb-ass little plans were secret, but he and Knox had anticipated every pathetic move. That stupid priest had looked for strong-arm help in the wrong places, and when they'd gotten past the main shaft's locks, they discovered all the explosives had been removed. They were driven down a tunnel plugged with a front-end loader and a dozen tons of dirt. Dead-end trap. Then Knox's goons had opened fire on them until the rebels had run themselves out of ammunition. Hell, at that point they were buried already.

It was still vivid in his memory—the low tunnel, he and Knox standing just around a tight bend beyond the mouth of the stretch where the doomed saboteurs were holed up. It had all played out underground, unknown to the outside world. Knox had insisted there be no bullet holes in the corpses, in case bodies were found years down the road. Daryl hadn't seen the point—a body is a body—but the boss had evidently wanted the option to claim no knowledge of how trespassers might mysteriously fall into mass graves. And it had been that way with the others who'd been killed and buried back in those tailings before.

He remembered how the tunnel had looked that night—the wandering beam of his belt-clipped flashlight as it swung randomly from his shoes to the dirt floor and back, Knox's aristocratic shirt collar sticking out from under a dusty miner's jacket, the boss's slender quivering fingers and stooped posture, his half smile, his hooked nose, his held breath...and how the others had been only too glad to take turns banging away at the trapped rats forty-odd yards down the dark hole, ducking behind a low embankment of their own. Target practice with orders not to hit anything more damaging than that weak-ass kerosene lantern.

He remembered the shuffle of his own boots and the echoes of the gunfire, and Knox's soft voice somehow commanding equal attention with the sounds of war. He remembered the instructions he was only too glad to hear: "Bring the two to me alive."

It had smelled good down there—gun smoke and kerosene fumes and mold. Fear.

But it was what came later that he lingered on most. He had gassed the pitiful pack of assholes, using coal smoke and a blower, until they were semi-conscious, and then had let the goons kill most of them with shovels. He'd dragged the bitch's Mexican, along with the weak little priest, into a cave further down, a place they'd used once before...and Knox had already been waiting there. The fuckin' place he called the grotto.

And there, they punished. They didn't ask any questions—no need. They simply punished, for sake of Knox's sense of proper order...and to kill.

And some day, just before he did the boy and the bitch, Daryl would tell her about it.

The two-way radio on the passenger's seat next to him crackled. Knox almost never slept.

"Where are you?" the thing hissed.

Daryl waited a moment before picking up the radio. He took another draw on the cigarette, exhaled fully, set the knife down, then keyed the mic without picking the transceiver off the seat. "Out at the half-Mex bitch's place," he muttered, "doin' what I please."

There was no reply from the other end; he didn't know whether his hand-held unit was out of transmit range or whether his employer, standing at the amped base station, had simply gotten the information he wanted. Didn't really matter, nor did he care that the Inferno bartender or anyone else with one of Knox's radios might have heard it. He put the radio out of his mind and returned to his prior thoughts.

The half-breed in that piece of shit house behind him could be waking up soon—that is if she was going to. Probably thought of herself as tough. Her husband had not really cracked, he recalled, and in the end he'd had to execute the wetback without hearing him beg enough for his life. That had been a disappointment. The skinny little priest had been a different matter, screaming every time a spike was pounded further through his toothpick arms. And crying like a woman when the Mex's head had been blown open. Probably pissed his pants before he died.

Daryl wondered what the new priest would be like, when his time came. Would he fall apart right away? Or after some hours of pain? No doubt they'd find out soon, especially now that the squaw had been done. He'd come looking for answers.

When it was time...maybe another biblical deal, or maybe just something that would hurt...start with limbs. There was something about the pious prick that needed to be put down.

At some point his thoughts were interrupted by the sound of an engine. Someone was coming on the road. Moving. Daryl didn't much care who saw him there, and let his truck continue to idle where it sat blocking the lane to the little farm. The car would just go on by...no, wait, it was slowing down. A Dodge...it was that old cripple who lived with the fuckin' priest.

Like a spider from the edge of the web he watched Elmer stop the car in front of his truck and stare past him toward the house for several minutes, then at him, then back at the house. Finally the old man pried his big frame slowly from his vehicle, went to the Dodge's trunk, and pulled something from within—a tire iron or something similar, Daryl assumed by the look of it. The big dinosaur lumbered toward the primer red truck slowly. Unbelievable...and too fuckin' good to be true.

*   *   *

Mick finished the morning service and quickly ushered out the few parishioners who had attended, then locked the door. He had far too much to

274

command his attention than to preside over rows of empty pews and banks of candles. He walked back to the porch of the priest's residence, but at the door changed his mind. He wasn't hungry and the cassock wouldn't impede his mission. Instead he turned and walked across town to the elementary school. The clouded sky began to rain as he went, and he hurried, wishing he'd thought to bring a jacket.

Hair dripping, he entered the main hall and again sought out the principal. She was not in her office; he found her in the first empty classroom he came to.

"Father...."

"Calahan," Mick finished for her.

"I understood you were planning an early return back east," she said, half in question.

"Yes, well...as soon as my work is done here."

"I'm glad it can wait."

"Anyway it's...it seems to be raining today, and I thought I'd read some books."

"Yes, the Lord sometimes sends us rain when we really need it."

Having admitted it was her library and not the school he'd come to visit, there was little sense in more delay. "I'm especially interested in the older books," he confided as they made the trip back to her office.

"Well they're all old," she said with a wink. She led him to the shelves.

"Any related to geology?"

"There are a few high school Earth Science texts there, but I'm not sure how much you'll get out of them." She scanned the wall of volumes. "Wait, I believe there's an older geology reference book up there...probably never been opened since we got it. And of course there's always the encyclopedia, but again it may be too general."

"Anything with a local slant?"

"Well we do have a small Montana History section—there. I say 'section' because I put those four books next to each other on the shelf."

They both chuckled.

"Anyway," she continued, "I don't know how old you mean, but those are far from new."

Mick thanked her and pulled a few volumes, and she left him to his research without further questions. He browsed the pages at a small table in the corner, occasionally taking notes on a scrap of paper he found in the trash can near her desk. He studied for several hours. At one point he quickly hiked up his cassock and pulled out of his jeans pocket an old newspaper clipping he'd borrowed from Elmer's collection, comparing it to something he'd discovered in one of the books.

It was mid-afternoon before he realized he'd gotten as much as he was going to out of the information available here. School had already let out. He thanked the principal and made the hike back to the priest's residence. Famished and realizing he'd not eaten since before his trip out to the mine, he made straight for the kitchen and began to toss together an uninspired sandwich. He slapped two pieces of bread onto the table and was reaching for the refrigerator door before he realized the piece of paper near which the slices had landed was a note from Elmer.

It took a moment to decipher Elmer's shaky hand, and another to digest his cryptic meaning. But it was enough. Mick ran to the door, leapt off the porch in a mad run to his truck, and sped out of town toward Gabriella's farm.

CHAPTER TWENTY THREE

He saw her car in the driveway, but not before he saw Elmer's parked on the road just out past the gate. Caution and former military experience—expert, they had called it—told Mick not to rush headlong into the house. And yet...it was broad daylight, and he didn't really know what the problem was; Elmer's note had been too vague, too abbreviated. "Gabrl may need help going now" was all it had said.

He stared a moment longer at Elmer's car; the old man was not in sight, so he pulled past it into the driveway, climbed out of the truck, and, watching and listening, slowly approached the house. The closer he got, the less he liked. The first thing he noticed was that he didn't see or hear Zeke, and a quick visual survey of the yard confirmed the reason. The faithful dog's body lay where someone had tossed it, partly visible in the tall grass near the fence. Another step and Mick noticed the screen door standing at an awkward angle, and the splintered doorframe behind it. Throwing aside all caution, he leapt to the porch and stormed into the kitchen.

Gabriella stood absently at the sink, wearing a long night shirt, her hands immersed in cold, empty dishwater. She was unresponsive, staring at nothing; she'd not even flinched when Mick had burst in.

Angelo stood behind her, holding onto her shirttail. He was crying. Mick picked up the child and carried him to a chair at the table. Returning to Gabriella, he took her gently by the shoulders and guided her away from the sink. She sat at his urging, and he knelt in front of her.

It wasn't hard to figure out what had happened, or to feel the vulgar, cruel horror of it, and he bit back hot tears when he saw. The left side of her face was badly bruised, where Mick knew she'd taken a heavy blow from a right-handed assailant. Her hair was matted in back in a small amount of dried blood. This immediately concerned him, and he started to inspect it, but she shook her averted head to tell him it wasn't as serious an injury as it appeared. Her night shirt was torn nearly in two; most buttons were missing. Mick reached slowly and touched the ragged edge of the fabric. It was more a question than anything, and she didn't flinch, pull away, or try to cover up. Harshly judging herself and at the same time begging him not to, she allowed her vacant gaze to rise slowly to his face, and in her eyes was the barest hint of pleading, and disgust, and shame.

He needed to know. "The cruel one...one they call...Daryl?" It was a name he knew shouldn't be uttered in her home.

She confirmed by not denying. In a voice not yet conceding to crack, she responded instead, "Now you know why I confess of hate."

There was another lapse into silence while she held a fiercely protective look on her son, and then in a wavering voice, clinging to a last finger-hold on dignity, she asked the priest, "Father, is it true that in sacrifice lies redemption?"

Without a word Mick enveloped her in his great protective hug, cradling her in secure, unconditional devotion. She cried openly at last then, releasing a cathartic deluge of fear, rage, and grief. They both let her tears flow and flow. The small child approached, and Mick opened the embrace and included him in the big circle of his arms.

To mother and son the priest brought some small comfort, some measure of peace...and promise. Unseen by them, his own face showed the tempest in his soul.

CHAPTER TWENTY FOUR

Sunset draped the valley in rose and pastel yellows. Soft, dreamy rays of light floated low and slowly, nurturing tiny songbirds and butterflies, and alighted angelically on all things. The entire valley was truly paradise incarnate.

Mick carried a small roll of clothing and blankets to Gabriella's car. "You'll feel safer staying with us at the Rectory," he'd told her off-hand. As he stepped off the porch, however, he scanned the roadside for signs of imminent danger. This thing was far from over, he knew; the serpent had tasted human flesh. And he couldn't shake the belief that he had helped draw this evil to this innocent family. Knox and his men, who had somehow singled him out as a threat to their supremacy, would have known that this crime would also strike at his own soul.

He also had another concern—Elmer's car was still empty and still on the side of the road out past the gate.

Gabriella emerged from the house carrying Angelo bundled in a few more old jackets. She kept her eyes on Mick and tried not to think about being out in the open. She would focus on protecting her child. Mick noticed that she carried the little .22 rifle under one arm.

She followed him to her car. "What about your truck?" she asked.

"It's a very cold ride at night. I'll come back for it later."

Mick got into the driver's seat of the Ford and started the engine; it turned over and came to life without issue. Gabriella put Angelo in the back seat and climbed in next to him. In the rear-view mirror Mick could see her glancing furtively back at the house and cradling the firearm across her knees.

Distrusting Knox's men, he opened the door and leaned his head out and down to check that all four tires still held air. They were in luck; her three, plus the old Landcruiser spare still on the left rear, were all okay. He backed the car, put it in drive, and pulled out the gate front-first. At the edge of the road, he paused to carefully scan the pavement in both directions. Seeing nothing, he eased onto the road, then stopped again.

"Elmer's car," he said, before realizing she'd already recognized it. "Have you seen him?"

Gabriella shook her head.

At a loss, he had no choice but to roll warily along the country road back toward town. They went slowly, and when the sun's illumination eventually failed they kept the lights off. No one passed them from either direction. Nearing the east end of the main street, they saw an unnatural glow down past the hotel. As they got closer they could see that the sheriff's office was burning; wildly moving human silhouettes revealed a group of people throwing objects. The noise of mob shouting carried to their ears.

Mick had expected something like this—an assortment of tribal militants, outraged over the Leake incident, counting the minutes until Aak's glorious return and leveraging their currently bloated numbers in town to raise some hell while they waited. Gabriella and Angelo needed no part of such destructive violence, nor could Mick personally afford to get too near the moth's flame. He steered his mind and the vehicle left down a smaller street, arriving at the church by a quiet route, and pulled around to the side in the shadows near the residence, hoping to keep Gabriella's car out of easy sight.

Angelo was asleep, and Mick carried him to the porch and up the steps. Gabriella followed, the jackets under her arm draped over the concealed small rifle. He could see she had good instincts.

They opened the door; on the slim hope that Elmer had experienced nothing worse than car trouble, Mick called out repeatedly to the caretaker and searched the rooms and behind the house, but found no one there. With increasing alarm Gabriella watched him move hurriedly about the house grabbing bits of food, extra blankets, keys, a dirty flashlight...and two small kitchen knives. He tossed the articles onto one of the blankets and wrapped it all into a bundle, shut off the lights and peered nervously out each window, then picked up the child again and led the way out, this time by the house's little-used back door. They stayed to the shadows and made for the church's side door. By the sound, the riot uptown had increased into a small-scale war; glass could be heard smashing, cars being overturned, guns discharging into the air. They opened the church door and slid inside. Once through, Mick locked them in.

He listened carefully for a full minute but heard no one inside the building, and leaving the lights off led them into the main chamber, where he dropped the armload of gear he was carrying onto the low step in front of the confessional, spread out one blanket, then lowered the sleeping child onto it gently. Gabriella set the jackets and rifle down nearby, but Mick picked up the firearm and handed it back to her. He said nothing, but she knew he was preparing for the possibility of a siege of the church...by which faction she could not guess.

She continued to watch him. She hadn't known exactly why he'd brought them here, to the church, or what he was expecting, until he'd put the gun back in her hand. Now, more agitated by the minute, he circled around all the doors and windows multiple times, checking locks, ducking to avoid the dim light of the candles casting his shadow on the glass. He listened for outside noise and verified the lock on the side and front doors a third time. It wasn't difficult to see where his mind was. Finally he came to a standstill, wringing his hands nervously, casting his eyes this way and that, trying to think of what to do next. He was a man of action, she knew, and he understood well the need to prepare for what might come, but was nevertheless unprepared for the task of sitting and waiting for what would be.

And she knew he was avoiding something he was trying to say.

She mounted the single small step. "I think this is where we first met," she murmured, touching the old wood of the small confessional booth, trying to open him up.

But he didn't hear. Pacing again ineffectively, muttering to himself, Mick shot glances at the windows and doors one more time. "This is not good," he said at last, breaking his silence. "I don't want to alarm you, but...I have to tell you things are coming apart, you can hear it out there coming to pieces, and...this is not good."

"You thought we'd be safe here."

"I thought you'd at least not be off alone, but..."

He looked around at the empty church and its shadows, then whirled suddenly to face her, his agitation spawning a hasty decision that had been a long time in the making.

"Thing is, I'm not sure I can protect you," he explained. "Yes, I think maybe you'd better take the child and leave town on your own. You can drive out, there's still time, you'll make it to Kalispell or wherever you think best before you know it, and I'll distract them here." His words were punctuated by a gunshot ringing out several blocks away.

"What are you talking about???" she demanded with a confused look. "I'm not going out there alone.

And I'm not leaving you here either. You're in as much danger as we are, and maybe more. You're right, it's coming unglued. And Knox fears you, his men hate you...and have you forgotten what they did to the former pastor?"

"No, now listen. I know what I'm doing. Just...."

"No. You're afraid for us and I'm grateful for that, but let's just...."

Mick grabbed her wrists and held them. "Mrs. Cielo, I need you to listen to me! It's the best way. I'll be fine, I'll be very careful! You have to take your son and go!"

She had never seen him in this state. "It's the tribe rioting, that's all," she said uncertainly. "Shop windows...."

"The others will take the opportunity to get rid of their obstacles and blame it on the riot," he said emphatically. "You know them! They'll guess who's hiding you all too easily. Believe me, he leaves no stone unturned; he'll know the child is key. For all we know they'll be coming for you any minute!" He tried to urge her off the low step where she stood, and toward the side door. "I'll carry the boy; it's still clear to the car."

She almost took the step, but froze decisively. "I told you I'm not going anywhere," she said, trying to pull her hands from his. "If they come, then I want you with me!" Tears welled up suddenly in her eyes; she shook them off defiantly. Her knuckles turned white where she clutched the rifle barrel in one fist.

Mick refused to let go; she pulled, and he held on, pinning her arms to her sides in a bear hug, holding her to him, pleading, while his own tears clouded his vision. "I'm no good for you, I can't even protect you, Gabriella, don't you realize that?"

Unknown to either of them, the child was awake, standing, watching them with round, silent eyes. With gifted timing he approached the priest from behind; tiny arms encircled Mick's knee and held the innocent embrace.

Of all solvents known, the most powerful is Trust. A moment of it applied and uncompromising resolve melts like candle wax. The big priest sagged against the confessional booth, sliding to a sitting position on the step in front of it. Gabriella, out of breath from struggling, eyes still wet with tears, sank with him. Slowly she sagged too, and leaned against his shoulder.

He knew it was fatigue speaking, but could no longer stop it. "I'm not the man you need here," he said softly, "not a man you can trust. I've let people down, all my life. And I've dealt my share of horrors. I'll let you down too if you don't get clear of me."

"Whoever sent you must have had faith in you."

"They don't know me," he admitted. "I'm no priest—not really. I just hid in the robes from what I know I am. Nobody knows the truth but me."

She listened to his tortured voice.

"I wonder if your boy will remember his father?" Mick asked softly. "I don't remember mine. He was a coal miner, like his Daddy before him and his before that. The family bounced around a lot. Rough life. But my Dad's Pa and Grandpa at least lived out their lives. They weren't cursed with a devil child like me."

His mind always saw it in slow motion and reverse order—a terrified seven-year-old boy surrounded by adults standing at the mouth of a mineshaft, black night, flashlights swinging until they grew dim. A wooden railroad water tank on its side, gushing water into the mouth of a small mine shaft. A useless rusted school bus coasting backward into the upright legs of a tall, stilted wooden water tank that stood by the tracks. His own child-sized hand rattling the gearshift lever of an old bus, where he played against his father's orders.

"I killed my father. I killed twenty two men...fathers, husbands, sons.... They died horrible crushing, drowning, suffocating deaths way below the surface...most of them alone, no one there to hear their last thoughts, see their last visions.

"He told me so many times not to play there...God, how it hurt! He never knew I was the one who'd killed him. Killed them all."

He tried to stop talking about it, but it had a mind of its own. "A mine needs water, you say. Well...." He told how water had shorted the ventilation wiring and washed out the shoring, and how most of the men were never found. There was little she could say.

"Nobody knew it was me. I crawled out of the bus and they thought the old gears had just given out on their own. They consoled me, told me and the other sons and daughters to be brave, at the funeral. But I knew. I knew who the devil had used to do his work."

Distant shouting from outside, now audible from where they sat, meant the violence was expanding. Another far-off gunshot echoed off the altar wall.

"Did you have other family?"

"My mother lasted another nine years, and finally succeeded in overdosing herself into a hole of her own. I was where I belonged—in hell—alone— nowhere to go. I fell in with some other sociopaths. And evil followed me. I got to know it."

The candles flickered against the far ceiling.

"It always follows me," he said in summary, "or draws me to it. It drew me here. You're better off getting clear of me."

Yet another gunshot, this time farther off to the north...and the muffled sound of a small or distant explosion. Mick tried to rise, but she didn't move. She knew him by now—knew this man could have overcome what sorrows he had told her up to now. A child could blame himself, but a man would know the difference between calamity and guilt. She knew in her heart there was yet a darker secret.

"Where did you go?" she pressed.

"Hell is where you bring it."

"Then...why did you stay there?"

The violence outside raged for a long time, and yet he did not answer. Her silence was as loud as any repeat of the question could be, and so he knew he had no choice.

"I had no future, nowhere to hide from myself. I was drafted, went to war, which changed nothing. Murder and decay moved as I moved, followed me—I was the hand of evil, the finger of death. Trained a long time in the deadly arts...they said I had a gift. I don't remember much else...I recall screams...but when I didn't see their eyes, that was a blessing."

She waited. And before he began another word, a river of tears began to fall. They both knew there was something coming that he had to confess.

"See, there was ...one...." He paused and composed himself. "One...time. My unit had been overrun, gotten separated, and I was taken alive. They put me in this...shack. It was the countryside, small post, probably were going to hand me over to the main army when it came through.

"There was a...family...of farmers, small family, lived right there. Soldiers of that post used to take food from them. The man and woman...they were given the job of sticking water in for me now and then, sometimes a bit of grain, and cleaning up my mess.

"One night, the farmer left the door open to the shack...you know only a farmer knows for sure if it's going to be really dark out. And I got out. I realized they were helping me. They led me around this stone wall, but...a bright light came on, a North Korean soldier was there, and he saw me...saw them with me.

"He laughed. He didn't take me seriously. I looked weak, looked like a bag of bones. And before he could pull his firearm I'd gotten some...length of something, piece of pipe, in my hand, and I'd killed him. I had to, if not for me, then for those farmers, who he had seen helping me. I destroyed him, so easily."

"That is not your fault," Gabriella reminded him softly. "He was a soldier. It was war."

But Mick hadn't finished, and now nearly gagged on what he was about to say. "The...farmers were...staring at the man's face, I remember. You see, they didn't see the danger, see it coming, any more

292

than I did! I reached across his body...I had seen the butt of his revolver, and was going to get it. I was actually going to give it to the farmers! And I...I heard another soldier's boot step behind me! By the wall...so close, and I didn't have time...I thought all three of us would be killed in the next second...and I grabbed the handgun and shot, turned and shot, so straight, and...killed."

"You don't have to feel...."

"It was their little boy. He'd wandered out of their hut looking for them. I killed their child, their little...headless...child."

Even the telling of it put her in shock. Gabriella went instantly numb. Torn between imagining tiny Angelo in that floodlit clearing and realizing what this priest had lived with in the decades that had followed, how he'd hidden himself away from the world, and how by doing so he'd saved the world from the evil thing he thought himself to be, she lost herself momentarily in the bouquet of horrors. Mick's voice, cracked but trying to recompose itself, brought her back.

"I never even looked them in the eye. I went straight back to the other enemy soldiers. I guess I wanted to die, I went in with such recklessness. I became this two-dimensional machine of revenge, making them all pay for what they'd made me do. Hoping to pay myself. But I killed them all. I don't ever want to remember what I did to them...and I don't ever want to forget the other, or be forgiven. It replays in my head every day, every night." He took a quivering breath. "They decorated me later...said 'that's war'...but I never told anyone the real story, the shame I carry, until now...until you."

She steadied her own voice. "You were not the man you have become. You were still a child," she said at last.

"I'm the conduit of hell. Nobody who relies on me makes it. I can do these horrible things, but I can't recall my own parents' faces...can't keep devastation from happening...can't stop myself from sliding back into what I am."

"And so you...disappeared."

"I thought I could bury my rotten soul in a seminary. I never told them. They saw my unfortunate childhood...my medals...and took my silent ways for holiness, and I was so keen to be one of them...I studied...mostly specialized in restoring the old cathedral, staying away from people with real lives. And keeping clear of temptation, of my own nature, was my only hope of any small piece of redemption. I've fooled them and I've locked myself up, but I don't want you fooled, because if you rely on me I'll fail you. Please. Please Gabriella, don't look to me to save you."

The mother of a small child considered for a long time. Then she laid her head against his chest, stretching her arms out to Angelo and hugging the boy to her breast. "Yes," she said softly, "I think you were not born a holy man. I think you are a warrior."

All but defeated by his private ghosts, Mick looked ashamedly and yet gratefully at the boy's cherubic face, then at Gabriella. She returned his gaze with eyes of fire, eyes that radiated no blame, no judgment, only defiant loyalty. He knew then, but still had to ask.

"So...I take it you're not going to get clear of me."

"You're part of us now, and we of you."

"You know I will fall again, back into hell."

"Into their lair. Only you know the way. Pursue them there, and triumph."

The priest nodded, set his jaw, took a deep, decisive breath, and rose. "Stay in the shadows on the floor then, away from the windows." He looked about the little church. "We're claiming Sanctuary. Maybe it will be enough."

He put the rifle once more into her hands and strode without a backward glance to the side door. He stooped to pick up a dark grey cloth bag from the floor by the door frame, then unlocked and opened the door. He slipped out, re-locking it behind him. Gabriella let him go; she took the child to the poorest lit area of the church's main chamber, near the center benches. They sat down in the shadow on the floor and covered themselves with dark blankets. She held the boy until he went to sleep.

Mick walked quickly and quietly to Gabriella's car, still hidden in the shadows where he'd parked it earlier. From there he stepped around behind it and slid quietly to the residence. The back door had latched shut when he'd closed it earlier, and he reached into the grey cloth bag, pulled out his hammer from the small collection of tools inside, and pried the door open with the claw. Once inside, leaving the lights off, he whispered Elmer's name several more times in another feeble hope of finding him home. Failing as he knew he would, he went to his bedroom and picked up the phone, hoping to hear a dial tone. The line was dead; the wires were evidently still down. As much as had happened since the night Leake died, it had only been a couple of days.

He got rid of the grey cloth bag and left the residence the way he had come. Going back to the church building and keeping to the side opposite the street lights, he made it unseen to the sidewalk, then set out with purpose on foot, heading west and north.

CHAPTER TWENTY FIVE

Keeping to the darkness wherever he could, Mick retraced the path over which the deaf Washokki boy had led him to the elders' meeting the day before the two Unit Rig diesels had come through. He arrived at the small backyard and waited, watching, staying out of sight beneath a tree behind the fence. A burly Washokki man loitered outside the back door of the house.

An old man, the same man who had lectured him during his last visit, came to the screen door and spoke with the guard. Suddenly there was a gnarled, bony finger pointing in Mick's direction. The burly man turned and looked directly at him. He'd been spotted.

Embarrassed, he stepped into the open, easily vaulted the low back fence, and walked up to the guard, who without ceremony opened the door and let him into the house. At least he knew the elder resident considered him welcome.

Mick found the old man in the kitchen, filling a glass with water. He could hear no one else in the house. He stood in the doorway to the room and waited, giving the master of the house first right of speech. The elder turned to face him, addressing him quietly and curiously, with no hint of malice or alarm.

"Why are you standing outside my house on a dangerous night?"

"I need your help."

"Yes, I think so." The old man paused to consider the priest's face, and to take a drink of his water.

Mick didn't have very much time, and so got right to the point. "When I was here before, I saw a boy with a radio transmitter."

"My grandson. He's very smart, and knows the modern technology. We use the radio to coordinate with our chapters who are far from the town."

"Will it reach Missoula?"

"It will reach people who can call Missoula on the phone."

They stepped into the small room where the radio transceiver sat. The old man did not ask questions. The transceiver was powered off, but on a word from the elder to the back door guard, the burly man disappeared across back yards and a minute later reappeared with the grandson. The boy threw a handful of switches and brought the control panels of several pieces of equipment to life.

"It should be someone you can trust," Mick said. "And someone who will understand me."

They selected the common frequency and quickly identified a radio operator on the other end whom the elder knew, then changed to a frequency they referred to only by private code. The operator on the other end agreed to make the Missoula call. Mick took hold of the microphone; he spoke earnestly as two faint gunshots from the center of town added their percussive noise to the staccato crackle and hiss of the radio.

"Yes, that's the number," the priest said loudly, "and ask for Vernon Greene!"

The reception was poor but he could make out the reply. The boy running the transceiver motioned for him to avoid shouting, and he dropped it a half notch.

"If he's asleep," he continued, "tell them they need to wake him! Tell them to inform him Father Mick Calahan says it's happening and he'd better get some help up here...."

He released the mic key; there was another marginally decipherable response.

"Yes, I spoke with him a few days ago."

The other end suggested a morning call.

"What? But that's not soon enough! It has to be now! And thank you very much."

This time the reply was garbled, but Mick pressed on; he was running out of time.

"One more thing: Please mention the gunshots, and that we fear people have been hit. I really appreciate it."

There was nothing more to be said. Mick dropped the mic roughly back on the table, and nodded to the old man and boy.

"Keep as much of your community safe and uninvolved as you can tonight," he cautioned them. "I will do what I can to stop this."

The old man caught him by the arm and looked for a moment into his eyes. "Take care of yourself, young man. Keep watch with your heart. There are demons loose."

Mick returned his piercing gaze. "I'm afraid I'm one of them," he replied.

He left the house by the front door, moving briskly toward the shouting and gunfire.

*   *   *

The riot had erupted within twelve hours of news of Leake's death getting out; it started with petty vandalism of street lights and traffic signs—the simple edifices of authority—and when repercussions did not materialize the affronts escalated and the participant numbers grew. The tribal population of the town was more than double normal levels due to the influx that had occurred for the Unification councils, and the crushing incident provided more than enough spark to ignite the keg of human powder. By the time Mick and Gabriella had arrived at the church, serious property damage had already begun.

Now the larger body of the mob continued to move up the main street, smashing shop windows and leaping through the shard-lined holes to loot where and what they could. They were mostly young Washokki and Tissoma men and boys, although the frenzy had spread to other elements of the tribal community as well. In parallel with the outrage over the death of one of their own grew the grass-roots rumor that Wayne Aak had returned from the state prison at Deer Lodge to Terradise Valley that day; his stature as a figure of defiance gave rise to high expectations for retribution. The mob had only to rail until it built its courage up sufficiently to overcome Knox and his armed mercenaries, and then they would inevitably surge on and take over the mine.

It was the time spent looting, mainly, that had slowed their progress up to now, but looting had also done something to fuel their zeal. Some buildings burned in the riot's wake. Smaller groups stampeded up side streets, but fewer, as there were fewer Caucasian-owned vehicles and businesses to target there. Guns, up to now mainly used as noise-makers and tools of vandalism, added to the mayhem, and everywhere the cry, "Wayne Aak is coming!" could be heard above the smashing and discharge of the firearms.

The main mob had built to sufficient size, confidence, and audacity that its members now crashed their way into the Inferno saloon, packing the dim space within, grabbing bottles and throwing chairs back out into the street, looking for Knox's men. Finding only the bartender inside, they beat him and turned to looting and destroying the few worthless items they came across. In a matter of a dozen minutes they had gutted the saloon completely. Using a bottle of grain alcohol, someone set the room afire even before most of the mob was out, and the blaze took hold quickly, belching hot tongues of flame out both shattered windows and sending rioters diving for their lives. The lethal suddenness with which the new blaze erupted and the peril it unleashed upon the crowd made them drunk with reckless frenzy, and they discharged shotguns into adjoining buildings and screamed, chanting Aak's name and arrival with new vigor.

"Aak is back! Aak is baaaaaaack!"

Here and there, white shop owners and their families living above their businesses streamed sparsely down outdoor staircases and across the backs of buildings, concealing their heads with jackets, desperate to evade both the fire and the mob. From homes near the business district, residents of both races peered terrified through thin cracks in drawn curtains, praying for divine intervention or blind luck.

One white man, believing his livelihood destroyed, leapt boldly out onto the wooden boardwalk in front of the smashed window of his shop. He held nothing but a rock in his hand, and hurled it back into the crowd, cursing in rage. It was more stupid than brave, but he was lucky; either no tribal militant nearby had a gun or none of them was quite prepared to shoot at a man. The rioters closest to him pelted him with stones and threats. He covered his head until the volley subsided, picked up another large stone through his smashed store window, and cocked his arm to throw, when his wife, motivated by an instinct to protect and a rage of her own, stepped out behind him brandishing a shotgun. The nearest portion of the crowd scattered and kept its distance, taunting her but soon choosing other targets further up the street.

On the edge of the boardwalk diagonally across from them, another white man stood leveling a rifle, trying to protect his shop, which was broken open but not yet looted. Up to now he had restrained himself from firing. Stand-offs began to form here and there, where the besieged had chosen to take stands. The hotel staff beat out flames with rugs and brooms in the historic old establishment's lobby. The gasoline pump at Hawkins' garage was burning. The mob continued to throw torches and let off gunshots into windows, cars, and the air, moving like a swirling, streaking organism, shrieking of Wayne Aak's sudden presence in their midst and feeding on the light from the fires they'd set.

Raam, Ofstedder and Thad had been in the Inferno saloon when the crowd first broke in. Keeping hold of their revolvers, they crawled on hands and knees back the dark narrow hallway into the filthy toilet room, then one by one stood on the bowl to reach and slide out the small high window there, into the back alley.

Ofstedder, last to attempt the window, almost did not squeeze through the opening. A large sheathed knife on his belt had hung up on the metal casement. "Hey. Hey! Pull my arms!" he whispered hoarsely.

The other two, unconcerned over his fate, were already on the ground and nearly to the rear corner of the building. They heard the hammer cock on Ofstedder's revolver and froze.

"Get yer fairy asses back here and pull me through," he growled. "Mebbe I'll hit you and mebbe I won't, but them fuckin' redskins will sure as hell hear the shot."

Raam and Thad came back and pulled him out, cursing his fat and ineptness. Then the three crouched behind a row of garbage cans, gauging the size of the mob and their best chance of getting clear.

"Fuckin' war goin' on," Thad said, trying through obscenity to sound manly and nonchalant.

"Gotta split up," Ofstedder muttered, realizing how visible three white men would be on any street in the town.

"Make up yer fuckin' mind," muttered Raam, referring to the small toilet room window.

"Maybe I'll make up yers," Ofstedder returned menacingly, and turned his gun momentarily toward Raam's head.

"Fuck you," Raam shot back at him, knowing a gunshot would be the last thing Ofstedder would risk right now.

"Whyn't we set up behind that fence, there?" suggested Thad. "Nobody's hangin' out on the quiet side of old fences tonight, an' we kin keep an eye on what's happenin.' Fer the boss. We're on duty, and he wants us to stay up here and handle it. Ain't gonna like it if his kingdom is in revolt and we're all like 'whereabouts unknown.'" He liked the sound of that phrase; his lobe-less ears tingled. And besides strutting his intelligence, he felt he was exercising leadership.

"If you make it I'll follow," Raam replied, unimpressed but with nothing better to offer.

Ofstedder said nothing, but motioned with the barrel of his handgun for Thad to lead the way. Although he didn't point it out, he preferred instead the looks of a partly-fallen-down lean-to shed, the near side of the fence Thad had spotted. The lean-to had a better vantage point on the main street anyway. And Ofstedder wanted little to do with these other two; they were fuck-ups as he saw it, and alone there'd also be no one to tell Knox Ofstedder had done nothing but save his skin until he could get clear. He would let the other two crawl wherever they wanted, and then never show up.

Thad nodded heroically, stuck his gun back into his belt, and began again on all fours. Twice he stopped and flattened out in the dirt, waiting on some sound or other to prove meaningless, but once he got to the near end of the fence, he was well concealed from the main street by wood planks and the slanted shadows they threw. Excited by his success, he motioned enthusiastically; Raam, muttering to himself, bumbled toward the same spot, through laziness or stupidity not getting nearly low enough to be very safe. He made it anyway, and melted into the darkness there with Thad.

Ofstedder waited a minute, then made his own move. More exposed than the other two but not having as far to go, the big man angled deeper across the back alley. He ducked into the only entrance the shed offered, and immediately put his eye and the muzzle of his revolver to cracks in the dry-rotted pine plank shed wall.

From where he stood, he could remain undetected and still see rioters clearly, some at very close range. Forgetting the tension he had felt when exposed, he recognized the opportunity for cruelty and instinctively began to scan the crowd for a likely victim. The cry, "Where's Wayne? Wayne's here!" came to his ears amid the regular firearm noise, and he grinned, aimed, and fired. A scream from the crowd confirmed that someone had been hit.

Some elements of the mob recoiled momentarily at this new threat, but most were unaware. It was difficult to determine where the shot had come from. A shop owner? An upstairs window somewhere? Accidental friendly fire from within the mob? Some tribal men with prior military backgrounds began to scan windows and corners of buildings. Whites defending their shops, up to now treated to something less than lethal force because they had also stopped short of human carnage, were now beginning to be regarded with more suspicion, more hostility. Rage escalated as gunfire increased with wild abandon into shadows and the air, and Ofstedder, pleased that no one suspected his shed, sought another opportunity.

Raam and Thad heard Ofstedder's shot; Thad snorted excitedly. "Oooo, that one musta hurt!" he snickered across to Raam.

Raam's participation wasn't far behind. He recognized the opportunity afforded by the heightened noise in the wake of Ofstedder's blast. "Watch me shoot somebody's nuts off," he bragged, and fired. "Damn, missed!" Muttering curses, he ducked back to a secondary crack in the fence and peered again.

"Well, I seen squaws out there," Thad retorted. "I'm goin' fer a tit!" He fired two shots before ducking back, chuckling to Raam as more screams rang out in the crowd.

A spray of twelve-gauge shot peppered the fence, and they cringed; but it was only a random blast into shadows from far up the street. No one had yet detected their whereabouts. They snickered with glee and looked again for another opportunity. Thad, imagining the glory of being the one to drop Aak himself, concentrated his attention on the denser pockets of rioters and the heads of columns. The hero of tribal hoodlums was out there, and he'd be the first to find him. Raam looked more for easy targets— loners who, if hit, would not be able to identify what they'd seen or heard.

Ofstedder could see the other two were aware he was firing, and had begun to realize there was too much mob noise for him to be heard easily from the center of the street. And if any of them were found out, Thad and Raam would likely be detected by the mob first. Encouraged by that thought, he picked out another target and fired again, then put his eye to the crack to see if he'd hit anything.

He too was aware of the possibility of meeting the returned prison hero face-to-face. More than a year before he'd been the one to arrest Aak for the trumped-up murder charge, and had had the pleasure of clubbing the injun into unconsciousness with his bare fist back then. If not for Knox's order to leave no visible injuries he could have done more. Now he'd be free to do as he pleased. And it would be sweeter knowing Aak would recognize him, remember him, and hate him.

A softly disturbing noise from behind made Ofstedder's pulse miss a beat. He turned slowly to confront what he sensed was a stealthy intruder; and he knew it was not one of Knox's men. Slight movement in the back of the shed belied a shadowy figure, unrecognizable in the dark but of somehow familiar stature, creeping up on him slowly.

Anyone not blinded by a lust to kill would have presumed it couldn't be Aak, but Ofstedder's mind was on a singular track. "Been lookin' fer you, convict," he hissed.

The sneaky bastard hadn't barged in brandishing some firearm, and was hanging back even now...so Ofstedder put that worry aside. He glanced at his own handgun and leered again. This would be sweeter than he'd imagined. He holstered the piece and pulled the large knife from its sheath. "Gut you like a fat red pig," he said, and took a half step toward the shadow, angling to cut off escape, knowing a knife of the size he held would make his victim want to get clear.

But his sneer changed as the feet of his intended victim took a step toward him rather than away. It wasn't until the stocky intruder came into a thin sliver of light that Ofstedder realized it was Mick, not Aak.

"What the fuck are you doin' here?!" he demanded.

"Cast out a demon," Mick responded in his own mind, without bothering to give an audible answer. He brought his right hand forward and up to shoulder level, and in it was the big claw hammer. Without wasting further time he did what he knew, getting to the necessary business at hand. In a panic Ofstedder transferred the knife to his left hand and with his right groped to re-draw his handgun, but the priest was faster. He pinned Ofstedder's arm to the holster with one hand and with the other brought the hammer down and through the forearm, head, and face. He delivered the blow with practical, machine-like purpose, and Knox's man fell with one loud whimper. It was done in a single stroke.

As more rioters went down with gunshot injuries, the mob began to realize they were under counter-attack, although from where no one was certain. From the hardware store they produced kerosene lanterns, jars and liquid fuels, and set about fire-bombing any cars, boardwalks and buildings they'd not destroyed up to now. Shop owners defending their stores were now suspected and in some cases being fired upon; they had to take cover and abandon their daring attempts at defense. Mob gunfire into darkened alleys and doorways increased as the tribal militants sought to flush out their assailants.

Two burly men felled a wooden utility pole near the destroyed sheriff's office with a chain saw. The pole and the wires it still supported toppled across the street. "Wayne Aaaaaaaak!" they yelled, and the mob took up the cry anew. They moved up the street to select another pole, this time with a transformer, up ahead of where the Unit Rig trucks had wrought their damage. The lethal gunfire had breathed new life into the contagion of destruction.

Jaycoxx appeared out of nowhere behind the fence. He had a two-way radio in his hand. "Where's Ofstedder?" he whispered hoarsely to Raam.

"Shut up! Over there in the fuckin' shed!" Raam hissed; he continued to peer anxiously out the crack in the fence, now more fearful of discovery as the mob intensified its search for assailants. The number of rioters had increased and his avenues of escape had suddenly dwindled. He dared not leave by the back alley or he'd have done so by now.

Thad leaned over to Jaycoxx. "Give me that thing," he said, snatching the radio from Jaycoxx's hand and pocketing it. "Who's on the other end?"

"The house."

"Get up here and keep an eye out, asshole," Thad commanded him, again relying on obscenity to appear manly and in control. Thad would let Jaycoxx babysit Raam, and would use this opportunity to fall back to Ofstedder's position while he could. He knew one man had a better chance than two or three, and he considered it intelligence rather than any kind of leadership failure to sacrifice others to save himself.

He dropped to his belly and slid feet-first across the alley to the shed, keeping his eyes glued to the main street and his revolver in his right hand. Once he thought he saw a shadow to his left, but it was gone before he could make anything out. He got to the shed, slid inside, and stood up, brushing the filth from his belly and chest.

It took half a minute before his fire-reddened eyes got used to the low light inside—before he saw Ofstedder's fleshy body lying in a pathetic heap, limbs splayed out in comical positions, revolver still in its holster, wide forehead reduced to mush. He vomited on himself before he could turn away.

He wiped his mouth on his sleeve, pulled the two-way radio from his pocket, and keyed it, calling out in a hoarse whisper to the man he knew was listening.

"Daryl! Daryl! They got Ofstedder!"

A voice on the other end took its time to answer. There was a moment of indecipherable crackling before words could be made out, and Thad turned the volume down in a panic before venturing a reply.

"The damn...Wayne Aak and the rest, who the fuck do you think?!" he hissed. "Get some people out here!"

More crackling; and he now had orders to go back for Raam. He swore without keying the mic.

Thad stole another morbid look at Ofstedder and shuddered, simultaneously horrified and fascinated by the gore. The sound of wild rioters suddenly close by outside made him step over the body and put his eye to the wood. The danger passed and he crawled out the shed and again slid to the fence to seek Raam and Jaycoxx.

As he neared the back of the fence, Thad stopped to listen. Rioters could be heard on the other side of the wood, close. He could make out only random gunfire coming from the street side—nothing from Raam's side. He turned the radio volume down lower and crawled to where Raam would be. Something was in the way of his movement, and he started to push it aside. It was Raam's head, joined to the body by only floppy neck and brain stem flesh.

Thad vomited again and wriggled quickly through his own spew to the fence. He could now see more of Raam's body, and the ragged rend where something blunt had torn right through the throat with tremendous force, parting the spine as it went. Fresh blood still pumped softly from one artery onto the ground. Thad realized he himself was covered in red sticky liquid.

He ripped his eyes away from Raam and looked for Jaycoxx. He found him ten feet to the right, unconscious but writhing, bleeding from a heavy blow to his temple.

"Holy fuck!" Thad croaked to himself. He slithered backward to lie in a low clump of weeds further from the fence, then fumbled to raise the radio volume imperceptibly. He keyed it and whispered wildly, "Raam and fuckin' Jaycoxx too! Aak...they...got 'em both!"

No answer from the radio.

"Where the fuck is everybody...?"

The radio crackled, too loud, too late. Someone on the street side of the fence hollered, "I think they're back here!" Rioters began to kick in some of the wooden fence slats. Openings appeared, the light of fires from across the main street showing where. Men carrying clubs and blades were prying themselves through.

Thad froze and flattened. He thought about faking death, using Raam's blood on his body to fool them, and for an instant was glad Raam had bled so much. But he'd have to roll onto his back to make it show, and opted to remain flat and still.

The rioters found Raam's body, then Jaycoxx, and recognized him. One older man killed him immediately by repeatedly crushing the head with his boot heel. Others swore and whooped excitedly, and Raam's head was parted from the corpse trunk and lofted over the fence into the street, where it spurred even more yells. Too scared to speak, Thad keyed the radio mic and held it so that the yelling could be heard by Daryl, both as a plea for reinforcements and to keep the staccato crackling from coming out.

A cry went up beyond the fence that Wayne Aak was on the next street over leading a hundred men. Triumphant, the rioters behind the fence picked up the two bodies and heaved them over to the street side, then kicked more slats out of the fence and stepped back through to the street side, picking up the corpses and parading them exultantly into the mob.

Thad prayed that he was going to evade detection. One brandishing a hand axe and the other a baseball bat, the last two men back through the fence stopped for a parting look. One of them stepped halfway through, then made a last cursory scan of the weeds offset from the fence line, and caught sight of what he thought was a peculiar dark shape.

"Over here!" he shouted, and the two of them leapt back toward the weeds in question.

Thad knew it was time to go. He tried to spring up, but his revolver, his single asset, accidentally slipped from his hand. He spent a fatal half second groping for it unsuccessfully, and squandered his final moment rolling onto his back, shrieking, hands and feet waving futilely in the air. The mic of the radio remained keyed in his grasp while the first tribal man to reach him hacked him to pieces with the hatchet as he screamed.

The two rioters lifted the butchered head along with a piece of shoulder attached to it, and returned to the street, chanting; but after a short distance they tired of the greasy load and elected to simply display the carnage for the rest, using a fire hydrant as a pike. Raam's and Jaycoxx's bodies had similarly been draped onto mailboxes not far up the street.

CHAPTER TWENTY SIX

The sheriff knocked on Lucius Knox's front door. He didn't pound on it, although he was in a panic. His office had been obliterated by fire, the riot was in full swing, and there was no sign of any of the mayhem coming under control, but it was Mr. Knox's severe expectations that gave him pause; whether the townspeople lost their businesses, homes, or lives was not a question that occurred to him.

He waited a long time. He knocked again. The door coasted open only enough to reveal Daryl Lievestro standing just inside. Daryl regarded him but said nothing.

The sheriff shuffled his feet involuntarily and tried to sound authoritative. "I need to speak with Mister Knox."

Daryl continued to regard him like a hunter regards his hound, then turned his head sideways and looked at something or someone inside.

The disembodied voice of Knox demanded, "What the devil does he want?"

Still silent, Daryl casually opened the door a bit more—enough for Knox, eyes partly glaring and partly wild, to see the sheriff fidgeting outside the door.

"Well?" the gaunt man demanded.

"They're...uh...killing your men. I seen it! They got the bodies hangin' on posts all over town!"

"Who is?"

"Wayne Aak and his gang! They'll have us all 'fore they're through! I told you we should have never done what we done to him, I wanted no part...."

"Shut up," Knox said coldly. Then he changed his tone, taking a well honed approach he'd found effective with men like the sheriff. "They know what you've done. They know." He laughed a wicked laugh.

"What I done???" the Sheriff echoed his words with alarm. "You all was the ones who done it all! Some was to go to prison, others was to disappear, you said for me to...." But he didn't finish; Daryl stepped through the doorframe and knocked him to the ground with his fist. The sheriff landed heavily on his back with a gasp and a thud, and elected to stay down.

Daryl stepped out of Lucius' way; the tall gaunt man strode to the doorframe and looked down at the Sheriff groveling there. "Do you want to die tonight?" he asked the fleshy creature lying prone before him. "Do you want me to lose this kingdom?"

The sheriff quickly shook his head as expected.

"Then go and stop them. Show me you're worth all that fat. Meet the rest of my men behind the gas station. I want a stack of Indian bodies at every corner! I want my streets, and my damn river, and my damn mining trucks in my hand by dawn, do you hear me?!" His voice had escalated back to where it had begun. Then he turned and breathed to Daryl, "I pay you. See to it. I'll show these squatters in paradise what hell is."

Daryl sneered.

Sheriff Andrew Silo rose in a grunting cloud of dust and scurried to be off. He didn't know what he'd do or how he'd fulfill the ghastly order, but he dared not disagree. He'd appear eager until he got out of sight, and then crawl in a hole somewhere to think. He was a survivor, not a hero.

Lucius, already deep into other thoughts, resumed his prior absent glare as he stepped back into the house. Daryl waited a moment, then stepped in after him and slowly closed the door, peering out toward the perimeter of the property as it creaked shut.

The riot raged on. Secondary streets were now falling prey to the madness of the mob.

*   *   *

Lucius Knox waited alone on the second floor of his house. He had turned out all lights visible from outside; only the dim stairwell torches remained lit. He stood like a looming statue in the dark, peering out the bare window at the austere grounds below, and at the streets and yards beyond them. The glow of the mid-town riot was easily visible from where he kept vigil, and he watched the dancing shadows of the tall flames, wild-eyed and fascinated. His ears tuned themselves to the shrieks, the rallying cries for Wayne Aak, the gunfire.

Around eleven he chanced to glance downward at his own property; suddenly he leaned forward, catching his breath. Was that a shadow gliding across the grounds? Was one of them coming toward his house? He'd fallen for his own eyes' tricks a few times in the last half hour, but this was different. There was definitely someone there—someone who wasn't using the employee entrance.

Had he been less blind than Ofstedder before him, he'd have assessed the threat more perceptively. But like Ofstedder his ego whispered that there was but one hothead with enough personal vendetta to come alone. "I thought Injuns were stealthier than that," he breathed to himself.

Heart pounding, he moved back along the hall and quietly down his winding staircase. He loved how the glow of the torchlight against the earth-red walls got brighter as he descended. At the dining hall on the main floor, he slipped through the secret sliding door hidden in the wall, closed the wall behind himself, and continued winding downward to his clandestine lower basement, to the great hall where he had researched and planned his entire scheme, where he had mapped out the shaft locations of the mine using countless scale models, where he and that priest had squabbled over such petty things as sacred burial ground claims and broken sports toys.

He was on his own turf; he had the advantage down here. How best to keep it? He plotted the defense of his castle as he had countless times, noting with satisfaction how the staircase wound clockwise as it descended, giving the advantage to right-handed swordsmen defending the lower depths. He imagined a classic face-off between himself and the brash, petty challenger—a clash in which the best man, the high-born man, was predestined to win.

Out of a more pragmatic sense he kept the electric lights off in the cellar and extinguished the staircase illumination, instead crossing the long room and igniting a dim kerosene lantern on the back wall. He then returned to the head of the room, took a small handgun from a hidden drawer under the table that held the model of the mine, and pocketed it. Only insurance, he thought; a man of his quality wouldn't need it against that rabble.

Finally, he pulled his chosen sword off the wall. It was the genuine Spanish Colonial weapon from the 1700's, over thirty inches of smooth straight steel, the handle wrapped in simple leather, the iron hilt split at the knuckle bow in twin curved branches. It would be a fitting messenger of death for Aak, its single blemish the sickening crater in the edge where it had rung against a fireplace poker swung by that priest. Knox left the beautiful implement in its scabbard and set it on the end of the table.

The house was an eerie kind of quiet, and he cocked his head, listening. He could feel something about to happen that was right now making no sound. He shifted his feet, the soft scraping of his shoes and his heartbeat the only things he heard.

There...there it was! A noise...somewhere up above. The ground floor? A creaking, from somewhere above him. Hard to tell where. He held his breath and tried to slow his pulse, to hear it.

The creaking sound, again. This time nearer, this time from the staircase! Lucius stared across the table, into the shadows at the base of the steps. He glanced at the sword lying on the table in front of him, and reached slowly for it as he peered again into the darkened alcove. His outstretched hand began to shake when a ghostly figure drifted in slow motion from the stairwell not quite into view.

"Aak," he breathed just above a whisper, certain in his paranoia that it was a Washokki face he'd see.

The intruder held something indistinguishable in his hand, and not knowing what it was struck an odd fear into Lucius. He could not move. An interminable second passed. It took the ghost reaching out to the wall and turning on the lights to reveal to him the obvious.

"You!" hissed Knox.

Haggard but resolute, Mick replied, "Avenging Angel of the Lord."

"You'd...side with...a convicted felon? Against me?"

"This has to end now, Lucius."

"End? What are you talking about?" the gaunt man tried to regain composure. "Nothing's ending, priest. I'm just warming up."

"No. The charade is over."

"No charade, priest. My world! My destiny! You think to change the course of history all by yourself? With a...what is that you've got there...a hammer?" It was the mocking, scoffing tone, more than the question itself, that he hoped would distract the priest.

"You can choose how it ends, but it does."

Knox was still off-balance over the priest showing up before Aak. He was hoping to settle scores with the tribal ruffian privately, first, without witnesses or explanations. Now he wasn't sure how it would play out, or who his primary enemy really was. He stalled, looking for a direction to take.

"I thought we agreed we were similar men," he tried.

"And we can aspire to better."

"Exactly what I've done here, priest. For the people of this town, not just for myself. Weren't you listening? Prosperity is knocking!"

"It needs to knock more softly."

"I've had challenges here! Yes, perhaps we've been a bit heavy-handed at times, but one must meet rough action roughly. Use the devil's own tactics against him, so to speak." Knox's fingers continued to twitch.

"Lucius, it's the tactics that make the devil who he is. Use them, and you become him."

"I see your hammer, priest. Are you one to lecture me on tactics?"

"Yes, I've become you. I'll never escape that now. It's the price I'll pay."

As if cued, there was a new creaking on the stairs behind Mick. He turned just in time to leap out of the way of something large sliding and tumbling down the spiral. It landed with a thud at the base, and Mick recognized it as the body of Elmer.

It was the reversal of fortunes that Knox, standing across the table, was looking for. "Well! My men have sent down the garbage," he beamed, recovering. "This is what happens to fools who side with convicted felons." His voice was more confident now. "I think you're paying your prices for nothing, priest."

Mick clenched his jaw but said nothing. His worst fear for Elmer had proven true. The wood plank the old man had used as a leg was gone, and the face and body showed the purple hue of horrific trauma. They'd felled the big tough man, and Mick knew it must have taken a lot.

Daryl sauntered down the steps slowly, smirking with pride over this new shock, and strolled into the room.

Mick ignored the henchman. Incensed, he looked from Elmer's brutalized body to Lucius' face, seeking a reason. Knox knew the look for the question it was, and shrugging, provided his answer.

"Tangled with my man here, out at the half-breed squaw's place. Can't have that. Bad for discipline." His gloating expression struck a sickening contrast to the suffering the old man must have endured, and Daryl matched it with his own standard sneer. But their expressions faded as the sound of an approaching mob floated down from above. There was a gunshot and a foul-mouthed scream as one of the remaining mercenaries went down—probably the scowling one they called Rowe, Mick thought, whom he'd slipped past some minutes earlier. Then heavy fists began to pound on the ground level outer door. It would be breached in a matter of minutes.

With war on the brink of entry, Mick sought to keep the focus on moral issues. "Why?" he asked Knox, pointing down to Elmer's body. "An old man. Are you that far gone? That far over the edge? What could you possibly gain by this?"

"I am supreme here, priest. I have dominion here. Lord of all this land! I will gut that mine and I will do what I please in my domain, and all the two-bit punks out of prison and their weak sympathizers will never change that...." He trailed off, drowned out by the stampeding footsteps of rioters swarming into the house above, his declarations of supremacy mingling paradoxically with the sounds of full-on rebellion. The boom of the hidden portal being flung open at the top of the stairs made him flinch.

Mick nodded toward Daryl. "Your faithful must have left the gate to eternity ajar."

Led by a handful of burly Washokki and Tissoma men, one carrying a heavy twelve-gauge shotgun, the mob charged down the winding staircase. When they got to the map room, Reuben Bitterroot elbowed his way to a position near the front. Ushered down the center of the column also to a point near the front was a much older man.

"Is Wayne Aak here? Where is he?" Bitterroot demanded.

"That stupid punk will do you no good!" Lucius shouted back. His hands were still empty, but with the shotgun waving about in the front ranks of the mob, he inched a hand toward his pocket, kept one eye on the sword on the table between himself and them, and mentally reviewed his options for control or escape. But what kept the tribe from shooting him and taking control was that Mick took control first.

"You're a fool, Lucius," the priest accused. "You're all fools. Wayne Aak isn't here. He isn't coming. He made it less than a mile from the prison gates." The bold statement drew a confused hush from incredulous faces; Lucius, Bitterroot, and the others stared uncomprehending as Mick continued. "If you weren't so busy knocking down phone lines and killing each other you might know these things! He's no savior of the people, and he's no threat to order here! He got drunk in the first bar he came across in Deer Lodge, got in a fight, and was back in a cell within ten hours!"

"Who says so?" Bitterroot demanded.

"I called the prison. Days ago. Evidently I'm the only one who checks facts. You're all being led by—or cowering from—a pariah! A ghost!" He aimed the accusation of cowardice at Knox.

There was a moment of silence as they digested the implications of that.

"But he killed my men tonight!" Lucius insisted.

Mick shifted the hammer in his hand and gave Knox a silent, leveled gaze.

"You...?" Lucius stammered in amazement. "Priest, you're killing my men?"

Even the mob leaders were taken aback. Confusion crept in. Jaws sagged as they stared at the big hammer, imagining death delivered by such a thing.

Silent up till now, awaiting his opportunity, Daryl seized the moment. Stepping right through the nearest intruder, he lunged for the shotgun in the second row and wrenched it away from its owner, brutally bashing heads as he jerked it free. Then he took a step back against the end wall, put his finger on the trigger, and began to swing the barrel back and forth from the mob to Mick, the leer returning to his face as lethal power returned to his hands.

The tables had turned yet again; the master of the castle had regained mastery. The mob, now suddenly captives, froze in confused shock. But Mick had known it would happen, because it was what he would have done. And now he waited for the error of ego he also knew would follow.

The scene under Daryl's control, the cruel man looked across, eager to see the pall of despair on the priest's face, but found none. He threw a taunting sneer at Mick.

"I did that," he boasted, nodding toward Elmer's body. "Did it to 'im with his own leg plank. Did yer girlfriend too. Been thinkin' 'bout doin' her for a year, off an' on. Waitin' till I got tired of white meat is all." He grinned the grin of fearless impunity, and added, "Used my own wooden leg for her."

It is a mistake to react to taunts from men like Daryl; the words are designed to tempt rash action. Mick hung his head in apparent defeat, out of the corner of his eye carefully watching the aim of the shotgun barrel swing from his own body to the mob and back. To Daryl's disappointment the moment passed. Mick raised a pious, imploring look to Lucius, and when the movement of his head drew the gun off the crowd and onto himself, he moved.

There was no hesitation—no doubt. His right arm swung in a concise, expanding arc, and the big hammer flew. The throw was so sudden, so powerful, that the finger on the shotgun's trigger had no time to twitch. The hammer spun in flight; its claw met Daryl's forehead and went through it like butter, cold blue steel ripping through bone and brain tissue as it decelerated.

Daryl's leer melted too gradually to seem real; with slow, raw finality, the cocky cruelty was replaced by an expression of gruesome horror. His corpse stood twitching for several seconds and then sagged into a widening pool of blood that oozed backward toward the wall. The shotgun discharged both barrels into the ceiling and rode his body to the floor.

No one knew what to do next. The suddenness and brutality of the spectacle left the room with no one in control. Revolted more by the loss of his deliverance than the grotesqueness of Daryl's execution, the aghast Lucius dropped his jaw in shock.

"We'll all be judged for our deeds this day," Mick said simply, breathing heavily, speaking without shame. He was telling them this should be the last act of violence.

Of the others, Bitterroot was first to effect a dispassionate tone. "We are...still taking back our land."

Lucius recovered next, half-heard Reuben's claim, absorbed it for a moment, and replied.

"Your...? That mine belongs to me."

"The wealth of Washokki land belongs to the Washokki," Bitterroot shot back.

"And Tissoma," a voice behind him added. Mick noted the undertone of rivalry still alive among the tribes.

Several young tribe members began to echo Bitterroot's claim, taunting Lucius with copycat emphasis, impressing each other.

"Nobody takes our land!"

"Our people have owned that place forever."

"Let's kill this white trash!"

"Shut up, all of you," interrupted Mick. "You want that mine? You want that wealth?" He reached into his pocket and pulled out stones he'd picked up in the underground shaft, tossing them like dice down the length of the scale model of the mine. The fragments wobbled and came to a stop. "There it is," he invited. "You want to die for those two stones? Go ahead. Kill each other for them. They're worthless."

Unsubstantiated, it was a risky play, but above all he needed to sow doubt. Once again those in the room were off-balance, as Mick's message continued to gain credibility. Reuben Bitterroot broke it with a quiet but ominous tone.

"What do you mean?"

"I mean there's a reason why that hillside was abandoned seventy years ago! Doesn't anybody read here? Does it take an outsider to teach you your own history? The Briskamph Lode land-slide was a cover-up. That hole in the ground was worthless from the day it was dug! The early hype was a scam, to sell partnerships at the turn of the century! The only person who ever got rich out of it was the accountant who snuck off to Panama with his partners' money!

And rumor has it the main...nugget...he ended up with was made of lead and lodged itself in the back of his head."

Lucius scoffed openly. "I did the research, priest, and the math. Yes, yes, there was never any real gold there. But where there's gold, there's always something else. I think you figured out what I found, priest, those deposits, right there on the surface! I read, I know what that ore would bring on today's market. You're bluffing...." But he spoke like a man trying to convince himself as much as his audience.

Mick cut him off. "You read, but not enough. Nickel isn't your personal epiphany, Lucius. It too was thought of when those shafts were worked...and when they were buried...especially after the gold scam risked being exposed. It just didn't get any real press. You should know by now that what's on the surface can be misleading. There never was enough ore in that dirt to pay for the transport costs, which by the way have risen, not fallen, since then, unless you still intend to use mules...and even if you did, what little is there isn't nickel oxide, it's nickel sulphide! Gotta be heat-processed to make the oxide version, and that takes energy and time, and that's all way before you ever start to pull out the pure nickel!" He paused. "They used to call it 'heazelwoodite,' and even if your Daddy wasn't a miner this information is easy to find if you wipe the craving from your eyes, people! Cracking that mud to get the metal out costs more than you could ever make."

Knox, Bitterroot and the tribe militants were silent—bewildered—staring from Mick's face to the stones on the table. His message, though uncorroborated, sounded painfully real. The elder watched the priest's face carefully.

"You want those stones?" Mick continued, taking advantage of the momentum he'd created. "Take them. They amount to low-grade tailings. About as valuable as fill dirt. And you're all out there killing human beings for that."

"But..." began one of the angry young rioters. Mick silenced him immediately.

"And I really doubt it's ever been a holy site of any kind, so shut the hell up! ...You're a handful of whiners and hotheads! Listen to your real elders for once," he admonished, glaring at Bitterroot, then back at the rest. "They've lived long enough to know what that place really is and how to tell truth from fable! Sacred ground, you say? That hole is a burial ground only to those who've died there at the hand of greed."

Serious doubt now replaced the motivations of all present, and Lucius looked for a way out.

"You lie, priest."

His fingers touched the small revolver hidden in his pocket; he pulled it into open view and aimed it at Mick. The rioters, having lost their reasons to die, and now weaponless except for clubs and blades, paled. One hot-headed teenager still looking for an opportunity to be heroic lunged across the table for the sword, but just as he touched it, Lucius dropped him with a single shot. He slid off the table; the rest heeded the warning. The sword clattered off the near end of the table at Knox's feet.

Mick had dropped his eyes to Elmer's body before the teen had made his lunge. When the report of the weapon rang out, the priest saw two of his caretakers' bruised and bloody fingers twitch.

The small gun in his hand injected one last breath of life into the gaunt man's courage; Knox swelled into an authoritative posture.

"You thought you could best me? It's like...rodents ganging up on God! You're no match for me. You imagine yourselves my equal? Any of you?!" He shot a mocking laugh in Mick's direction. "I am Prince here! I am Law! Now, we're going to move forward as before. You're all going to get out of this house, and I will come visit each of you in your homes and let you know how you can help me with my plans, and how you can apologize for this imposition. And," he leaned to the right and turned specifically to Mick, his face side-lit by the yellow glow of the lantern on the far wall, "your friends who are in a position to contribute more will enjoy...visitors...tonight." A look of crazed cruelty crossed his face. "In fact it's probably all falling into place as we speak."

"You're aware of course that I called the National Guard." Mick's voice was cold steel. "Phones aren't the only way to reach the outside."

"You...called the...." Lucius tried to chuckle, to conceal the harsh impact of the revelation. Then he simply gave up hiding it. There were at last no more rabbits to pull from hats, he knew; this was truly the end. The bastard priest would have done it; his damned holiness had played the final card.

He had no more clever things to say. Gun still trained on Mick, he simply slid right, along the side of the table, angling for the back wall. He stooped and grabbed the sheathed sword from the floor as he moved. "I have men out there," he mumbled incoherently, "already following my orders...you'll be the ones hunted down...you and yours...."

As Knox stepped sideways, he reached a point where Mick stood roughly between the tribe and himself. Shielded momentarily from the line of fire, the temptation to act and the fear of being cheated of their revenge proved too great for the mob. They sprang to life, surging forward and throwing knives and clubs. Knox fired his handgun. It was Mick this time who fell.

Feeling a momentary flash of pleasure from that, the gaunt man made it to the end of the room, swung around, and swatted the dim kerosene lantern off the wall. The fuel splashed onto the heavy tapestry hanging behind the wall-mounted pick-axe and shovel, creating instant flames and smoke. The tribal mob recoiled, then swarmed forward again over and around Mick, peering through the choking cloud. Knox was gone.

They looked under the table and sought through the black fumes for hidden doors in the walls. The blaze quickly consumed the already charred tapestry cloth; one of them yanked the fabric down to stamp out the flames and put an end to the smoke. The thick cloth fell, revealing a crude three-foot-wide hole in the cement wall, and a dirt tunnel leading to several plank-on-cement-block steps a dozen yards away, at the base of a hatch door. The door was swung wide. Some rioters bolted immediately through the tunnel and out the hatch, in hopes of catching Knox. They saw only a black pickup truck racing across the grounds and up onto a side street at the lot's far edge, gone in a squeal of tread on pavement.

The elder who had stood silently with Bitterroot at the base of the stairs now knelt beside Mick. He found a shoulder wound; it did not look good. Mick had regained his senses and was trying feebly to rise.

"You must lie here now," the old man said, placing a hand gently on Mick's good shoulder. "You have done enough."

But the priest would not. Fighting unconsciousness, he rolled up onto his knees. Before attempting to rise, he pulled himself close to Elmer's ear. Elmer partly opened his eyes, and Mick grasped one of the old man's hands.

"Can you hear me, my friend?"

Elmer turned his eyes weakly toward Mick's face.

"There's something I still need to do," Mick whispered.

Elmer closed his eyes and reopened them in answer.

"Pull this town together," Mick said.

Elmer's eyes closed and reopened a second time.

The priest struggled to his feet and staggered through the ranks of tribal militants; they parted as he passed, watching him disappear out through the smoky tunnel, alone into the darkness.

As he went, the tribal elder knelt again and took Elmer's hand.

CHAPTER TWENTY SEVEN

Mick made it back to the residence, blocking out the pain by focusing on what must yet be done. He pulled a jacket from inside the door and covered his torso; he didn't want Gabriella to see the wound.

Approaching the side door of the church, he was aware of a small shadowy figure standing there. It was the thin Indian man.

"You're...standing guard," Mick realized aloud.

"No one has been here yet. But they will come, even though he has been run off."

How this anonymous little man of mystery and few words knew things was a wonder to the priest. He weakly nodded his appreciation. Before turning toward the church door, he lingered an extra moment with a listener's eyes.

The thin man understood the question, and said simply, "The boy they said Mr. Carlo had killed, two years ago. My son."

Last piece of the puzzle.

The thin man melted one last time into the night. Mick knocked softly on the door and waited to hear Gabriella's muffled voice from inside.

"It's okay," he murmured simply; she unlocked and opened it.

"Men are coming," he said, once inside. "We should leave now."

They moved quickly to where Angelo lay asleep. Struggling but determined to get it done, Mick picked the child up with his good arm, hiding the extreme pain, and let Gabriella wrap the blanket around them both. Gabriella gathered up the armload of jackets and other articles, including the .22 rifle.

Her car was still where they had left it. Mick eased the child into the back seat and asked Gabriella to drive. She placed the bundle of jackets in back as padding for her son as the priest settled into the front passenger's seat. She set the small rifle across his knees.

"Take the old road, over the mountain," he said in a haggard voice. She started. He hoped he'd be able to relax once they were on the move.

She drove in silence. Something was wrong, she knew, but exactly what wasn't clear. He had had a rough time, but he had returned. After a while she inquired quietly, "Where are we going?"

"Just go east and keep going. We'll get you to Kalispell for a little while. Maps say this comes out on the other side." He remembered how the road looked on a topo map; a 'nice little getaway' he'd thought at the time. He realized the jostling had awakened the child, who had his little thumb in his mouth and was watching Mick quietly but intently from the back seat. Best not to show any pain.

"Yes, I know," Gabriella replied about the old road. "No one uses it much anymore." Then she asked, "What about Lucius Knox?"

"He's finished now," Mick sighed, reaching down to remove the tiny .22 shell from the little rifle's chamber and putting it in his pocket. "State militia will pick him up within a day; he can't get very far—he has a thousand witnesses and even more enemies." He moved his shoulder, hiding a wince of pain; it was swelling and the bleeding had reduced. "And I suspect they'll find more bodies," he added. "The radicals who met with your husband, and others—out at the mine."

She nodded.

"Knox will shiver in the cold wet woods somewhere out in the Kootenai until they hunt him down with dogs," he predicted with comforting assurance. He took a moment for a slow breath, then added another detail of interest to her. "And...his 'demon' has been sent to its...reward."

Gabriella's eyes narrowed, but the news was welcome; she felt grateful to the priest for that deed. "And what about you?" she came around to asking.

He considered hiding his condition, but now that they were safely on the road, good sense prevailed. "I...think I'm going to need some medical attention." He touched his jacket.

So he'd been hurt...and it must be bad or he wouldn't have mentioned it. She could do nothing for him on a lonely country road, and decided to concentrate on getting to Kalispell quickly rather than pressing for details.

After a pause, she asked, as much to keep him awake as anything, "What about the town?"

"Have to rebuild, but they're going to be all right. The town is in good hands I think."

They drove on several more miles; the bends in the road became less painful as time went on. Mick was surprised to find himself strangely awake, strangely introspective. He must be weak from loss of blood, he thought.

He heard himself rambling. Confessing. "I think I've led a poor life...a coarse life. I once thought that was being strong, but it's weak. I hid from that for awhile...hid in the robes...but...nothing really changed. He was right...we can't declare Sanctuary from the truth. And tonight I killed—people no more coarse than myself. I...I don't even know how to redeem that. I've slid into...."

Gabriella gave the silence a moment to mature, then finished his sentence.

"Into Hell?" Her tone was skeptical. "Because evil retreats there and you must chase it down, does that damn you?" A tired smile crept over her face; she looked at Mick with admiration.

"What?"

"Ever since we met you," she observed, "you've doubted your credentials. But you have completed your mission."

He thought about that, and smiled weakly in reluctant acknowledgement. "Only by a fool's luck."

"No," she mused half aloud, half to herself. "From your heart. They chose the right man. You are the warrior Angel sent by God to deliver us." She smiled again, and stole a glance at Angelo in the back seat, still awake, still absorbed with watching the priest.

The lonely road straightened out for a quarter mile. They didn't see the eyes that saw them. A third of the way through the stretch, a ghostly dark shape lunged from the right down a sloping dirt hollow in the trees. The black pickup truck had known they would come this way—had been waiting for them. With deft timing it rammed their moving car hard at the passenger's side door, and they spun, back wheels swinging wide to the left, off the pavement. Gabriella screamed; they skidded to a stop facing sideways, front tires on the road, rear resting in the ditch on the lower edge of the steep, loose gravel shoulder. The engine idled softly as though nothing had happened; exhaust curled wispy thin and white behind them and disappeared in the still cold air.

Across the road, a dirty black pickup truck sat stalled where, after full frontal impact, it had rebounded into its own ditch. Its bent hood had sprung open, exposing the engine; the carburetor squirted an intermittent thin, fine spray of gasoline into the air from a ruptured fitting. Oil leaked heavily from the pan down below, mixing with gasoline dripping off the bumper and fenders and trickling in a delicate serpentine line inexorably toward the center of the road.

Like the car, the truck's headlights were still on; the two vehicles faced each other, together illuminating the open space between them.

Gabriella righted herself and looked around. The passenger-side door of the Ford was crumpled. Mick was slumped low, head and right leg against the inwardly protruding metal, groaning from the pain of the impact. She whirled to see her son. Cushioned by the armload of jackets and blankets she'd dumped onto the seat beside him, the boy had miraculously escaped injury. No sooner had she breathed a sigh of thanks than the rear door behind her opened suddenly. A long arm reached in, seized the child's wrist, and dragged him out, his soft voice trying unsuccessfully to scream.

Gabriella knew whose arm it was, and she wasted no time with words. Mick, in bad shape, had not reacted yet. She reached for and seized the empty rifle from the floor at his feet, and tore herself frantically from the car.

Lucius Knox stood in the center of the road, illuminated by the car's headlights. He held the boy against his hip, off the ground, with one arm. His other hand clutched the sword in its scabbard. Gabriella stepped to the front bumper of the car and trained the small-bore rifle on him. She had seen Mick unload its single-shell chamber, and knew that pretense was all she had. She pulled the hammer back.

"Put him down!" she screamed. "I swear I will do this. Put my baby down now!" She tried to sight down the shaking barrel at the man holding her child.

From behind her she could hear Mick attempting to open his door. It was seized. He crawled across and fell out the open driver's side door. Groaning, head bleeding, he staggered to his feet and limped to join her at the front of the car. His body was failing but his eyes remained focused intently on Lucius Knox, exultant where he stood.

"Stand up and be a man, priest!" Knox taunted. "That's all I want. You think to put me on the run? You think you've bested me? I'm a rich man! I am Prince of this valley! You're a...transient! Hiding behind a skirt, for Christ's sake! Confront your enemy, coward!"

Mick did not react. His face was that of a man who knew his enemy.

Knox grew instantly impatient, and sought to arrange the meeting more to his liking. His long gnarled arm let the scabbard fall from the sword and he held the blade to the child's throat. "Drop that dishonorable piece of rust!" he commanded the mother.

Tears streaming down her face, Gabriella refused with a defiant shake of her head. The small empty firearm was the last high card she held. Mick limped forward and grabbed the barrel, wresting the gun away from her. Reluctantly she released her vice-like grip. He put the barrel to the pavement and leaned against the rifle like a cane, whispering so that only she could hear.

"Take the boy," he instructed her. "Walk into the woods. Put as much distance as you can between you and this place. It's me he wants."

She started to shake her head, but he coughed in pain and continued. "You can do it. For your son. Just keep...going. Do not look back."

She reached out to touch his wounded shoulder, then his face. "He'll kill you," she cried softly.

His own tears didn't stop his smile. "My mission," he reminded her. Straining forward, he kissed her forehead. "Now save the child."

He pushed her behind him and hardened his face; he had to draw Lucius' intentions away from the mother and child. "In sacrifice lies redemption," he muttered to himself, trying to steel his nerves.

Lucius had not moved, and now Mick took a step toward him, speaking softly.

"Do you intend to face me from behind a boy?"

The priest was in a feeble condition, Knox could tell. Revenge would be certain. His eyes grew wilder yet, and a lightly demonic laugh erupted from his lips. He cast the useless child roughly aside. "May the best man win," he crowed.

Gabriella dashed forward and picked up her son. She backed up to the front of the car again; the boy squirmed out of her grasp, ran to the driver's side door, and hid inside the vehicle. Simultaneously terrified and entranced, he stood on his toes on the transmission hump, pulled himself taller on the steering wheel and dashboard, and peered above the vinyl at the two men in the center of the road.

Lucius was beginning to circle Mick slowly, seemingly deciding on his first strike; the priest leaned on the rifle stock and sought to keep the gaunt man in front of him—sought to keep him blinded by the lights.   Gabriella backed up along the darker, shadowed passenger side of the car, where the truck's impact had crushed the metal inward.   She felt strangely frozen in indecision; she had to keep her son safe, yet...the one in mortal danger now was Mick. She cast a sideways glance into the front seat where Angelo stood, then back at the road, at the priest limping in a small circle, buying her time.   He had said she must abandon him.   Her hand groped blindly for the car door handle; she couldn't breathe.   Rattling the chrome grip, she tried in vain to dislodge the crumpled door, to pry it open, but it was hung.   Her eyes could not be torn from the death dance before her.

Lucius paused, still a dozen feet from his prey, and Mick matched the hesitation.   The gaunt man appeared to be at a crossroad of choices.   He firmed his grip on the sword; but, eyes flickering, instead of lunging forward he began to speak.

"You could have been part of it all!" he blamed, his voice a mixture of hostility and lament.   "I offered you the hand of friendship."

"You asked for approval."

"Ahhh.   And the Holy Ordained don't spare that vintage on sinners, do they?"   He was mocking the priest, but still there was the glistening hint of tears in Lucius' eyes.   "Instead you peddle that cheap tin cup you call Forgiveness."

"You can still have it."

Knox stared, nostrils flared, the moment his to define. Then, eyes refilling with madness, he chose, and screamed.   He leapt toward Mick, taking a massive cut through the air with his sword. The thin edge whistled; Mick barely got the rifle barrel up in time to block the blade. Steel rang against steel, shattering what the moment could have been.

Mick balanced on his good leg, now holding the rifle upright by the barrel with both hands, wincing at the shooting pain the added weight put on his injured shoulder. He tried to take a step to one side but stumbled and had to drop the gun's stock to the road to catch himself. Knox saw the obvious opening. With a yell he lurched in aggressively, gracelessly, his boot heel shove-kicking Mick in the front of the hip. The priest went down.

Knox was strutting; it was far too easy! He laughed. From where he lay, Mick could see Gabriella still lingering in the shadows by the car. She needed to run; he needed to buy more time. He'd fallen just past the edge of pavement wet with gasoline and oil, and the smell alerted him to get up. He struggled and mostly regained his feet, climbing the rifle to rise, one hand weakly trying to motion for the woman to go.

He didn't have a chance to straighten before Knox stepped in again, delivering a rising, swinging kick to his stomach. The pain to his bullet wound was too much to bear, and he went down again. Knox bellowed, turning away to raise the sword to the sky, smiling to the low cloud that had begun to form. Gabriella and Angelo both gasped.

And the mother and child saw the gaunt man come back yet again to the place where the priest lay bent. Mick knew too, although his head was turned the other way. He gathered his remaining strength and with his good arm swung the rifle butt at his assailant's knee. As weak as he was, he could still remember how to deliver power.

Lucius fell, cursing. He had underestimated the priest. He rolled out of reach of the rifle's length and rose a few yards away. He was smeared in black, his face and clothing coated in the thinned petroleum mixture from the road's surface; he looked like a creature from foul depths. Realizing his knee was not seriously injured, he laughed; then using more caution, he stepped back in to deliver another vengeful kick to the priest's rib cage. That one was for the rifle butt, he said to himself, enjoying the deep groan he heard from the pavement.

He addressed his victim. "You're pathetic, priest! Is that all you have left? ...maybe a little of your Master's own fate, eh?" He set the point of the sword against Mick's side and pushed it in, loving the way it punctured and then slid through living flesh, drinking in the tortured cry of pain that rose to his ears.

The big man circled his fallen nemesis once again; he held the red point of his sword high above his head, exulting, speaking to the darkly clouding night sky. "Oh yes, I have killed!"

Tears streamed openly down Gabriella's face. Time stood still. Her hand rattled the door handle like a machine stuck in a perpetual repetitive cycle; her eyes remained riveted to the grisly scene playing to its inevitable conclusion on the illuminated road.

His contorted face on the pavement, Mick could no longer see the mother and child. He didn't know where Knox was, or why he'd not been executed yet;

he hoped for the sake of the tiny family that the intention was slow death, but his weakness as a man begged inwardly for an end to the pain. He tried to gather a knee under himself, and again, but fell prone each time.

Eyes level with the road, he saw the strange beauty of the pavement's coarse texture, side-lit as it was by the floodlights from the low stone wall...no, they were headlights, that's right. And now tiny splashes, tiny fountains...was that the cool drizzle of soft rain? And there was deep, rich darkness beyond the points of light. Peculiarly fascinated by the beckoning peace of that richness, he managed to heave his torso onto one forearm and began to drag his body lethargically toward the light's edge, up the center line of the road, leaving a smear of blood as he moved.

Knox stopped circling and took a step toward the crawling man.

"The best man always wins, priest," he intoned. "Is this your best, priest? Is this it? Well, let's make an end of it."

Angelo watched with eyes wide. Lucius took a moment to kick the scabbard out of his way, then returned to within a few feet of the priest. He raised the blade high above his head. He would speak in tongues now, he decided; it would be fitting, for the execution. He began to chant a pious gibberish, eyes rolling back into his head.

Gabriella backed further into the shadows; Angelo's fingers dug into the vinyl of the dashboard. The idling sound of the car's engine mingled with the chant's senseless rhythm. The sword wavered at its apex.　　　Time slowed surrealistically as the unintelligible voice of the gaunt man muffled and faded to lip-twitching silence.

Years later, Angelo as a young adult would remember in indelible, high resolution graphic detail, and write, "He was evil the way Father Mick had explained evil. And I remember the bad one had said the best man would win. But...what is a man's best? Is it only what he can do on that day, in that moment? Or is it the full path of his life? ...and all the deeds that have won him the loyalty, and the gratitude—the love—of those he had protected, those whose lives he had affected...or saved?"

Sound returned; the moment transformed back into real time. The fair young child still strained to see. Below, on the car's floor, his tiny toe tapped, reaching, searching with a delicate, innocent purpose. It recognized what it sought, and stood down onto the car's accelerator.

The old engine sputtered and came to life, roaring to lay claim to the night. The rear wheels spun wildly. The Landcruiser spare tire mounted on the left rear wheel sprayed loose gravel...and grabbed. The old car lurched, and lunged like a wounded animal up and out of the ditch.

Thrown backward into the bench seat, Angelo continued to reach; he kept his small foot on the pedal. Gabriella's car charged across the headlamp-lit arena, narrowly missing Mick by inches where he lay. His sword still raised, the charging car struck the astonished Knox full-on, carrying him screaming toward the front of his own vehicle, pinning him with a sickening crash against the black truck's distorted grill.

Like the eyes of beasts locked in mortal combat, the headlights of the two machines glared at each other at close range. Wide-eyed with surprise, Lucius bellowed and cursed, struggling to get free. His stomach and legs were pinned, and the delayed pain now rushed him, momentarily overwhelming him until he cried out. He grunted, stopped straining, and took a deep breath. He was alive. He could see the priest's broken body still lying on the road to the car's side, and laughed with demonic glee. He had won!

Sword still in one hand, he renewed his straining against the wreckage, pushing down around himself in an effort to raise his body. The steel blade of the weapon he held angled backward, momentarily bridging across the terminals of the battery; a series of white-hot electrical arcs instantly sizzled and sparked. The fumes from the gasoline that had been spraying throughout the engine compartment ignited immediately in a deafening ball of fire, and the liquid fuel on his arm and body were quick to follow. Lucius watched in horror as the fire rampaged up his sword arm to his chest and face, and Gabriella witnessed him suddenly engulfed in a towering inferno of yellow flame.

From within the flames there came horrendous screams; the torso writhed. She saw that he was still conscious! ...and that he began again to babble incoherently as he burned alive, his eyes bulging like the eyes of the defeated angel Lucifer in Angelo's little bible. For a terrifying moment she feared the interminable torment and the madness it surely caused would make him turn the flaming blade inward on himself and run the hot steel through his own heart. She feared seeing it, for she could not tear her eyes away.

But the weapon only quivered in his hand and finally dropped to the road, and then his charring body slumped and went silent. The flames continued to consume him, sizzling in the onslaught of miniature droplets from the clouds above.

Mick was semi-conscious, dimly aware of a fire and Knox's screams. He did not try to turn his head to look.

Gabriella ran to the car window; she saw that her child was safe. Immediately she rushed to where Mick lay, now damp from the gentle wash of soft night rain. The car continued to idle, its white exhaust curling delicately upward. The boy climbed out of the vehicle's front seat and walked to his mother's side. She turned and hugged him to her with both arms, and he looked at the priest with the innocent eyes of a child.

Mick was floating in and out of consciousness; Gabriella's tears fell, mingling with the rain on his eyes and cheeks, and it seemed to her his face showed no pain. She pressed his big hand in hers. "Rest, Mick Calahan; we're with you now," she whispered in an angelic voice, "and all is well."

Far to the east, the calm, clearing sky was just beginning to lighten, heralding the break of dawn.

ABOUT THE AUTHOR

Michael Vorhis was born to a large farm family in Midwestern USA. He has resided in or extensively traveled Australia, New Zealand, Italy, France, Germany and other parts of Europe, the New England states, and Colorado, Wyoming, and other stretches of the Great American West. Most recently he makes his home in Northern California with his wife and daughter. His passions include high alpine mountaineering, the paddling of free-flowing rivers, soaring flight, fly fishing, string instruments, cartooning, baseball, volleyball, the martial arts, photography, the open road...and writing.

He has developed and published fiction and nonfiction, including novels, short stories and screenplays, for more than three decades; some of those works are described on the following page.

Contact information:

Email: Freeflight-Publishing@vorhis.com
Archangel@vorhis.com

URL: www.vorhis.com/FreeFlight-Publishing/Archangel.html

Look for these and other fine works by Michael Vorhis:

Open Distance (Novel)

Within a daring, fantastic world of competitive soaring flight, an old distrust breeds jealousy, calamity, hatred, sacrifice...and love.

Stick Riders: Of Men whose Keen Wits Miss Naught, and with Glory
(First published in Insider Magazine, Cincinnati, Ohio, 1988)

A larger-than-brains tale of rugged high adventure that lionizes two swashbuckling young explorers--tougher than biker gangers, more clever than sixty two percent of marsupials--as they straddle the unlikeliest of manly machines through the dry and deadly Australian Red Centre.

An American Sporting Man Goes to Hell

A hilarious (sadly also true) tale of gloriously misguided athletic expectations and how they can instantly wither to so much overcooked gnocchi when steeped in a small town Italian soup.

Real Heroics from the Less Than Renowned
(First published in Hang Gliding Magazine, 1997)

The story of a Regional Cross Country Hang Gliding Championship in the high deserts of the American West.

Flying in the Face of the Gods
(First published in Hang Gliding Magazine, 2001)

The story of the first and only World Hang Gliding Slalom/Speed Championships, and the American team that took home the gold.

www.ingramcontent.com/pod-product-compliance
Lightning Source LLC
Chambersburg PA
CBHW020823180626
46814CB00001B/83